The children of a savage frontier

MEG KINCAID O'HARE

Escaping a violent husband, she must now seek the protection of an enemy . . . or surrender to a life of peril and degradation.

JIM KINCAID

His search for his own identity leads him to a high mountain wilderness—and into the murderous path of a relentless killer.

KITTY KINCAID ADAMSON and BEN ADAMSON

On the merciless frontier, they must fight to preserve what is theirs—or see everything they love destroyed by one man's treachery.

MARCUS HUNT LYNDSAY

Brilliant and bloodthirsty Captain of the First Dragoons, the West is his for the taking—and he will crush anyone who threatens his glorious destiny.

BOOTHE CARLYLE

The aging, legendary frontiersman, he abandons a life among the Nez Perce for a fateful, foretold confrontation with the "black wolf."

THE KINCAIDS

MOUNTAIN FURY

TAYLOR BRADY

AVON BOOKS ◆ NEW YORK

THE KINCAIDS: MOUNTAIN FURY is an original publication of Avon Books. This work has never before appeared in book form. This work is a novel. Any similarity to actual persons or events is purely coincidental.

AVON BOOKS
A division of
The Hearst Corporation
1350 Avenue of the Americas
New York, New York 10019

First Avon Books Printing: April 1993

AVON TRADEMARK REG. U.S. PAT. OFF. AND IN OTHER COUNTRIES, MARCA REGISTRADA, HECHO EN U.S.A.

Printed in the U.S.A.

RA   10   9   8   7   6   5   4   3   2   1

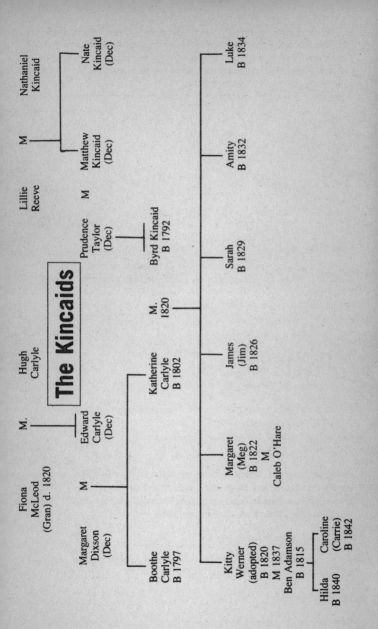

The Kincaids

Fiona McLeod (Gran) d. 1820 **M** Hugh Carlyle

Margaret Dixson (Dec) — **M.** — Edward Carlyle (Dec)

Lillie Reeve **M** Nathaniel Kincaid

Prudence Taylor (Dec) — Byrd Kincaid B 1792

Matthew Kincaid (Dec)

Nate Kincaid (Dec)

Boothe Carlyle B 1797

Katherine Carlyle B 1802 — **M. 1820** — Byrd Kincaid B 1792

Margaret (Meg) B 1822 **M** Caleb O'Hare

James (Jim) B 1826

Sarah B 1829

Amity B 1832

Luke B 1834

Kitty Werner (adopted) B 1820 **M 1837** Ben Adamson B 1815

Hilda B 1840

Caroline (Carrie) B 1842

Prologue

The Rocky Mountains,
1843

Boothe Carlyle looked up from the stream and the wolf was there, watching him from the opposite bank. Its eyes were keen and observant, and its coat was black as ink.

Boothe had spent most of his life in the wilderness, navigating the rugged rivers of the lowlands and wandering the high mountain passes, and he was not an unwary man. He had knelt beside the stream and cupped his hands to drink, his long rifle no more than an inch from his foot, within easy reach of his fingers. It was twilight, the time of day when other animals besides man were apt to feel a thirst, and he kept a cautious eye out for the big cats that were known to roam this part of the country. He heard no sound, felt no warning. He simply looked, and the wolf was there.

Instinctively, his fingers slid toward the rifle. But they never closed on it.

There wasn't much in this world Boothe Carlyle had not done or seen. He had never seen a black wolf before, but he had dreamed of it many, many times. He had spent the past six years of his life waiting for this wolf to appear.

Boothe possessed the gift of second sight, of dreams that never failed to come true. Long ago he had dreamed of death at the teeth of a black wolf. In the dream, he raised his rifle, but did not fire. Just as now, his hand touched the rifle but didn't lift it. The wolf watched him with keen, intelligent eyes. Boothe looked back, his heart beating slow and hard.

He had never even heard tell of a black wolf before, nor until this moment believed there was such a creature. Was the animal's coat truly black, or was it just a trick of the dying light? Neither had he ever known a wolf to attack a man, except in times of great famine or sickness. The stream was less than three feet wide. The animal could be across it before Boothe got his rifle to his shoulder. Why did it just stand there, looking?

He always dreamed true. And he had come into the mountains to die as he had lived, a free man in the last of this untamed country, close to the heart of God. His time had been rich and full, and he was ready.

Yet a man will cling to survival, and instinctively Boothe dropped his eyes to his rifle for an instant, measuring the time it would take to lift and fire. When he glanced up again the wolf was gone, having melted into the shadows from whence it came.

After a time Boothe stood and shouldered his rifle and continued on his way, moving from the stream to make his camp for the night. But his sleep was troubled, and he felt as though something fundamental inside him had been shaken.

The Indians would say it was a sign. Boothe had no doubt they would be right. But a sign of what?

He did not rest easy that night, or for many nights to come.

Chapter One

To travelers heading west from Missouri, the Flint Hills were always a surprise. They rose out of the plains, some as high as three hundred feet, flat-topped and green, wooded with oak, slippery elm, cottonwood, hackberry, walnut, and sycamore. Creeks and rivers cut through the sheltered bottom lands and secluded valleys. The meadows, the true *prairie* that the French explorers had named, were lush and thick with grasses and wildflowers; not the short grass of the western plains, but the tall bluestem grass of eastern Kansas that could reach five, six, and even seven feet tall.

The Flint Hills cut a swath through the plains of Kansas Territory north to south two hundred miles long and twenty to eighty miles wide. They took their name from the nodules of flint embedded in the limestone that was their foundation. Limestone formations thrust out the green and gave sanctuary

4

to ground squirrels, fox, and rabbit. Otters swam in the clear streams; deer and elk roamed the valleys.

By 1843, few white men had made their homes in the hills even though the two most important trails west crossed them—the Santa Fe to the south, the Oregon to the north and west. Some people thought the thin top soil of the hills wasn't rich enough to be farmed; others decided it was foolish to plow land riddled with outcroppings of limestone rock; but most who passed through were simply on their way somewhere else—to the rich trading center of Santa Fe in Mexico or to Oregon, the promised land. The hills were only of passing interest.

Ben and Kitty Adamson were the exception. Traveling through with a small caravan of missionaries headed for Pawnee country in 1837, Kitty had fallen in love with the rugged hills. When she and Ben married, she chose to make her home nowhere else, and the Adamsons became one of the first white families to receive permission to settle in the hills.

Ben and Kitty had seen the possibilities others had ignored. The crossroads of two important trails meant the Indian territory would not stay empty of settlers forever. And while the rocky soil was not suitable for large acreage crops, it was rich and arable in small patches, and a man could feed his family from it if he wasn't afraid to break a sweat.

The Adamsons had immediately seen that westward-bound travelers, as well as settlers who were lured into the hills by the abundant game and rich bottoms, would all need one thing: horses. Kitty's skill with the animals was renowned, and when the time came she expected to supply the entire territory with her own sturdy stock. In the meantime she and Ben made a steady living for themselves and their two children by trading for horses with the Cheyenne and selling them to the army. More important, they had made a home.

On a late May afternoon, Kitty Kincaid Adamson brought her little pony Snow to a halt and rose up in the stirrups. The bluestem was so high where she and the horse had stopped that only by standing could she see over the grass. She was gazing east, and her expression was troubled. Perhaps what troubled her most was that she did not know what she was looking for.

She rode astride, her faded blue skirt trailing down the flanks of the little horse. Her face was shaded by a round-brimmed grass hat that she had woven herself using a technique taught her by a Cheyenne woman, and it was tied onto her head with a strip of braided rawhide. Her freckled, sun-browned face testified to the fact that the hat did not often stay atop her head, despite the rawhide tie.

She stood for a moment, her eyes narrowed in the sun, searching the landscape. As far as she could see there was emptiness—rocky hills, trees just beginning to come into spring bloom, multicolored grasses stirred only by the passage of some small animal or an errant breeze. Once the emptiness of this place, the vastness of it, had threatened to overwhelm her, and she had felt lost within it. But over the years the rugged, undulating landscape had become familiar and the emptiness became a friend. Still, she wondered how many more years it would take before she learned to look over the landscape without expecting, or even hoping, to see another human being somewhere upon it.

Abruptly, her frown sharpened into one of pure irritation, and she resumed the saddle again, jerking the reins. This was more than ordinary foolishness. No one was there, no one was coming. She was a grown woman and far too busy to listen to the fantasies of her little sister. She gave the pony a light kick and headed back toward the farm.

Snow was an Indian pony, solid white, given to Kitty by her foster mother, a Shawnee woman, six years ago. The little horse had served her well over the years and knew his way unerringly back to the stable. Snow picked his way confidently out of the tall grass, across a carpet of bright wildflowers, and along a stream.

Near the source of the stream, a spring that bubbled out of the limestone, stood the Adamson farm. It topped a small rise above the valley and the meadow, sheltered in a stand of cottonwood that kept the house and outbuildings cool in the summer but admitted the sun's warming rays in the winter.

Kitty had wanted a stone house, one solidly carved from the limestone that was nature's gift to the hills, but even she realized that without a stone mason such an undertaking could consume a lifetime. Skilled craftsmen were not to be found so far away from civilization, and when she and Ben settled, their closest neighbors of any kind were the soldiers at Fort Leavenworth, some four days' ride away.

Together, she and Ben and their hired hand had felled and stripped the trees for their log cabin, using their pack mules to drag the tree lengths out of the woods to the cleared homesite. They had leveled the logs by sight and set them on a dirt foundation, with the result that the little cabin leaned in several places and was constantly losing big chunks of its mud chinking. The mud chinking was also a perpetual invitation to bees and hornets, which liked to drill into the walls and make their nests, and every spring Kitty took several days to smoke out the bees and rechink the walls.

The first chimney they built had been of the stick-and-mud variety, which used creek rocks and mud mortar up past the firebox, then wooden slats and thick clay the rest of the way. It was quick and economical and got them through the winter, but it drew so badly that the slightest breath of wind filled the cabin with smoke that was often so thick it drove them from the cabin out into the cold. Kitty was almost relieved when it caught fire and was destroyed—along with a good portion of the roof— down to the mortar.

The next chimney they built was more ambitious, using fieldstones all the way up, and thick lime clay mixed with grass chaff and animal hair to make it set up harder. This one drew much better and lasted almost two months, until a hard rain loosened the foundation. Kitty and Ben were awakened one night by an enormous crash and ran into the main room to find a gaping hole in the rear wall, the chimney lying scattered on the ground behind the house.

Building, like so many other things on the frontier, was a matter of trial and error for the young couple. Kitty had not completely given up her dream of a stone house and a barn to match, but for now she was satisfied with a straight tall chimney that drew deep and didn't leak smoke through the chinking, with a roof made of split-oak shingles that kept out the weather, and with a strong storm cellar lined with stone.

Both Kitty and Ben had seen what a cyclone was like on the plains, and had begun digging the cellar before their first summer was done. It had been Ben's idea to line it with the flat limestone he dragged from the bottomlands, which not only reinforced the dirt walls and floor and made the cellar more secure, but also kept it cooler in the summertime, providing a convenient place for Kitty to store her preserves and cheese. Once or twice fierce storms had blown through the hills, uprooting trees and knocking over fences, and they all had been grateful for the cellar in which they could take refuge.

The most recent additions to the cabin were a small front porch with a sloping roof, and at the rear of the house a small stoop of a back porch. Most of the windows were covered with oilskin so highly polished it was very nearly translucent and fitted with shutters that could be tightly closed against inclement weather. But two of the windows had panes of real glass that Ben had obtained in sharp trading when his path crossed a wagon train headed down the Santa Fe Trail. Ben managed to get the glass, a looking glass for Kitty, and a small volume of poems for the price of a spotted Indian pony. The horse had been a favorite of Kitty's, but the gifts Ben presented to her made her forget the loss of the animal. Sometimes she had to be reminded they were in the business of trading horses for profit.

Like her mother and her mother's mother before her, Kitty planted flowers near the front porch. Mostly they were native flowers that she transplanted from the meadows and the woods. She knew the names of some of them—yellow-centered asters and daisies, downy purple ironweed, pale pink verbena, and white and purple phlox. The others were a mystery to her with their lavender and blue flowers and delicate scents that hung on the summer air. Her little sister Sarah had brought seeds from Illinois when she had come to stay last year, and Kitty hoped to grow some of the flowers she remembered from her childhood around her own front door.

Like all farm families, the Adamsons had a kitchen garden near the house where they grew pumpkins, sweet potatoes, carrots, cabbage, beans, and peas. Billy Threefingers, their hired hand, tended the corn, which was in a larger patch that he and Ben had cleared among the trees behind the barn. The husks were used for fodder for the livestock in the winter if the grass was scarce, and the ears were enjoyed by humans and animals alike.

The barn was made of oak, sturdy and strong, and the corrals were of split rail, laboriously erected by Kitty and Ben with the help of Billy Threefingers. There was a springhouse, clumsily made of stone and not pretty to look at, but thick enough to keep milk and butter cool on even the hottest days.

The homestead was not grand or even very big, but already Kitty had more than her mother had had at her age, and her needs were simple. As long as her children and her animals were sheltered and well fed, Kitty rarely took time to wish for more.

Kitty swung down from Snow and in a few deft movements divested him of saddle and bridle and turned him out into the corral. She returned his tack to the barn, then crossed the yard to her husband, who was loading the wagon for their trip tomorrow.

In the morning the family would depart for their semiannual trading rendezvous with the Cheyenne. Usually Kitty's spirits were high before such an expedition, her anticipation strong. The uneasiness she felt now annoyed her because it was totally unfounded and because it threatened to spoil one of the highlights of her year.

Ben looked up from his work as she approached, and smiled sympathetically when she came close enough for him to see her expression.

"Nothing, huh?"

Kitty gave an impatient shake of her head and pulled off the grass hat. Her blonde hair spilled untidily from beneath it, a tangled braid that gleamed golden in the afternoon sun. "Of course not. That Sarah, what an imagination. Why do I listen to her, anyway?"

Ben carefully wedged white blankets, which the Cheyenne coveted, around jugs of New Orleans molasses. Kitty hoisted herself onto a spoke of the wagon wheel and leaned over the side to help him.

"That's what I've been wondering," Ben said. "That letter from your ma is over three weeks old. What makes you womenfolk think young Jim will come riding up just as soon as we leave the house is beyond me. It could be months before he gets here, and probably will be." He shot her a grin. "You know how those Kincaid men are, wandering feet, every last one of them. Jim's liable to see something that strikes his fancy and take off in another direction altogether. Myself, I'm not going to start looking for him 'til the snow flies, earliest."

But Kitty was not coaxed by his grin, and her eyes were still shadowed as she looked toward the horizon. "I know," she admitted. "It is foolish. But Sarah is so sure, and . . . there's something between them, Ben, that's hard to explain. I love my brother—I love all my brothers and sisters—but there's a bond between Sarah and Jim that's different from anything the rest of us have. Sarah's always been able to—well, *know* things, and if she's worried about Jim, I reckon it's with good cause."

"Or," suggested Ben gently, "it could be she's just lonesome for her brother and wishing him here."

Kitty's eyes returned to Ben's, and after a moment she smiled. "You're probably right. It hasn't been easy for her since she came out here, and she does have a mighty big imagination." She shrugged. "Besides, if Jim does show up while we're gone I wager he'll have sense enough to sit and wait a spell for us to get back, after riding all this way."

"It's not like the place'll be deserted. Billy will be here."

Kitty cheered. "That's right, he will. And he can use all the help he can get with the rest of us away."

Slowly she allowed the tension to leave her shoulders and the familiar anticipation for the adventure ahead to warm her with its glow. She had missed the autumn expedition because Carrie, her last born, had been too young to travel. Ben and Billy had gone without her, and it wasn't mere sour grapes that caused her to observe that they had made some very poor bargains, too. But now she was back, doing what she loved best, and on this trip she would make up for losses they had sustained last autumn.

Reading her thoughts, Ben reached across the short distance and squeezed her hand briefly. "You're glad to be on the move again, aren't you?"

Kitty smiled. "I remember my mama always said God had planted her feet right there on the banks of the Ohio and nothing was ever going to move them. But I guess I'm more like Pa, or Uncle Boothe. Even though I'm only an adopted Kincaid, I've got the wanderlust too, and there's nothing I like better than to be going somewhere."

"Well, I can't complain about that." Ben turned to pick up a stack of buffalo hides, and Kitty helped him spread them over the trade goods in the wagon. "If you hadn't been so all-fired set on traipsing after me and Boothe when we set out for the Platte, I might not have ever found myself a wife."

"You might not have *made* it to the Platte if it hadn't been for me," Kitty retorted, and just in time she saw the twinkle in her husband's eyes.

Together they finished securing the hides over the wagonload. Tomorrow, before they left, Ben would load the bags of rice, cornmeal, and dried corn. The spring trade was always weighted on their side because the Cheyenne were anxious for the goods they had done without during the winter; nonetheless, Ben made sure to offer them only the best and in fair quantity. He was well aware that their own existence here was dependent as much on the Indians as it was on the fort, and only by dealing fairly with both sides could he guarantee a long-term relationship.

Kitty inquired softly, "Are you ever sorry, Ben Adamson?"

And Ben replied without hesitation, "Never, Mrs. Adamson."

They shared a smile and a quiet moment at the end of the day. Then Kitty sprang down from the wagon wheel and together they started toward the house for supper.

But she couldn't resist one last look over her shoulder, toward the empty horizon.

Jim Kincaid hadn't eaten anything but corn pone and hard jerky since he'd left Cairo, Illinois—or at least that was how it seemed to him. His diet had been supplemented on occasion by rabbit, muskrat, or prairie hen, sometimes accompanied by a handful of wild onions or Indian potatoes, but such feasts were few and far between. The truth was, a man who spent all his time hunting didn't have much left over for traveling, and as far as Jim was concerned there was far too much to see in this world to waste any time at all.

But his supplies were running low, and so was his taste for jerked beef. The buck he had pinned in his sites made his mouth water.

Jim had turned seventeen years old the day the snow melted on the front steps of his ma's house late that March. The restlessness had been building all winter—longer than that, really. There were times when he thought if he didn't get out and do something—anything—he'd explode.

He was a man surrounded by women and children, and that was part of it. It wasn't that he didn't love his brothers and sisters, and his ma was the finest woman he'd ever known. God knew there was plenty to be done on the farm, what with fences to mend and crops to lay by and little ones to keep from falling in the fire, and he knew he was needed. But Jim's father, Byrd Kincaid, was one of the first men to head across the great Missouri into the wilderness beyond; his uncle, Boothe Carlyle, had mapped the Great Divide with John C. Fremont and Kit Carson. Jim Kincaid was not cut out to be a farmer.

And so on that day that the snow melted off the front steps he stood outside, looking toward the river, and he was not thinking about the plowing that needed to be done or the barn roof that needed patching, or the trade goods he'd be bartering for at Sherrod's store. When he looked around, his ma was coming toward him, leading their best chestnut, and she had his rifle in her hand.

She handed him the reins and the rifle. Her eyes were narrowed toward the sun, and she didn't look at him directly. Jim was grateful for that, because if there were tears in her eyes he didn't want to see them. She said, "It's time, I reckon."

She said it quiet and steady-like, but that was his ma. She wasn't one for letting on to what she was feeling, especially when those feelings might hurt somebody she loved.

But Jim's throat was husky as he answered, "I reckon."

"One of these days I'm going to raise a child that'll see fit to stay home and take care of his ma, like children ought to do."

And Jim smiled. "No, Ma, you ain't. We're Kincaids, ever' last one of us, and the only way to make us stay put is to nail our feet to the ground."

She smiled back. "I don't even think that'd do any good."

Then she reached into her apron pocket and took something out. Jim's throat tightened when he saw what it was. She said, "You are my oldest son, Jim Kincaid. I wish your pa was here today, or your Uncle Boothe. They'd both be proud of the man you're growing up to be."

She lifted her arms, and Jim's throat seemed to close up entirely as she dropped the pendant over his head. He was a tall boy, and she had to stand on tiptoe to kiss his cheek.

"Go with God," she said softly.

The pendant was an iron cross surrounded by a circlet of bronze, and it was old, ancient. Jim had heard his mother speculate it might even have come from a time before Christ, but he found it hard to imagine anything that old. He knew that it had been in his mother's family since before memory, passed down from father to son, son to daughter, mother to daughter, for as long as the Carlyles had been a family. It had gone from Ireland to Ulster, when the Carlyles were exiled to Scotland. It had crossed the ocean to the New World, traveled this big country and come back again. Stirring tales of heroism were built around it. Lives had been saved because of it.

Almost thirty years ago, when the country was new and the land was wild, Jim's great-grandmother Fiona Carlyle had sent his Uncle Boothe across the Blue Ridge Mountains with the ancient talisman around his neck and those very words to guide him. Boothe Carlyle had become a legend in his own time.

Now Jim was entrusted with the talisman, and the footsteps of those who had gone before stretched long and wide in front of him. The pendant was heavy around his neck.

Jim's hand closed around the iron cross and for the longest time he couldn't speak; he couldn't even move.

Katherine Kincaid said, "You stop off and see your sisters, you hear? Kitty'll be hungry for news, and you'll need a change of horses."

He nodded mutely, still holding the cross.

"And Sarah—I worry about her. You check on her for me, won't you?"

"You know I'll take care of Sarah, Ma."

Her expression gentled. "Yes. I know."

For a long time they looked at each other, and it hurt Jim, even frightened him a little, to think he might never see this woman again.

Katherine turned away abruptly, but not before Jim saw the glint of tears in her eyes. Her voice was gruff. "Go on, now. Get."

Jim had mounted the chestnut and ridden west.

That had been over a month ago, and he had never looked back, or even thought about it. Sometimes he got homesick, sometimes he got hungry, but the world was waiting for him, and he was impatient to find his place in it.

It was twilight, and the big buck—an eight-pointer—had come to the stream to drink. Jim was upwind of it ten or twenty yards, but his line of vision was partially obscured by the wooded landscape that separated him from his quarry. He dared not move for fear of alerting the buck. He waited patiently for the animal to shift its position—a fraction was all it would take—and give him a clear shot.

Both his pa and his Uncle Boothe would've had his hide if they had caught him drawing bead on a buck that size with nobody but himself to feed and no intention of spending the time it would take to smoke and pack the extra meat. Leave it to them and they would've cured the skin for a shirt, scraped out the rack for powder horns and stretched the bladder into a canteen—all right there before breaking camp. But his pa was dead and his Uncle Boothe was far away. These woods were full of deer, and Jim was hungry.

The buck looked up, seeming to sniff something on the wind. The movement gave Jim the clearing he needed and he squeezed the trigger. Jim Kincaid was the best shot in the county where he came from. The buck fell.

Jim didn't even wait for the smoke to clear. He let out a yell of self-congratulatory triumph and started down the hill toward the stream.

He took the stream in one bounding step and dropped down on one knee beside the carcass, pulling his knife out of the scabbard on his thigh. He felt the shadow fall across him in the same moment he noticed the feather-tipped arrow protruding from the buck's neck. The whole world went still around him.

His rifle was on the ground near his foot, not even an arm's length away. But it didn't matter. He hadn't reloaded after he'd fired; a foolish mistake that no man with real wilderness experience would have made. Now it was starting to look as though that mistake might be his last.

He lifted his eyes slowly. The Indian wore moccasins and buckskin leggings. His breechcloth was made of deerskin, too, and his torso, naked and hairless, was streaked with blue and red paint and draped with a multitude of feathered charms and amulets, metal chains and stone decorations. His face was brightly painted, too, and his head was shaved except for one sharp peculiar tuft at the very top, the greased distinctive scalp lock.

He was a Pawnee. And he had his bow drawn back, arrow aimed for Jim's throat.

A great many thoughts raced through Jim's head at that moment. *Pawnee.* There was no mistaking it. The fiercest of the fighting tribes, more apt to wage war on each other than the white man but possessing no scruples about flaying a man alive just for the sport of it if the mood struck them, or so Jim had heard. But there shouldn't be any Pawnee this far east. How deep was he into Indian territory anyway? Jesus God, why hadn't he paid attention at that last trading post, why hadn't he been more careful . . . Because if this Indian wasn't part of a tribe, he was a renegade, and Jim was now living out his last few minutes on this earth. And what were the chances of his bullet and a Pawnee arrow striking the same deer at the same time? Rapid thoughts, senseless thoughts really, just something to occupy his mind while he prepared to die.

He had really counted on seeing his sister Sarah one last time.

And then the Indian said something in harsh, rapid Pawnee. The sound was startling, unexpected, and it frightened Jim so badly that he froze in place, not flinching a muscle or changing his expression. That was probably the luckiest thing that could have happened to him.

He thought the Indian was speaking to him, issuing a command Jim had no way of understanding or obeying. At that moment three other braves appeared from the underbrush, all of them with bows. They moved toward him.

But only the scowling brave who stood over him had his bow drawn, and suddenly Jim understood. It was a hunting party. The three Indians approaching were less interested in him than in the deer, and the drawn bow was only meant to guard the kill.

Two of the braves grasped the deer and swung it between them. The third swept up Jim's rifle, and shared a grin with his comrades over the prize. And then they were all grinning, even the big one with the drawn bow, laughing at the boy on the ground. Jim felt a cry of outrage rising in his throat as they moved away, still grinning, his supper swinging between them. But the bow was still drawn and the big one kept his aim true, walking backwards to the cover of the woods. Then he turned and disappeared.

Even then it was a moment before Jim could lurch to his feet, his heart pounding so hard it felt like it was shaking his whole body, and shout, "Hey!" But even indignation was swallowed by the thundering of his heart and what should have been an angry cry instead sounded hoarse and querulous.

He stood there for a time, breathing hard, letting the sweat of fear dry in his shirt and hair. In the distance he heard the sound of retreating hoofbeats. *Indians,* he thought, and the word seemed to echo through his soul with a kind of awestruck wonder, tinged more than a little with the residue of fear. He had survived an encounter with Indians.

Stories of such encounters were legion in his family. His grandpa Hugh, struck down in an Indian uprising. His mother, bargaining with the Shawnee for the lives of a band of women and children in the wilderness. His father, Byrd Kincaid, held prisoner by them, and his sister Kitty wet-nursed by a Shawnee woman. His Uncle Boothe, friend to many tribes and worshiped by some. His sister Kitty again, leading the renegade Shawnee in an attack upon white men who would have murdered the ones she loved.

And now Jim Kincaid, adventurer, explorer, trail blazer . . . robbed of his supper and his gun by a bunch of laughing Pawnee. That was one for the campfire, wasn't it?

It was then that he looked down and saw the knife still gripped in his hand, and a wave of incredulity and self-disgust swept over him. It had been there all the time. All the time he'd sat there with a weapon in his hand and hadn't once thought to defend what was his. No wonder they'd laughed.

With a grimace of contempt he threw the knife, hard, piercing the ground ten feet away. He wanted to swear, he wanted to cuss up a blue streak, but his ma had never allowed cussing in the house and he didn't know any words suitable for the occasion. So he dragged at his hair in frustration, kicked the ground, spat, and at last strode over to pick up the knife and started back up the hill toward his horse.

Later, after he'd choked down another supper of dry corn pone and coffee, he started to think about how much trouble he might really be in. He had always fancied himself a woodsman, like his pa, and though that great man had died long before Jim was ready for him to, he had grown up in that legacy, followed in those footsteps. He'd been the man of the house for over six years now and that meant something. He was ready to strike out on his own, find his own way, break the trails that others would follow just as his pa had and his Uncle Boothe and both their pas before them.

But here he was, miles from he knew-not-where, hungry, cold, and alone. Tomorrow would see the last of his coffee, and the bottom of his provisions sack didn't hold anything but a few dried jerky strips and half a handful of meal. He didn't have a gun. A man couldn't hunt without a gun. And if the Pawnee came back he'd be easy pickings.

He wondered how far he was from Fort Leavenworth. He wondered how many hunting parties, scouting parties, or war parties he might expect to run into before he reached it, and how far off course he'd have to wander before he was in the heart of Indian territory.

His sister Kitty's homestead was only a couple of days away from the fort. Surely he couldn't be more than a week away. He'd make do 'til then somehow. It would be good to see family again, though. And Sarah. He spent some time picturing in his mind how he'd tell her the story of the Pawnee to make her laugh, and that made him feel a little less lonely for a while. But he did miss her. He surely did.

The sky had never seemed so big, the dark had never seemed so thick. The iron cross felt heavy around his neck. Jim Kincaid leaned back against a tree and tried to get comfortable, but it was a long time before he slept.

Chapter Two

Dearest girls,

Once again I send one of my children west, this time my firstborn son. I knew the day would come, but foolishly hoped it might not be so soon. But he's too much like his father, my Jim, and nobody will ever be able to tie a rope on him. He should reach your part of the country by summer, Kitty, and will be looking for a resting place. He's a good boy and will be a help to you on the farm. We miss him already.

All is well here. River flooded and the snakes are bad. Expect a good crop. Sarah, mind your sister and read your Bible. Give my love to the little ones and to Jim when he arrives. Remember who you are and that your mother loves you.

Katherine Carlyle Kincaid

The letter had arrived less than a week ago, brought by one of the soldiers at the fort. Sarah Kincaid had memorized not only the words but every curve and line of her mother's thin, spidery handwriting. Sometimes when she held the sheet of paper close to her face she thought she could smell home.

When she left Cairo last year to attend the birth of Kitty's second baby, it had seemed like such an adventure. At age fourteen she felt she had already outgrown the small backriver village of Cairo; as the oldest daughter left at home it was only natural that she should be the one to go to help her sister when Kitty wrote she was expecting again. She had felt so grown up and important, setting out for life on the frontier.

But the frontier was a horrible place, and now all she wanted was to leave it as far behind as she possibly could. Now, like an answer to a prayer, Jim was coming. Jim would take her away from here. He would take her home if she asked him . . . and if he could.

Very carefully she refolded the letter that was already so creased and soft from its many readings that it threatened to fall apart at the touch, and replaced it in her small wooden keepsake box. "Should be in your part of the country by summer . . ." It wasn't summer yet, but Jim was close, she could feel it. Close and—this was what Sarah had difficulty understanding, or even admitting—in some kind of trouble.

Sometimes she knew things that she had no way of knowing, felt things that didn't make sense, but always those feelings turned out to be right, especially where Jim was concerned. And she knew, as clearly as if someone had written it on a slate, that if they left tomorrow as Kitty was so insistent they do, Jim would come while they were gone. Jim would come, and he would need them, and they wouldn't be here.

The plaintive cry of a baby dragged her attention back to matters at hand, and she peered over the railing of the small sleeping loft that was her only private space. Baby Carrie was awakening from her nap in the cradle beneath the window, already scrunching herself up to pull up on the sides. Carrie was just learning to stand and had already taken two tumbles out of the cradle. Sarah caught up her skirts in one hand and hurried down the loft ladder to prevent another accident. She was halfway down when three-year-old Hilda came toddling out of her parents' room where she had been napping on a pallet, rubbing her eyes and whining that she was hungry. Sarah's brief respite was over.

Kitty's and Ben's cabin was smaller than the one in which Sarah had grown up, though it wasn't quite as crowded. There was a big stone fireplace that dominated one end of the room that served as kitchen and living area. Ben and Billy, the half-breed who worked for him, had made the furniture out of oak and walnut. Some of it was rough hewn and ragged; other pieces, which the men had worked on during the winter months when the cold kept them inside a good part of the time, had a more finished look. There was a long rectangular table with six stools pulled up under it, and a corner cupboard for storage.

There were two big chairs that Sarah, in her spare time since coming here, had outfitted with straw-stuffed calico cushions. Kitty didn't care much for such niceties and in fact had seemed surprised when Sarah once asked her why there were no curtains on the windows. She simply hadn't thought of hanging any. The windows, even the oilcloth ones, were now decorated with muslin curtains made out of old petticoats that Sarah had sewn with her own hands. Sarah had also made it her responsibility to keep the mantelpiece supplied with fresh flowers and the tabletops and stools free of dust. Kitty wasn't much of a housekeeper, and, though she was a loving mother, she seemed to prefer spending her time out of doors with her horses rather than inside with her children.

"Poor baby!" Sarah scooped Carrie up just as she pulled up to her knees, her weight tilting the cradle at a precarious angle. "You want your supper, don't you? Well, me too."

Sarah looked around in disgust at the empty cookpot hanging beside the nearly dead ashes of the fire. Well, *she* wasn't getting supper, not again. Even if it meant eating seconds on that awful Kansa soup the crazy half-breed Billy kept going on his own outdoor cookfire all the time. It was a bland-tasting concoction of dried buffalo meat, boiled corn, whatever beans he could find, and a dribbling of bacon grease all simmered together in a pot of water. It was always hot and filling, and Kitty claimed that if the Kansa Indians had survived on it for years it must be good for a body. But Kitty didn't seem to care much what she put in her mouth—or on her family's plates, for that matter. Sarah's preferences were a bit more refined.

"Hungwy, hungwy!" wailed Hilda, also stretching out her arms to be picked up.

"All right, Hilda, but I can't pick you up now."

The thought of Billy's soup sent Sarah to the cupboard in search of something to pacify her own stomach as well as keep the children quiet. The baby snuffled in her ear. Hilda dragged at her skirts. Through the glass window she could see Kitty and Ben crossing the yard arm in arm, and Kitty did *not* look as though she was thinking about supper. Two big brindle dogs of no known breed danced and barked around them as though welcoming them home from a cross-continent journey. Dogs, Sarah decided with a downward twist of her lips, were second only to horses in stupidity.

But as much as she hated the frontier, the Flint Hills, horses, Indians, and her sister's careless house-keeping, Sarah did love the children and she'd miss them when she left. "You'll miss me too, won't you sweetheart?" she crooned to Hilda, kneeling down with the baby on her hip to search the bottom shelf of the cupboard. "Won't you miss your Aunt Sarah?"

She found a jar of dried apples and pried off the cork lid, scooping out a handful. She gave a slice of apple to Hilda, who examined it querulously before testing it with her teeth. "I'd bake you some tea cakes if I had butter. At least in Cairo I could get butter," Sarah grumbled.

She tossed a couple of apple slices into her own mouth and chewed quickly as Ben and Kitty came in, accompanied by the chaos of the two big dogs and, not far behind, Billy Threefingers with a load of firewood.

"Mama, Mama," wailed Hilda, running toward her mother with sticky fingers and crocodile tears. "Hungwy!" The apple slice was trampled under foot.

Kitty picked her daughter up absently, glancing around. "Didn't you make any bread?" she asked Sarah. "I thought I asked you to make some bread."

It was entirely possible that she had. The one good thing about Kitty was that she paid so little attention to domestic details she was as unlikely to remember what she had told Sarah as Sarah was.

"There's nothing for supper," Sarah announced.

Hilda stretched out her arms for her father, and Kitty gratefully passed the child to Ben. Baby Carrie started whimpering again, and Sarah jostled her soothingly as she continued to search the cupboard.

"We'll make some fried pies," Kitty said, pushing up her sleeves. "We'll enjoy them on the trip. I remember the first time I left home, Mama sent us off with a stack of fried apple pies and they tasted mighty good between Cairo and Westport, didn't they Ben?"

She was bustling and full of energy as she opened the flour barrel and reached for the molasses. Sarah felt her spirits sink, just watching her.

"A little bit of home," Ben agreed. He sat in one of the big chairs by the fireplace, bouncing Hilda on his knee. She was laughing now, fat tears still clinging to her rosy cheeks.

Billy dumped the firewood on the hearth and Kitty said, "We'll fry up some bacon, too, if you didn't pack the last of it, and maybe Billy has some stew going?"

"Yes'm, just like always. You want I should bring it in?"

Kitty smiled at him benevolently. "That'd be a big help, Billy."

They'd met him five years earlier, in 1838, at the Fort. Kitty and Ben, six months married, and not wanting to return back east to family in Cairo, Illinois, were attempting to make their case with the commanding officer of Leavenworth that they should be given permission to settle in the Flint Hills in Kansas Territory.

To the army, it was still Indian territory and for that reason not open to white settlers, but Kitty and Ben knew there were settlers in the territory already; they'd seen them. In fact, many lived on the Kansas side of the Missouri River within sight of the fort and supplied the soldiers with milk, cheese, bread, meat, and vegetables. They were called squatters and, it seemed, were allowed because it was convenient for the soldiers.

As for the threat of Indians, the chief tribes between the Flint Hills and the fort had been dealt with and pacified. Treaties allowed the passage of travelers along the Santa Fe and Oregon trails, and the Indians who'd either been bought off by the government or frightened by the presence of the soldiers at the fort were no danger. The United States government was negotiating with the Kansa for two million acres of their land, which meant that soon settlers would be pouring across the Missouri. The Kansa, who'd been trading with white men since 1800, were not known for being bloodthirsty. The Osage had been paid off by the government to let the Santa Fe trail pass peacefully through their land, and the Pawnee, farther out on the plains, were more interested in fighting with the Sioux and the Cheyenne than taking on the dragoons at Fort Leavenworth.

Kitty and Ben argued with Colonel Stephen Kearney of the First Dragoons that it would be of great benefit for the soldiers if they had a ready supply of horses, fast Indian horses that could run like the wind all day and were used to the rigors of travel on the plains and in the mountains. Kearney was interested but skeptical, but still willing to strike a bargain. If the Adamsons could bring in a string of good horses that passed the quartermaster's muster, he'd be persuaded to give them permission to settle on a temporary basis in the hills.

Kitty and Ben had only to find a way to get the horses. Their first thought was to trade with the Pawnee, perhaps making contact with the Indians through the Presbyterian mission where Ben had once hoped to serve. They knew some of the missionaries there who might be willing to help, but still they needed an interpreter and that led them to Billy Threefingers, who occasionally appeared at the fort and hung around the stables helping with the horses. He was said to have an extraordinary way with animals, and when a horse came up lame or off his feed, Abe Moore, the sergeant who was in charge of the animals, looked for Billy.

It was serendipity that led Kitty and Ben to Billy. When Kitty and Ben went to inspect the horses of the First Dragoons, Sergeant Moore said Billy had shown up the night before and was somewhere around the fort. Ben and Kitty waited for two hours until he reappeared. He was in his late thirties or early forties; it was hard to tell, and Billy, if he knew his age, never revealed it. He told Kitty the first time she met him that he was the son of a Pawnee woman and a French missionary. He had a French name, but liked to be called Billy, and he'd added the Threefingers part himself because of an accident to his left hand with an ax.

Later, over the years, Billy's stories changed. Sometimes his mother had been a Kansa and his father a member of the Lewis and Clark expedition that had passed through the territory in 1804. Sometimes he said his mother was an Osage and his father a white trader on the way to Santa Fe. No one really knew.

Billy was tall and thin, with weathered coppery skin and pale gray eyes. He wore moccasins, leggings of animal skin, a faded army shirt, and a rusty-looking army jacket, buttons missing and the chevrons removed. His hat was leather, broadbrimmed, and shielded his face from the wind, rain, and sun. His black hair fell in two plaits below his shoulders. Billy walked with a swagger that gave him an air of ferocity that was completely at odds with his gentle nature.

Billy had assured them that he could trade with

the Pawnee if they had a mind to do business, but the
Pawnee would rather fight other tribes than trade.
The Cheyenne had the best horses, beautiful animals
from Texas and Mexico, traded from their allies the
Kiowa and the Comanche. Billy knew all about trading with the Cheyenne. He swore his grandmother
had been a Cheyenne and he knew some of the
language. He knew where the Southern Cheyenne
would be camped; he knew when they'd have their
horses from trade. All they needed in exchange were
trade goods and those Billy would leave to Ben and
Kitty to come up with.

The young couple stayed up all night, sitting at
their campfire outside the fort. Ben prayed a great
deal; Kitty thought about the past and worried about
the future. Was this what she was meant to do? Was
this where she was meant to be? Her own parents—
her birth parents—had left Germany in 1820 to make
the long journey to America. They had died in the
wilderness as they went west, and Kitty had been
reared as a Kincaid by Katherine and Byrd Kincaid.
She had been wounded by a Shawnee arrow when
she was still in the womb and bore the scar like a
birthmark on her shoulder to this day.

Kitty had left home when she was seventeen in
search of her own freedom, her own life. She had
found it here in the Flint Hills. She didn't want to
turn back.

She felt the round hard edge of the gold coin
in her pocket and wished she had Ben's faith to
pray for an answer. Katherine had gotten nine such
coins from her grandmother Fiona back in Kentucky.
They'd been brought by Fiona's family from Scotland and had strange markings on them that no one
could read, but they were real gold and people had
died because of them. Each time a child left home,

Katherine pressed a gold coin into his hand and Kitty, though not born of Carlyle blood, had gotten her own coin. It was a link to the only family she had ever known. Could she give up her coin?

Dawn broke slowly across the Missouri River, glazing the water with strokes of silver and peach. Kitty had made her decision. She shook Ben, who'd fallen asleep only an hour before.

"We're going to Weston with Billy today. We're going to buy a wagon and trade goods. We have enough gold for that and more. We're going to use the coin that Mama gave me."

Kitty had never regretted that decision.

Billy Threefingers had guided them through their first trading expedition with the Southern Cheyenne. On the strength of their success, Kearney had granted them permission to set up their farm in the Flint Hills. It seemed only natural that Billy would go with them, help build their log house, and remain to work on the farm, accompanying them on trading forays and breaking and training the horses on their return. Kitty and Ben paid him what they considered a fair wage, but Billy seemed uninterested in the money. He and Ben built a one-room cabin near the barn where Billy slept and kept his few belongings.

He showed no interest in leaving the Adamson farm and they were content to let him stay. Kitty knew very well that without Billy she and Ben couldn't have lasted in the Flint Hills.

Sarah filled a big bowl with water and dumped the apple slices in to soak. Carrie started to squeal and kick to be let down, and nervous unhappiness made Sarah snap at her. "Oh, all right! See if I care if you get stepped on!"

She set the baby soundly on the floor, but Kitty's

youngest was of such a generally cheerful temperament she didn't even notice the rebuff. She crawled off happily toward one of the dogs.

Kitty looked at her sister, surprised. "What's got under your hide?"

"Well, if you think it's any fun minding those two all day—and that's with a roof over my head! What's it going to be like on the trail? Let me stay here, Kitty," she pleaded. "The girls are too young to be traveling that far, and you know I'll take good care of them here—"

Kitty was already shaking her head, one fist immersed in piecrust dough up to the elbow. It was a familiar argument.

"We'll be all right by ourselves," Sarah insisted. "And we won't even *be* by ourselves! That Indian will be here—"

"Billy," Kitty said sternly, and for a moment her eyes flashed a cool warning. "His name is Billy."

Ben spoke up from the hearth, where he was spinning a wooden top for Hilda. "We've been through this, Sarah. You're not staying behind. We're going to be gone too long. Your sister would worry."

Despite the voice of male authority, Sarah turned back to Kitty. "But I don't *want* to go!" she cried, a little desperately. "Who wants to go see a bunch of dusty old Indians and chase horses and sleep on the ground—"

"They're not 'dusty Indians'," corrected Kitty calmly. "They're Cheyenne, probably the finest horsemen who ever lived, and I'll thank you to remember it's only because of them that we have a roof over our heads and food in the larder."

Sarah knew she had lost the battle. She had lost it days ago. But she was still young enough and stubborn enough to keep protesting. "I don't know why

I have to go. I hate traveling. I won't be any help to you at all—"

"Is that a threat?" Ben put in mildly, and Sarah scowled at him. Sometimes she thought her brother-in-law took her entirely too lightly.

"I *want* you to come," Kitty said, turning the pie-crust out onto the tabletop, which was smeared with flour. "It'll be a real experience for you, and everybody deserves at least one adventure in her life, even a woman." She thought about that for a minute. "*Especially* a woman," she corrected herself.

Ben grinned at his wife from across the room, and Sarah muttered, "I don't want an adventure," as she ladled out a generous dollop of lard into the deep skillet, which she hung on a hook over the fire. But her grumbling lacked any real malice and she knew she was wasting her time. She couldn't argue with Kitty when she put it like that, especially since she knew her sister meant every word.

Kitty put a flour-covered arm around Sarah's shoulders, surprising her with a little squeeze and a smile. "Don't look so gloomy. This'll be something to tell your grandchildren about. And," she added, lowering her voice just a little, in the way sisters have when they're sharing confidences, "we're not going to miss him. He'll wait 'til we get back."

Sarah's throat tightened. Suddenly she loved her sister very much. She wanted to tell her about the bad feelings she had been having about Jim. She wanted to tell her how very important it was for her to be here when he arrived. But just then the dog snapped—irritated, perhaps, at having the hairs of its tail systematically removed by a curious toddler—and Carrie started to cry and everyone rushed forward to investigate with suitable noises of comfort and alarm.

Sarah, having ascertained that Carrie was more scared than hurt, turned to the piecrust her sister had abandoned. The chaos faded into the background as she turned her eyes toward the window and the faint wagon track of a road that faded off into the meadowlands beyond. An involuntary shiver gripped her.

Oh, Mama, she thought. *All I want is to come home . . .*

More than anything in her life, Meg Kincaid O'Hare wished she could go home. She stood over the body of her husband with the carving knife weighing heavy in her hand, and she knew that she had to get out of this place tonight. And that she would never see home again.

The sounds and smells of the riverfront drifted in through the broken window of their room, and with them the raucous noises from the saloon below. Thick and humid and fetid, something slowly rotting in the fog—that was what St. Louis smelled like to Meg. And it sounded even worse.

Caleb O'Hare was not dead, just drunk. But as Meg stood over him feeling the heft of the knife, watching with a kind of fascinated detachment the glint of moonlight on steel, she knew that if she lingered much longer, she would kill him. And that was why she had to leave.

She crossed the room silently on bare feet and, using the point of the knife, pried out the loose wallboard behind the bed. It made a slight squeaking sound, and though she knew Caleb, passed out in the chair across the room, couldn't possibly hear, her muscles froze instinctively, as did her heartbeat, her breathing, even the blood in her veins.

When her body started working again, it was with

a rush that left her dizzy. Thundering heartbeat, explosive breaths, shaking hands. She reached inside behind the wallboard and drew out a silk reticule. It was empty except for a single gold coin. And it could mean the difference between life and death for her.

She went back to her husband and this time didn't hesitate. While her courage was high, and still holding the knife ready in one hand, she dipped the other hand into his pockets. He had for once quit while he was ahead and tonight those pockets contained something besides lint. She dropped the money into her reticule, and he didn't stir.

The reticule was large enough to hold the knife, though the handle protruded. She slipped it inside and tied the bag around her waist by the drawstring. Then she picked up her shoes—a pair of battered cloth slippers twice turned and lined with newspaper at the soles—and left the room. After five years of imprisonment, it was that easy. She just walked out. The simplicity of it, the relief, the overwhelming power of it, struck her all at once and left her so weak she almost stumbled; she had to brace her hand against the wall before she could go on. But she recovered quickly, for recovery was something she had a great deal of practice with. She slipped her shoes on her feet and hurried down the back stairs without looking back.

In 1843 St. Louis was fast becoming the queen of cities; no city in the United States was growing faster. Her location was strategic, at the mouth of the Missouri River, the Big Muddy, where it met the Mississippi. For years the city had been well known to beaver and other fur traders whose pelts were sold in St. Louis to be shipped to the eastern seaboard and then on to Europe. But the coming of the steamboat into St. Louis in 1817 dramatically affected the growth of the city. It was still a center for trade, but it also became an important jumping-off place for westward migration.

The steamboats brought settlers west along with trade goods and luxuries for the new class of wealthy businessmen that had been spawned by the city's recent commercial success. Miles of wharves lined the riverfront, and hundreds of steamboats were docked there. St. Louis made its living from the river, and even the most casual of observers was knowledgeable about the steamboats that clogged the waterfront.

The elegant sidewheelers that dominated the Mississippi were docked side by side with their Missouri River counterparts, the hardworking western riverboats. The big Mississippi sidewheelers were unsuited to traveling the Missouri; they were too wide, too deep of draft, and too unwieldy for the often narrow and turbulent Missouri. The western riverboat was broad with a flat bottom for shallow water and a spoon-shaped bow for climbing over sandbars. Eighty percent of its bulk was above the waterline: passenger decks above cargo decks with the wheelhouse perched on top, giving it its nickname, "wedding cake."

Large warehouses, some wooden, many brick, radiated out from the St. Louis waterfront. Trade goods of all kinds were brought up the Mississippi River from New Orleans and down the Ohio from Pittsburgh and the East. They were stored in warehouses, awaiting transfer to boats going up the Missouri to the newly established settlements like Weston, Bellevue, and Fort Union. In addition to the myriad warehouses and shipping companies in St. Louis, there were banks, hotels, taverns, livery stables, schools, apothecaries, newspaper offices, butcher shops, and fine bakeries. The streets were cobbled and led to residential areas, where two-story houses of red brick overlooked neat parks and garden areas. In 1830 St. Louis had a population of less than five thousand. By 1843 there were over twenty-five thousand citizens in the city.

As in any large bustling city, not all the citizenry was upstanding. There were con men and thieves, prostitutes and villains, who hung around the tavern and the seedy hostelries near the waterfront. Meg feared none of them. She walked down the mist-shrouded pier and heard the occasional catcall or drunken shout from the taverns behind her, felt the lascivious gaze of narrowed eyes following her. She walked with her head up, her steps purposeful. She was free, and she feared no man.

Staying close to the water, she moved as silently as a wisp of the fog that shrouded her toward the shadowed end of the pier. It was quieter here; voices and music were distant and muted by the dampness. The slap of water against hull was audible. She saw what she wanted and slipped toward it. She was as much a part of the shadows as the night itself.

The *Katherine K.* was a stern wheeler tied close to the dock. The name itself seemed an omen to Meg. Surely a boat with her mother's name could only bring good luck. Meg had spent the afternoon watching from her high broken windows as boxes, barrels, and crates were loaded and tied down for the trip upriver. The last consignment had been strapped into place just before sunset, and the *Katherine K.* would leave before dawn. Meg didn't know where the steamboat was bound, and it didn't matter. All that mattered was that it would be away from here.

There was a short, fat man standing by the gangplank, checking his pocketwatch and looking official. Meg hurried up to him. "I'd like to book passage," she said.

"Where to?"

"Upriver?" she asked hesitantly.

"How far?" He was exasperated. "I only got a few minutes, miss. We're pulling out soon."

Meg thrust a handful of money at him. "How far will this take me?"

He counted it quickly. "If you share a cabin, and that's the only space we got left, this should take you to Bellevue."

Bellevue. Beautiful view. "It sounds nice," she said.

"Names can be deceiving. Make up your mind."

"Yes, I want to go."

"Then tell the first mate to put you in a cabin with a lady traveling up to Fort Pierre. Her husband's a trapper with American Fur Company. You don't mind sharing with children, do you?"

"I don't mind anything," Meg answered.

"Luggage?"

"I don't have any." Meg looked him in the eye, daring him to ask questions. The captain's face was lined and wrinkled, his eyes tired.

He looked back at her. "I don't care as long as your money's good. Step aboard."

The first mate was thirty pounds lighter, forty years younger, and a lot more curious than the captain. Meg was tired and nervous, and she found it increasingly difficult to answer his questions—and to remember to lie.

"Name?" the first mate asked.

"Mary . . . Mary Louis." The first lie came easily.

"Going to Bellevue, eh? Right popular place this trip. Guess you're going to meet your husband?"

"That's right. I am." He gave her the answer, and she gratefully took it.

"Most of the time nobody gets off there. We just take on pelts from American Fur, but this trip we got half a dozen traders and their goods aboard. They're gonna head along the Platte and then hit the Oregon Trail. They're planning to stock up tradin' posts along the way. Probably sell to the overlanders, too."

Meg nodded, eager to get to her cabin, but the young man kept on talking.

"I hear there're more than a thousand goin' out along the trail this summer. Fort Laramie and Fort John'll be runnin' out of food and supplies 'fore long. Lotta money to be made; wish I could get a cut of it, but Cap'n Dakins would kill me if I jumped ship."

"My cabin number," she said firmly and held out her hand for the key.

"Oh, yes, Miz Louis. That's nineteen. You'll be sharin' with a real nice lady, Miz Henley. 'Course she does have those babies . . ."

Meg took the key, got directions, and walked along the deck. Thousands of people heading west along the Oregon Trail. It would be easy for one woman to get lost in the crowd. If she could get to the trail, join in a train, and then . . . vanish . . .

She'd spent all the money she'd stolen from her husband on passage, but she still had the gold coin her mother had given her. Perhaps that coin would buy her a new life in a new land.

Chapter Three

Oliver Sherrod stopped the buggy under the shade of a willow tree and gestured toward the few buildings that made up Cairo, Illinois.

"It's hardly changed in twenty years, Katherine. The streets aren't paved, there's no decent store. The Mississippi still floods its banks as soon as you get a crop in, and the mosquitoes will eat a man alive in the summer."

Katherine Kincaid was unperturbed. "It's home, Oliver."

Oliver's eyes swept the waterfront. "I'll admit the taverns probably do good business, river rats and seamen from the riverboats—"

"And good decent settlers who want to cross the Mississippi and need a place for a meal or to spend the night," Katherine put in. "Lots of people on their way west come down the Ohio to Cairo and then cross the Mississippi to go west."

"On the way, Kate," Oliver said deliberately. "They're on their way somewhere. That's my point."

Katherine smiled. "It's a futile argument, Oliver.

I'm not going to desert my home and my family to move across the river to Cape Girardeau, even if the Sherrods do own the most prosperous store on the west bank of the Mississippi."

Oliver slapped the reins on the horse's back and the carriage bumped down the rutted road along the Ohio River.

"I guess subtlety isn't my strong point, Kate, but you know what I want. I want you to marry me and bring Luke and Amity to Cape Girardeau. I can give them a good life, all the things they're missing here."

"They're missing nothing here," Katherine said stubbornly.

"Except a father." Oliver waited for her reaction.

"They have a father. At least the memories of the best father children could have." Byrd Kincaid had been dead for six years, but his memory burned as strong as ever in Katherine's heart.

Oliver couldn't control his irritation or his anguish. "You're a young woman, Kate. My God, you're barely forty years old—"

"Forty-one," she corrected, "and still three years older than you, Oliver."

"You're still a young woman," he persisted, "and you're beautiful to me. It's inhuman to think of you spending the rest of your life alone without a man."

"I've done pretty well these past six years," Katherine said. "I have a good tenant to help with the livestock and the farm; I do a fine business with the settlers selling my goods—"

"I'm not talking about the damn livestock, Kate. I'm talking about companionship and love. You know I've loved you since I was fifteen years old."

Katherine put her hand on Oliver's. "I know, Oliver, and you know I care for you, too. You're part of my past, an important part. If it hadn't been for you and your mother, we never would have survived that awful trek along the Ohio to Cairo. Just women and children in the wilderness."

Katherine had lead a group of women and children, the survivors of a flatboat crash on the Ohio, through the treacherous wilderness to Cairo. That had been twenty-three years ago, but in her mind and Oliver's it was as fresh as the smell of spring. And Oliver, who'd been a gangly fifteen year old in the throes of first love, was now a man with the lines of a life hard lived on his face. He had loved her then, and he loved her now.

"But we did make it, and you met Byrd Kincaid, and I lost you forever." Oliver couldn't keep the bitterness out of his voice.

Katherine's laugh floated on the sultry air. "Oh, Oliver, you always were dramatic. You had your own life to live, your own future to find across the Mississippi, and now you've had your adventures and come home to your sister and the family store. Just like me, you've found your home."

The way was more shaded now by elm and cottonwood trees as they made their way toward Katherine's farm. Oliver was quiet for a while and then he said in a low voice, "That's it, isn't it, Kate? The road I took, the life I lived. What happened out on the plains with Boothe and Kitty."

"You saved their lives, Oliver," Katherine said gently.

He shook his head, his lips compressed into a thin line. "But if I'd've done what Sheldon Gerrard paid me to do, they'd be dead by now. And I set out to do it; I never tried lying to you about that. I reckon you're right. There's a streak of badness in me that'll always be there, and I'm no good for you."

Katherine chose her words carefully. "Lots of people do things they're ashamed of later. Sometimes we do what we have to to survive. None of us is perfect."

"To think of hurting Kitty and Ben . . . I was a weakling and a coward, Kate, and I have suffered for it."

"But you couldn't do it, could you Oliver? You couldn't let Boothe Carlyle down. You stranded them on the prairie and then you went back and helped save them. The goodness inside you outweighed the bad. I've always known that about you, Oliver."

"Anything good is because of you, Kate."

She shook her head. "No, it isn't. It's because of you and what's inside you, Oliver Sherrod."

"Well, I learned then that I'll never be the man that Boothe Carlyle is."

"I miss him," Katherine said. "It's been six years since I saw him."

"They're all scattered, aren't they?"

"Boothe is God knows where and Kitty's in Indian country and Jim—"

"Jim and Kitty and Sarah should all be together soon, and that'll ease your mind."

"And then there's my Meg in St. Louis." She tried to hide the concern she felt.

"They *are* all scattered, but that's the way they're supposed to be. My grandmother Fiona told me long ago that my seed would spread across this land, from the shining mountains to the thundering waters and beyond." Her smile was distant, but not sorrowful as she added softly, "And Moses never saw the Promised Land, you know."

She looked at Oliver, and her smile deepened as she closed her hand briefly atop his. "All is as it should be, Oliver, and I am content."

Oliver was scowling. "And did your grandmother

tell you to spend most of your life in widowhood?"

Katherine laughed softly. "No, but she set an example. After my grandfather died, she never remarried. She raised me and my brothers and sisters back in Kentucky after my parents died, and she did it alone. She was the strongest woman I've ever known."

The horse, sensing home, began to quicken his steps, and Oliver gave him free rein. "No, Kate, she isn't the strongest woman. You are." His expression grew warm as he looked at her. "And I guess that's my misfortune."

Katherine squeezed his hand briefly and released it. "My purpose in life has been served, Oliver, and I'll be happy just to rest a while. It's up to my children now." And she smiled. "Let's go home."

But as the buggy turned down the lane that led to her house, Katherine Kincaid's eyes were on the setting sun, and her thoughts with those who had gone that way.

She could tolerate her cabin mate, Callie Henley, but her two small children soon got on Meg's nerves. She'd always thought she loved children; maybe, she decided wryly, in wide open spaces, not in a tiny six- by eight-foot cabin.

Meg began spending most of the daylight hours on deck. The decks were piled high, not just with flour and sugar, coffee and tobacco, but with wagon wheels, horse shoes, coils of rope, bolts of canvass, anvils, harnesses, crowbars, and tools of all kinds. One of the men traveling to Bellevue, she learned, was a blacksmith. Like Meg, he and his wife seemed cut off from the other passengers, and they too walked the deck at all hours or sat on a bench, shielded from the wind, talking in a language that no one else could understand. Even though Meg never exchanged words with them, only nodded as she passed, she felt a camaraderie with them; they were outcasts, too, it seemed.

Lionel, the first mate, who could spend most hours of a day talking, told her that the most valuable man on a wagon train was a blacksmith. Wagons broke down or the mules threw a shoe, and a blacksmith was the only man who could handle the problems. Lionel wasn't exactly sure where the blacksmith and his wife were from. Maybe Germany. Or someone said they were Turks. He himself thought they were from Russia.

They didn't talk much, hardly spoke English, so he hadn't really had a chance to find out. That disappointed Lionel, since learning the life histories of the passengers on the *Katherine K.* was his major pastime.

When Lionel was called to his duties, Meg walked the deck and watched the river flow past and tried not to think of what lay ahead or what she'd left behind. Sometimes early in the morning, before the rest of the boat stirred, she'd find Captain Dakins alone on the bow. Once or twice he invited her into the wheelhouse for coffee and talked about his life on the river.

He'd been a pilot on the Ohio and the Mississippi, but he liked the Missouri best. "You can never tell what Old Muddy will do," he said with a chuckle. "It's something new every day, and the *Katie K.* and I have to work hard."

She asked him about the name, and he shook his head.

"Don't have any idea where her name came from. I was just hired on to pilot her. She's a fine one though, one of the best of the breed."

The Missouri riverboats were lighter and shallower

of draft than their sisters on the Mississippi, the big paddle wheelers. The new high-pressure steam engines were twenty times lighter than the old models and could double the power of a boat, and all that power was needed on the upper Missouri to fight the fast-flowing rapids. Steam was generated by wrought iron boilers, not below as in the old boats, but fore and aft on the deck, to keep the boat as shallow in the water as possible.

Like all the boats, the *Katherine K.* used river water to make steam. The water was filled with mud and silt, and at the end of the day a fireman would shovel out the steaming mud from the boiler. If the boilers weren't cleaned out, the mud would work its way into the engines, and a crew's nightmare was to be stranded on the Missouri with a broken engine.

That was only one of Captain Dakin's problems on the Missouri. There were no gauges on the boilers, and the steam could build to prodigiously dangerous temperatures. Explosions were frequent and deadly.

The river itself was quick and fast, filled with rapids and snags, followed immediately by sandbars and shallows. It took a brave man and a smart one to pilot a boat up the Missouri, and Meg decided Captain Dakins was both. She liked being with him because he wanted to do all the talking. He asked few questions and accepted her for who she said she was. He was a man and by rights believed his life and stories were more interesting than hers.

It was different with Callie Henley. She wanted to know all about Meg's husband, why he was in Bellevue, and where they were headed. Meg got tired of lying, and her short answers hurt Callie's feelings. Meg was sorry, but she had to protect herself. Caleb might try to follow her, and if he did, he'd kill her. Unless she killed him first.

She knew that the passengers talked about her; she didn't care. Captain Dakins provided protection of sorts, and at night she had her cabin and the company of the Henleys.

She was determined to keep to herself; but one of the traders, a tall man with a mane of blond hair and a clean-shaven face, was equally determined to keep company with her.

Vincent Matoon was over six feet tall and handsome in a weak kind of way. *Like Caleb*, Meg thought. Each time Matoon approached her, Meg turned away. She answered his greetings with a curt nod; she deliberately never met his eyes. Yet he persisted. He was subtle in his pursuit. He never came near her when others were around, but always when she was alone, going down the stairs to the lower deck, or making her way along the narrow passage to the small dining room, or taking a last turn around the deck at sunset. He would manage to rub up against her or touch her breast with his arm or stand blocking a door, forcing her to squeeze past him. And when their bodies touched, he smiled, a self-satisfied grin that made her want to scream and slap his face.

She began to hate him, the smug look on his handsome face, the cut of his well-tailored plaid suit, the disgusting scent of violet pomade that he used in his hair. She tried to talk to Captain Dakins about him, but what could she say? That Matoon passed her in the hall? He stood in a doorway?

When she quizzed Dakins about him, the captain knew little to report. A trader from back east with goods aboard, Matoon had paid full price with gold. He was taking wagon wheels and harness pieces and other supplies to sell on the Oregon Trail. Matoon was a real go-getter, Dakins said. He'd paid passage for those foreigners, too, though Matoon never had much to do with them. Dakins wasn't sure where Matoon had met up with the blacksmith and his wife, but he'd heard they were indentured to Matoon for passage west.

So, Meg thought after her talk with the captain, Matoon was ambitious and a go-getter. Part of her admired that. A secret part of her longed for success and money and the nicer things in life. She knew Matoon was attracted to her and that if she smiled at him instead of turning away, if she touched his cheek or shoulder, his wagon could be a passage west for her.

Meg felt a surge of disgust at herself. She thought of Caleb. He'd been handsome and charming. He'd promised her the world. He'd told her of the saloon he owned in St. Louis, how she'd be his partner. They'd have a big house on a fine square; they'd have a carriage and servants—

And so she'd left Cairo and run away with him. He'd worked for a saloon all right, she'd learned. Several, in fact—driving a wagon that delivered barrels of ale. He soon lost that job because he'd rather drink the ale than deliver it.

She'd left Cairo and married Caleb in her search for love and adventure. She'd found neither.

Now all she wanted was anonymity and a place to hide. All she wanted was to survive.

Sarah woke suddenly, choking back a strangled cry. She lurched to a sitting position, drenched in sweat, her heart thundering. The dream followed her into the waking world: the black wolf, its teeth bared and glistening, lunging for her brother Jim. It was so real, so clear and immediate, that even now she had to clench her teeth together to keep from screaming out a warning.

Squeezing her eyes closed did not help, but eventually the vision dissipated of its own accord, leaving behind a queasiness in her stomach and a clamminess on her skin. She pushed aside the blanket and drew in several slow deep breaths, as though the cool night air could cleanse her memory of the taint the nightmare had left. Slowly she forced her eyes open, half-expecting to see a wolf looming over her, its fangs dripping.

There was, of course, no wolf. Around her the night stretched as clear and empty as a still lake, and the sky was filled with stars. Above her in the wagon, Hilda and Carrie slept nestled on soft grain sacks and woolen blankets, and the sounds of their gentle breathing and soft murmurs were reassuring. On the opposite side of the wagon slept Ben and Kitty, their forms as still as shadows on the ground.

Sarah shivered in the darkness and got up, stumbling to the back of the wagon where she slid the lid off the water barrel and drank thirstily from the dipper. She dunked her fingers into the water and splashed it on her face, trying to wash away the residue of the dream. It helped a little.

This was not the first time she had had the dream. When she thought about it, realized she had been dreaming about black wolves since she was a child, but such a long time had passed since those childish nightmares that she had forgotten them. Now they were back again, only different. This time the wolf threatened Jim.

The dreams had begun when the letter first arrived from her mother telling them Jim was on his way west. Sarah had been so excited and eager at the prospect of seeing her brother—of possibly even talking him into taking her home—and then the nightmares began. At first the wolf had been in the background, a silhouette on a hillside, eerie but not bothersome. In another dream Sarah had seen the wolf slipping through the tall grass while Jim was unaware, moving closer. Last night the wolf had circled the campfire where Jim lay sleeping. Tonight he had lunged.

When next she dreamed, would it be to see her brother torn apart before her eyes?

Again Sarah shivered in the cool night air, blotting her damp face dry with her skirt. She couldn't go back to sleep. But she didn't want to wake the children with her restlessness. She moved away from the wagon, looking out into the vast emptiness of the prairie.

Never before had Sarah realized that space could be terrifying in its hugeness. Back in Cairo she had fretted for a room of her own, for privacy, for spaces that were open and uncluttered. Everything was dense there, close with trees and shrubs and livestock and crops, and it was impossible to walk for long without running into someone she knew.

Here a person could walk for days, for weeks, and never meet another living soul. Here the sky was so big, the land so featureless, that it was easy to imagine a person could walk and walk and eventually just walk right off the face of the earth.

She hated it here.

She heard a footstep behind her, and such was the state of her nerves that she jumped involuntarily before she recognized her sister.

"I heard you get up," Kitty said softly, drawing her lightweight knit shawl around her as she moved closer. "Are you all right?"

"I thought I heard something," Sarah lied. She darted a quick glance at her sister. "Maybe a wolf."

Kitty chuckled, low in her throat. "I doubt that.

There aren't any wolves in this part of the country. A coyote, maybe."

Sarah scowled in the dark and wished she had kept silent.

Kitty tilted her head back, looking at the sky. "My, it's pretty out tonight, isn't it?"

"It's big, and it's dark, and it's empty," Sarah said flatly. "I don't see anything pretty about it."

Kitty smiled. "I remember when I felt the same way about the plains. When Ben and I came across with Uncle Boothe, I thought this land was the most terrifying thing I'd ever seen. There was a hailstorm that I thought would kill us all. And a cyclone that ripped up chunks of earth and crushed a wagon like matchsticks. And a buffalo stampede that turned the day black as far as you could see. But the worst was the bigness of it all. Sometimes you can stare into the sky and it just seems to go on and on and on, you know, and that foreverness, the *sameness* . . . well, it can get to you if you're not careful."

Slowly Sarah began to feel more charitable toward her sister. She did understand, in a way.

"It never seems to bother men that way," Kitty went on thoughtfully. "But women—I guess they need a roof over their heads, something to anchor them. Of course, after all this time I've kind of gotten used to the country, but I never really got to like it. That's why I made my home in the hills."

"That's not much better than this," Sarah said.

Kitty smiled and slipped her arm through Sarah's. "Let's walk."

Sarah did not want to walk. She was afraid to move too far away from the wagon. But she didn't want to admit that to her sister, and Kitty didn't seem worried. They walked, but Sarah made sure to keep the wagon in sight.

After a time, Kitty said, "When I was fourteen I never dreamed I'd be living out here on the plains. I never thought I'd be trading horses with the Cheyenne either."

Sarah glanced at her anxiously in the dark. "Ben said we'd meet up with them tomorrow."

"Or the next day," Kitty agreed. "The Cheyenne are a wandering people and they don't tell time like we do. But if we reach the rendezvous point first, we can wait."

Sarah couldn't entirely keep the worry out of her voice. "I've never seen an Indian. Except Billy, of course, and the ones around the fort and Weston, and they always look so dirty and tired. But I've never seen a wild Indian."

Kitty repressed a smile in the dark. "The Cheyenne aren't particularly wild."

"You know what I mean."

"I guess I do." Now Kitty's tone was serious. "I remember the night we camped outside the Shawnee mission, right before I was going to meet my first 'wild' Indians. I was scared to death. I was so worried I was sick to my stomach."

Sarah's eyes flew to her in astonishment. "You? You were afraid of Indians? But you were raised by the Shawnee!"

"I was wet-nursed by a Shawnee woman," Kitty corrected. "And don't forget, my real mother was killed by Shawnee. I still have the scar on my shoulder that I got from a Shawnee arrow before I was even born. I'd never met the Shawnee nurse who saved my life, or even knew much about her, until that day at the Shawnee mission."

She fell into a contemplative silence, and Sarah prompted, "What was it like?"

"Nothing like I expected," Kitty answered. "Just as,

I suspect, the Cheyenne won't be anything like you expect. Her name was Mirawah," she added softly.

"Who?"

"My Shawnee mother. She called me Warrior Woman and gave me Snow. I'm glad I got to meet her."

"So that's why you're not afraid of Indians."

"I didn't say that. It's wise to be afraid of some Indians, and I was sure afraid of the Pawnee when I first saw them on the plains. Their faces were painted red and blue, and their heads were shaved, and they looked so fierce . . . but it turned out they were more honorable than some of the white men on the plains."

Sarah frowned. This was one of the things she didn't like about living on the frontier. Things that you expected to be one way were often another. Indians were more honorable than whites, the emptiness of the plains was more frightening than the darkest forest.

"How do you stand it, Kitty?" she burst out suddenly. "How can you stand being out here all by yourself with nobody to talk to and nothing but the same horrible chores day in and day out and not even fresh milk when you want it? Don't you ever wish things were different, that you could live in a fine city like St. Louis with so many shops it'd make you dizzy just to look at them, and fancy clothes and music halls and—"

Kitty gave her an odd look and Sarah broke off. "Music halls? Where in the world did you hear about things like that?"

When Sarah remained stubbornly silent, Kitty said, "You sound like Meg, and nothing good ever came to *her* for daydreaming, I can tell you that."

Sarah knew that her older sister Meg had run off with a ne'er-do-well and everyone disapproved.

Rumor had it she was living in St. Louis. Sarah thought it sounded like a grand life, and she wanted to know more. But no one talked about Meg.

Now if *Meg* should ever have a baby, Sarah would be more than glad to go to St. Louis to take care of it. But that kind of good fortune did not appear to be in the cards for Sarah.

As they walked, Kitty added, "I'm a country girl born and bred, Sarah, just like you are, and I always knew my life lay across the river, out here on the frontier. Besides, if this trade goes well, Ben thinks we might be able to get a cow through the fort this fall."

"Well, my life is *not* on the frontier."

Amused, Kitty glanced at her. "How do you know that?"

"I just do."

Kitty squeezed Sarah's arm in a sisterly fashion. "Don't be afraid of the Cheyenne, Sarah. I promise it won't be anything like you think."

Sarah kept her eyes on the ground. "I'm not afraid."

Kitty stopped walking. "What is it then?" she inquired gently. "What's bothering you? You're not still worried about Jim, are you?"

Sarah drew in a deep breath, hugging her arms tightly as she looked out into the darkness. She wanted to tell her sister. She wanted to tell *someone*, and she wanted it so badly that it seemed as though the words would just come bursting out of her in a torrent that would flood the countryside. But the truth was, there were no words at all. How could she make Kitty understand? No one would understand . . . except Jim.

When at last she spoke, the words sounded feeble. "Sometimes I have dreams."

"Bad ones?"

Sarah nodded mutely. The vision of the wolf loomed fresh in her mind, closing up her throat. She knew Kitty was waiting for something more, but Sarah could not give it to her.

In the end, though, her sister's perception surprised her. "Uncle Boothe always dreamed true," Kitty said thoughtfully. "It was a gift, this second sight, passed down from your mother's side of the family, usually to the daughters. But this time Uncle Boothe got it. Is that what worries you, Sarah? That you'll dream true?"

Sarah wanted to cry, *I know I do! I know I dream true! I don't want to, but I don't know how to stop it.*

Instead she said, "I wish I could've known Uncle Boothe. I was just a baby when he went away."

Kitty put her arm around Sarah's shoulders. Her voice sounded a little thick as she said, "You never know. He's liable to show up anywhere. You might get to see him again yet. I have a feeling you two would have a lot to talk about."

Sarah thought so too. But she doubted if even Uncle Boothe could make this burden easier to bear.

After a while Sarah let her head rest against her sister's shoulder, and she stood there looking out at the darkness, trying not to think about wolves.

Jim Bridger was the most famous mountain man of his time. He'd been a trapper, a trader, a scout, and an Indian fighter. He was the first white man to lay eyes on the Great Salt Lake, when he'd been only twenty years old. Now in the year before his fortieth birthday, he'd taken on a new enterprise.

Fort Jim Bridger.

It was located on the Oregon Trail west of the South Pass, across the Great Divide, high in the Rockies, beyond the valley of the Platte River, west of Fort Laramie, past Chimney Rock and Independence Rock, and all the other markers on the trail from the East. It wasn't much of a fort. There was a palisade of sorts, a stockade of small tree trunks honed to a fine point on top and daubed together with mud. There were a couple of low log cabins, smoke filled most of the time, hot in summer, damp in winter; some barns for the livestock and good forage pasture.

But mostly there was Jim Bridger, tall and flinty-eyed, ready to take worn-out oxen from the tired settlers and sell them fresh, "recruited" oxen that Bridger had gotten from previous travelers and fattened up again. He also knew more stories about the West than any man living, and he could recite from memory each turn and twist of the trails that led west.

Boothe Carlyle and Jim Bridger had known each other for almost twenty years. Theirs was the kind of friendship that could pick up after years of not seeing each other as if it had been yesterday.

On a warm spring day Boothe tethered his horse at the hitching post and stepped into the smoky log house. An Indian woman bent low over the fire, stirring a pot. Jim Bridger had had three Indian wives that Boothe knew of and a series of mistresses in between.

"Mornin', ma'am. I'm looking for Jim."

"And you've found him." Bridger strode in from outside, taking off his wide-brimmed hat and hanging it beside the door. "Boothe Carlyle, Ole Firebird. Back from your travels." The men shook hands warmly. "Heard you didn't come back with Fremont."

"Decided to winter with the Nez Percé up near Canada. Got a little tired of the army way."

Bridger laughed. "Ain't a one of them who knows his tail from his ear." He called across his shoulder,

"Bright Moon, fix something to eat for Firebird here. We'll step outside and smoke."

Bridger offered Boothe fresh tobacco from his own pouch, and they filled their pipes. Bridger lit his with a long stick from the outdoor fire where a washpot now bubbled slowly, then passed the stick to Boothe.

In the bright sunlight Bridger squinted at Boothe. "Hell, you ain't much of a firebird now. Lots of gray in that red hair."

Boothe chuckled, sucking on the pipe as he tossed the stick aside. He took off his hat and ran his fingers through his long hair. "You're looking pretty grizzled yourself, Gabe."

"I'm old, Boothe."

"I'm older than you."

"We've both done a lot of living."

The two men sat down on the steps of the wooden porch. Boothe looked out over the mountains. "This is a mighty fine place you've got here, Gabe."

Bridger drew on his pipe. "Yep, I guess so. Though it ain't turned out like I thought. Seems as though there's a cutoff 'bout a hundred miles back east. The Sublette, they call it. Goes across about the damndest country you've ever seen, dried up alkali lakes, sand, rocks. Nothing for fifty damn miles until they hit the Green River."

Boothe puffed thoughtfully. "Sounds like a crossing for fools. This here's the trail we surveyed with Fremont last summer."

"And that's why I built my fort here. Yep, the Sublette's for fools, but that's what these damned wagon trains are full of. They'll take any risk to get to Oregon quicker. Even if it kills 'em." Bridger broke off quickly. "Sorry. I remember you had your troubles on the trail."

Boothe shrugged. "No one said I wasn't a fool."

"Let's drink to that." Bridger went into the cabin and came out with a jug of whiskey that the two men passed back and forth. The air was still and in the trees they could hear the raucous chatter of a squirrel.

"Mighty peaceful, Gabe."

"Until those damned fool wagons start rolling in. This summer I hear more than a thousand overlanders may be coming. Sometimes I wonder what the hell we've started, Boothe. All these folks—maybe it might be better if they stayed where they belonged."

"Folks aren't like that. Look at us. We couldn't stay east. Neither can they."

"I hear Fremont's taking out another exploring party."

"I won't be with 'em," Boothe said.

Bridger grinned. "Once was enough?"

"Fremont's a smart man. Just turned thirty with a lot of years ahead of him. Doesn't hurt that his father-in-law is a U.S. senator from Missouri. Doesn't hurt that Fremont's wife is the darling of old Senator Tom Benton's life. But what I find real interesting is that guides like me and Kit Carson were concerned with breaking trail and telling the truth about how hard it is to cross the Rockies, especially in a wagon, while Fremont has another way of looking at it. Seems he wants to make it seem real easy, like going to a Sunday school social. I get the idea that no matter what we found, he and Benton are determined to get settlers moving west with a lot of pretty stories."

"You hear what that dang fool Fremont did on his way back to Fort Leavenworth?"

Boothe shook his head.

"Seems he got to the Platte and it was in flood. So he sends half his men back overland and then he and some others decide to go down the Platte in some kind of toy boat—"

Boothe laughed. "Oh, I know that boat. We carried the damn thing all over the West. John C. Fremont's little India rubber plaything."

"The end of the story is that they shot the rapids in it and then capsized. All of 'em, thrown right in the water, splashing and shouting. Story's all up and down the trail from Fort Laramie to here."

"And I'll bet Fremont turned it into a great adventure, with him the hero. Like I said, the man's got gumption."

Bridger took another drink of whiskey. "Carson gonna sign up with him again?"

"Probably. Kit's at loose ends now. His Cheyenne wife died and left him with a little baby. In fact it was that baby that got him hooked up with Fremont He took her to his brother in St. Louis and met Fremont while he was there. Fremont signed him on to explore the trail to Oregon. I met up with 'em in Fort Laramie. I guess I was at loose ends myself."

"Kit Carson and John C. Fremont. Now there's a pair. Neither one of them bigger than a prairie chicken." Bridger laughed uproariously. "How tall you'd say Fremont is?"

"No more than five and a half feet," Boothe answered. "Same as Kit. But they make up in gumption what they lack in size."

"Still it don't seem fair that such little fellers have such a big name in the West."

"They ain't as big as you, Gabe. Everybody in the West knows your name."

Bridger shrugged. "All I ever wanted was to live my life the way I saw fit. Just like you. Just pick up and go whenever the spirit moved me."

They sat quietly, listening to the sounds of the day, of the oxen lowing in the pens behind the fort, the shuffle and whinnies of horses, the noises of a meal being prepared inside the house.

"Where you headin', Boothe?"

Boothe was silent for a while, long enough to make Bridger turn to look at him curiously. There was an odd, distracted look on Boothe's face, and he tamped his pipe without looking at Jim.

"Funny thing," he said. "I never expected to be this old. Never expected to have to make plans this late in life. Leaves a man feeling at kind of loose ends, if you know what I mean."

Then he shrugged. "I reckon I might head on down to the prairie to see my family. I've got a little niece settled back in the Flint Hills somewheres, and it surely would pleasure me to see her again. She's probably got young'uns by now. And my sister Kate, back on the Ohio. It's been a long time."

"Sounds like a mighty dull plan to me. The kind of plan that suits old folks."

Boothe glanced at him, grinning a little at the glint of challenge in his friend's eyes. "You got a better one?"

The woman's voice called from within. "Supper, Jim."

The men got up. Bridger put his arm across Boothe's shoulder.

"We go back a long way, Firebird. I remember when the Indians first called you that. Saw that red hair of yours and were sure you were some kind of spirit. Those were the times, eh?"

"There'll be more good times, Gabe."

A crafty smile appeared above Jim Bridger's grizzled gray beard. "If you'll stay a while, Boothe. Lots of wagons coming through this summer. Some'll take the cutoff, but some won't. I could use a good man here. Just for the summer."

"Now, what can I do that you can't?"

"You know damn well, Boothe. You can read and write and I can't. My woman can cipher a little, but I could use the help of a good man, a man to ride the river with. This is the first time I've ever done more than wad a bunch of cash in my pocket. They want maps too . . . not just drawings like I can do, but maps with names on 'em. Soda Springs, Fort Hall, the Snake River. I know this country like the back of my hand, but I can't write it down for them. Hell, Boothe, your family don't care if it's July or Christmas day when they see you."

Boothe followed his friend inside the house. Bridger was right. There were possibilities here. Challenges unmet, adventures not yet thought of. Things to *do*. Boothe knew he was living on borrowed time, and he wanted to see home again . . . but maybe not just yet.

His family would still be where he left them. Katherine would never leave Cairo, and Kitty and Ben were just settling in the Flint Hills. There was no hurry.

"You know, Gabe," he said, "I think I can spare you a little time."

Chapter Four

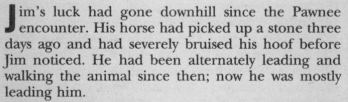

Jim's luck had gone downhill since the Pawnee encounter. His horse had picked up a stone three days ago and had severely bruised his hoof before Jim noticed. He had been alternately leading and walking the animal since then; now he was mostly leading him.

Yesterday he had snared a prairie hen, his first meal in thirty-six hours. It was starting to look as though it might have to last him another thirty-six.

This country was not like home. Jim had grown up believing he could make his way anywhere, living on his wits and his knowledge of the land. But he had grown up in the flat bottoms and tangled woods of the Ohio River; that was the land he knew, the land he had mastered. This country was flat and empty and endless, and sometimes he thought its sheer bigness was his fiercest enemy.

It was hard to stalk game when the sound of his footsteps seemed to carry half a mile. Hard to conceal a cookfire with no trees to filter the smoke through. Hard to find good shelter in this open, godless place, and hard, most of all, for a man to keep his nerve when the sky was so big and so close it seemed ready to swallow him up. He knew for a fact he was the only white man for a weeks' ride in any direction, and the shadow he cast on the land was so small he felt like an ant moving across a giant tabletop. The whole of it was a sobering experience, indeed it was.

Still, he might have been all right if he had been able to follow the stream a little farther. But on the day his horse went lame he had seen signs of Pawnee, and he had been forced to veer far off course to avoid them. Now he was beginning to wonder if it might not have been smarter just to ride right up to their camp and ask for food.

Now he had no idea where he was. He was heading west, that much he knew. But where the nearest trading post or settlement was, how far he might be from Fort Leavenworth or Kitty's farm—or even in which direction either of them lay—he could only guess.

Worse, he couldn't think of a way in the world to turn his situation into an entertaining story for Sarah.

He had heard talk about the tall grass as you came into Indian territory, not far from the fort. He had been wading in grass up to his knees for two days now. That could mean that tomorrow, or a week from tomorrow, he would walk right up to the fort. It most probably meant that he was walking right through the heart of Indian territory with no gun and a crippled horse. But all it meant for sure was that he was walking in tall grass.

The air was thick with chaff and bugs—gnats that buzzed around his face and clung to his sweaty skin, chiggers and fleas that crawled up his pants legs and down the back of his shirt. It was hot, too, for May, and the sun baked through his leather hat and turned his hair into a steamy helmet beneath. He was light-headed from undernourishment, and the sameness of the landscape blurred his vision and impaired his judgment. Or at least that was what he told himself later. He never would have made such a stupid mistake if he had been in his right mind.

All he knew was that he was trudging along one moment, pushing aside grasses and wiping the itchy chaff from his face with the back of his sleeve, and the next time he put his foot down, the ground gave way beneath his feet.

He stepped right off the edge of the world, and tumbled into the abyss.

Fort Leavenworth stood high atop imposing bluffs that overlooked the Missouri River. Established in 1827, the soldiers of the fort, the First Dragoons, had a threefold mission for the Indian territory that lay before them—to protect travelers on the Santa Fe and Oregon trails, to pacify the Indian tribes, which for the most part were friendly to whites, and to explore and map the territories west.

Over the sixteen years that the fort had been in operation, it had changed from a few rough buildings into a settlement of some sophistication. There was triweekly mail service from Liberty, Missouri, and a chaplain had arrived in 1838 to conduct religious services. A dozen whitewashed cottages offered housing for the officers and stood along a three-sided square. A large brick house had just been constructed on the north side of the quadrant for the commanding officer. The fourth side of the square was open and afforded a view across the plains, where groves of fruit trees and the squatters' small log cabins dotted the prairie.

Weston, across the river in Missouri, was a trading town of some one thousand people, and its claim to fame was the large illegal whiskey trade by undesirables who sold liquor to the Indians—and sometimes to soldiers. In the spring of 1843, there was relative peace in Indian territory and other than the illegal whiskey trade, Colonel Stephen W. Kearney, Commander of Fort Leavenworth, had little else to occupy his mind—except, of course, this problem with deserters. That was why he'd called Captain Marcus Hunt Lyndsay to his quarters.

Kearney was all army. He'd fought in the War of 1812 and acquitted himself bravely. He was a stickler for detail, and he liked his commands to be obeyed. For that reason he had an affinity with Lyndsay. Compared to most of the soldiers at Fort Leavenworth, Lyndsay was too good to be believed. He was professional, dedicated, and ambitious, a cut above the riffraff that seemed to fill the ranks of the army. But even to a man as ambitious as Kearney, there was something about Lyndsay that bothered him . . .

"So, Captain, you'll take a small detachment of men, say no more than five, and ride after this last bunch of yellowtails." It was late in the evening, and Kearney had poured glasses of brandy for himself and Marcus. "I don't know why a man would sign up with the Dragoons only to hightail it out of here for no good reason."

Marcus sat in a leather campaign chair across the table from Kearney. The colonel's gray hair glowed in the lamplight and Marcus reflected upon how much his commander resembled the likenesses of the Roman generals he'd studied in school. There was the same squareness of face, penetrating eyes, and look of determination. In fact, Marcus had requested to serve under Kearney, knowing that his command would be tough and orderly, not slack and undisciplined as on some of the posts where he'd served.

Marcus took a sip of brandy and pondered the question thoughtfully before answering. He knew Kearney didn't like men who were impetuous in word or action.

"I think, sir, because they have no idea what the army, the real army, is like. They believe it will involve killing Indians and the glory of battle. Perhaps they imagine balls with lovely ladies admiring their heroic deeds. Instead, they find themselves in a fort on the edge of nowhere with very little to occupy their time but drill, care of their horses, and an occasional scouting party. And the only admirers they have are Indians begging for money outside the fort. Not their romantic dream of soldiering at all. Added to that, these men have no discipline and no understanding of the role of the soldier in society."

Marcus considered saying more but decided not to. He knew he and Kearney agreed on certain aspects of a soldier's role, but he also knew that on some points their views diverged.

Kearney's scowl concealed agreement and no small amount of admiration. Lyndsay was an educated man, and he appreciated that. He was also a thoughtful one, which was rare in these parts. He had what it would take to go far. But Kearney did not like to give approbation freely. It was bad for discipline.

"Whatever the cause of the men's desertion, I want them brought back," he said briefly. "I want them alive, Captain. I plan to make an example of them. So tell your men to watch themselves. No shooting out of turn, no taking this into your hands. This is a matter for army discipline and court martial."

"And maybe hanging?"

"And maybe hanging. Any questions, Captain?"

Marcus knew that he was dismissed. He put down his glass, got to his feet, and saluted. "No questions, sir. I'll choose my patrol tonight and ride out at daybreak."

"Good luck, Captain."

Marcus didn't immediately search for his sergeant to round up a patrol. Instead he walked to the edge of the bluff and looked out across the wide Missouri River, glimmering faintly in the moonlight. The night smelled dank and musky—there'd been rain recently—and a swarm of gnats circled Marcus's head. He ignored them. He had schooled himself to ignore trivialities like gnats, mosquitoes, sleeping on the ground, eating cold food, going without sleep for twenty-four hours. All the things that other soldiers complained of, he reveled in. That's what set him apart. That's what made him different. Mind over body. Intellect over situation.

Like Alexander the Great.

Alexander—soldier, scholar, ruler, philosopher, dreamer, forger of a new world order.

Marcus had first read of Alexander when he was eight years old, a precocious child living in Boston with his parents. Shanna and Philip Lyndsay were wealthy, indulgent, and selfish. They were interested in little except themselves and were happy to give over the rearing of their son to a tutor, who in turn was happy to teach Marcus whatever would hold his interest and pacify the temper that had raged in him during his childhood.

The Lyndsay fortune was based on old money and their standing in Boston society was impeccable. Philip Lyndsay was the son of Gerald Lyndsay, whose father had been the old British baron of

Whitman, land rich and greedy, whose family had owned most of York and Lincolnshire. The family money was founded on timber, shipping, and mining. Gerald, the third son, had no claim to a title, but his father bestowed on him one of the larger shipping lines, which Gerald decided to run from Boston. Thus the American line of the Lyndsay family was founded.

Philip inherited the shipping line and was smug enough in his own position to scandalize the family with his marriage to a Scottish heiress, Shanna Boyd, who, although she brought with her the wealth of her father's vast holdings in Scotland and Ireland and could trace her ancestry back to William the Conqueror, never seemed to make a place for herself among the elitist Lyndsays. She compensated for this by spending a great deal of money and developing some rather odd pursuits. She made it a habit to ignore her son. Marcus remembered her only as a remote, slightly fey figure in the background of his life.

While Shanna and Philip pursued their twin interests of money and society, their son pursued his own. By the time he was twelve, he knew everything about Alexander the Great. He began to read Greek so that he could study the philosophies of Plato, as his hero had. He knew all the battles from Chaeronea, when Alexander was only sixteen, to the defeat of the Persians.

Marcus read the exploits of Alexander again and again, and he knew that his destiny was to be a soldier. He was accepted at West Point and graduated with honors in rhetoric, engineering, and philosophy. With his father's influence and money, an incident of his attack on another cadet was overlooked.

Marcus told his father the argument had begun over a gambling debt. This his father could understand and forgive, but in truth the incident had a more personal basis. There were some men who simply weren't fit to be soldiers, and the army was better off without one Cadet Carl Jenkins.

As a second lieutenant, Marcus was sent first to Fort Moultrie, South Carolina, where he spent a miserable year, seeing little action. He wasn't interested in the ladies of the nearby town and their attempts at entertainment . . . and flirtation. In fact, Marcus had little interest in women. Few of them could do anything for his career, and he found their company boring and exasperating. Only someone with the luck of John C. Fremont could have the good fortune to marry a senator's daughter and thereby insure his career. At Fort Moultrie he met no senator's daughter, but he did receive his commission as first lieutenant and he asked for a transfer.

Fighting was going on in only one place—Florida, where troops were vainly trying to subdue the Seminole Indians, who, unlike their brothers the Cherokee and Shawnee, had refused to be moved to Indian territory in the 1820s.

The Seminole still fought in swamps and bogs and creeks, and they would not be subdued.

Marcus loved fighting the Indians. He loved the feel of his horse surging into battle beneath them, the sounds of gunshots, the clash of swords and bayonets. Most of all, he loved the killing. He took no quarter; he spared no lives—not women or children or old people. When he was made a captain on the field of battle at twenty-six, he knew that some said he was too young. But he knew he wasn't.

Alexander had conquered a world at twenty-five.

Marcus requested the post at Fort Leavenworth. It was as close to the frontier as he could get. Like Alexander, Marcus knew a world lay to the west, unexplored, unconquered, waiting for the men with the courage to master it. He was that man. He would make his name and he would establish his empire.

But every campaign began with one battle; every battle began with one raised sword. The assignment he had been given tonight might not sound like much, but it was exactly to Marcus's taste. And there were no small jobs in the army.

He was looking forward to the battle that would begin tomorrow.

It had been absurdly easy. They had been on patrol—Rafferty, McClellan, and Leo Jones—and they had simply ridden away. Rafferty, who'd been in the army for five years and was up for sergeant, felt kind of bad about it, because he knew the other two wouldn't have done it without him. McClellan was a big, good-humored fellow who was so unsuited to army life that he would have ended up in the brig sooner or later, and Leo was an eighteen-year-old boy so green and scared that he was as likely as not to shoot himself during target practice. Hell, the army wouldn't miss any of them, when it came to that. And Rafferty hadn't exactly held a gun to their heads to get them to follow him. Still, desertion was not something you could take lightly. And he felt kind of bad.

They were two days on the outlaw trail now, and the mood was a little more solemn than it had been yesterday. Rafferty supposed it had started to sink in for all of them, what they had done. There were few things a man could do that couldn't be undone. Deserting from the army was one of them. There was no turning back now, no changing their minds.

This was something they'd have to live with for the rest of their lives. That's what they were all thinking as the day wore on, and that kept them quiet.

They were moving southeast, vaguely toward New Orleans, a place they'd all heard of but never seen. A smart man would have turned his steps west and lost himself in its vast open spaces, but the West was the one thing Rafferty was trying to escape. If he had wanted to stay in the West, he never would have left the army.

He hadn't asked for the posting to Fort Leavenworth and probably wouldn't have chosen it if the Army had consulted him before cutting his orders. Nonetheless, it had sounded exciting, being stationed in Indian territory, and he had envisioned many a glamorous tale to be told of his Indian fighting days when he returned home, perhaps with a battlefield commission or two under his belt.

But there were no Indians to fight. What remained of the fighting tribes had either been subdued or bought off long ago, and the only Indians he had seen in his eighteen months at Fort Leavenworth were the beggars he tried not to trip over when he left his barracks each morning. Boredom was standard fare. Boredom, stale provisions, endless pointless patrols across flat, featureless country . . . when Rafferty thought of the West from now on, he would think of nothing, for that was what it was composed of in his mind: a lot of nothing that went on forever.

He wasn't cut out to live outside civilization. He was twenty-six years old and he had never been married. He missed the company of women. He missed their smell, their gentle voices, the way they moved, their *softness*. He would never put it into words for any other living male, but if he had to sum up what he missed, it would be candlelight, tablecloths, the rustle of petticoats. *That* was what he missed. Civilization.

And he missed the sounds of wheels turning, the sight of neat clapboard houses, children playing, cattle grazing, trees. He had almost two years left on his term and he didn't know if he could stand staring at that same big empty sky day after day for that long. The truth was, he hadn't known how much he'd hated it, how badly he'd missed the life of the East, until yesterday, when, instead of turning his horse back toward the fort, he had ridden south and kept on riding.

He wasn't sorry. Nothing could make him turn back now. But he worried about Leo and McClellan.

McClellan, who was slightly ahead, drew up suddenly. "Holy sap and stump water," he said. "What the hell is that?"

Rafferty saw what he meant immediately. He tried to keep his voice as calm as McClellan as he drew up beside him. "Could be," he drawled with every appearance of disinterest, "it's a horse."

McClellan shot him a dry look. "I know that, you jackass." But his tone wasn't quite so easy as he added, "What d'you reckon it's doing way out here?"

The horse was about a hundred yards away, fully saddled and outfitted, contentedly munching grass. Rafferty was keenly aware of how exposed they were, slap in the middle of this tall grass meadow with no place to hide for miles around. If the rider of that horse was concealed in the tall grass, sighting them down the barrel of a long rifle while they sat here talking it over . . .

If he was, there wasn't a damn thing they could do about it.

Leo spoke up uneasily. "You reckon the rider got kilt? Indians mebbe?"

McClellan spat on the ground and said cheerfully, "Ain't no Indians around here, boy. Leastwise, not the killing kind."

Rafferty glanced at him. If there was one thing he had learned in his year and a half on the frontier, it was that any Indian could be a killing Indian if the circumstances were right. He didn't really trust the Osage or the Kansa. The Pawnee roamed wide and deep, and there were always renegades.

"There ain't no rifle in the scabbard," Rafferty said.

McClellan didn't answer. Leo swallowed hard and looked around uncomfortably. The horse just stood there, munching grass.

"We could just leave it be," McClellan said.

"Yeah."

"But there might be something useful in that bedroll. Foodstuff. Even money."

"Yeah."

"It don't look right to me," Leo said tightly. "It just don't look right."

Rafferty released a long breath. "You're right about that, son." He lifted the reins reluctantly. "Well, come on. Let's have us a look."

Chapter Five

Jim Kincaid had never considered himself of a philosophical bent. But when a fellow was standing at the bottom of a hole surrounded by sheer dirt walls with nothing but the changeless face of the sky to look at, there was plenty of time for thinking. And what Jim thought about mostly was dying, and how little he had to show for his seventeen years of life.

He remembered his pa telling him once that the only advantage a man would ever have over the animals was his brain. "Now," he had drawled in that low, quiet way of his, "you try going hand-to-hand with a cougar or a bear, and more'n likely you're gonna come up on the losing end of that fight. Your teeth ain't sharp enough, your fingernails ain't long enough. You can't outrun a cougar. You can't outsqueeze a bear. But what you can do is outsmart 'em. It don't pay to try and fight the wilderness on its own terms, son. What you got to do is use what God gave you to come out ahead. You think about anything long enough, you'll generally come up with an answer. That's how come man got to be the boss of the animals. The only reason."

Jim remembered it as clearly as if it were yesterday. He and his pa had gone down to the river and cast their lines for mud-cats, and his line had gotten snagged on some underbrush. He looked forward to times like this alone with his pa, without the little ones hanging on to their coattails and clamoring for attention. Just the two of them off alone somewhere doing what men did to fill the table for a hungry brood. It was a perfect spring day, the river was quiet and lazy, and until his line got snagged Jim thought nothing could spoil it. But he had worked and tugged and snapped and pulled, trying to jerk the stubborn fishing line free; he was sweaty and tired and close to tears with frustration. It was beginning to look as though he'd have to cut the line and he didn't have another hook. He'd have to go home, the fishing trip ruined.

Then his pa told him to take his time and think about what he was doing. He started to work the line instead of fighting it, and eventually he freed the snag. He thought his pa was the smartest man who had ever lived.

Three days later Byrd Kincaid was dead, shot through the throat by a madman in a church.

Jim wondered what his pa would think of him now and had a feeling it wouldn't be much.

The edge of the pit was less than a foot above his head. He probably could have pulled himself over without much trouble at all if he'd had two good legs, but he'd taken the fall hard on one ankle; it was already swollen to twice its size and hurt like white blazes. Nonetheless, he'd given it a stern try, digging his fingers into the earth walls, bracing his feet against the side and ignoring the torches of pain that exploded behind his eyelids. He'd almost made it too; his fingers were within inches of the top when he lost his handhold and tumbled backwards. This time the pain of the blow on his injured ankle was so severe he actually lost consciousness for a time.

When he came to, dizzy and sick, staring at the sky from the depths of his open grave, he remembered his pa's words, and he started to think. The pit was obviously man-made. He'd heard the Indians sometimes dug such things to trap antelope and elk and some of the larger game. He couldn't remember what kind of Indians, but he was certain that whatever kind they might be, he did not want to be here when they came to check their trap.

He could hear his horse wandering close by. Sometimes he could even see its legs as it passed into view. If only he had the rope from his pack. If only he had something to stand on, a rock or a log.

He stopped thinking about what he didn't have and started to think about what he did. He took out his knife and began to hollow out narrow steps in the earth wall.

He placed his good foot on the shallow ledge he'd carved and stabbed the knife deep into the earth, using it to hoist himself up. Almost immediately upon bearing his weight, the shelf crumbled. He dug another. It fell too. He tried again, and again he failed. He tried piling the accumulated dirt into a pile upon which to stand, but with no moisture to hold it together it failed to hold his weight. The exertion and the pain left him light-headed and drained. He sat back against the wall and looked up at the sky and wondered how long it would take him to die down here.

That was when he heard the footsteps.

He stiffened, but only for a second. Ignoring the mushrooms of fire that blossomed from his ankle, he edged around the wall, out of a direct line of sight, gripping the hilt of his knife tightly. He knew he couldn't avoid detection for very long, but the few extra moments might gain him the advantage of surprise.

He was too exhausted and too inexperienced to register the heaviness of the tread or the cautiousness with which it circled the pit. He braced himself for the appearance of a fiercely painted red man's face. When he saw the barrel of a rifle edge over the pit instead, he was too stunned to react.

In a moment the rifle barrel was joined by a florid, red-bearded face. Blue eyes swept the pit, then stopped and focused on Jim as he pushed himself slowly to his feet.

The two men stared at each other in equally matched astonishment for a moment. Then the red-bearded man turned his face and spat tobacco juice.

"Boy," he demanded fairly, "what the hell are you doing down there?"

"I can see the smoke from their fires," Kitty said, pointing across the sea of prairie grass. "See, against the sky."

"Ummm," Sarah answered and tried to quiet Carrie, damp and squirming on her lap. Kitty was driving the wagon with her Indian pony, Snow, tied behind. Ben had ridden ahead, balancing Hilda on the saddle in front of him.

The spring sun was hot and bright, and Sarah, holding Carrie with one arm, pulled her straw hat lower over her eyes.

"I don't see why we're bringing corn to Indians. Don't Indians grow corn? That's what Mama always said. White men got corn from the Indians."

"Not all Indians grow corn. Some are like the Cheyenne and move from place to place and follow the buffalo, but they still like corn. In fact they love it. A long time ago, the Cheyenne used to grow corn—or so they tell me. When they lived further east, across the Missouri somewhere. They were farmers then." Kitty was unsure of her details of geography. "But they lost the corn—or so their story goes."

"Lost the corn? Really *lost* it?" Sarah was almost interested.

"I don't know. Maybe they lost the seeds when they crossed a river or maybe they don't remember how to grow it."

"Growing corn doesn't seem that hard to me," Sarah said.

"They don't stay in one place long enough to plant and harvest. Anyway, the Cheyenne were farmers before they got their horses and started hunting buffalo."

Sarah was thoughtful for a moment, watching the smudges of smoke against the intense blue sky grow larger. "Didn't they always have horses?" Sarah was sure that horses were like buffalo and wolves and foxes—they'd just always been on the prairie.

"The only reason the Indians have horses is the Spanish. They brought the horses here, oh, hundreds of years ago." Kitty was as vague about her history as geography, but she'd heard her Uncle Boothe talk about the Indians' almost magical alliance with the horses that the Spanish conquistadors had brought to America. "I guess the Indians stole some horses, and maybe others escaped and turned wild, and the Indians caught them and tamed them. Just like the horses we're trading for. Uncle Boothe says no one can ride like an Indian. No one."

Carrie was squealing and tugging at her mother's

hair, despite Sarah's somewhat half-hearted efforts to hold the baby still. Kitty pulled the wagon over and handed the reins to Kitty. "Here, let me have her."

Sarah traded the baby for the reins reluctantly. Driving the team was hard work, and she wished she had paid more attention to Carrie. "These reins hurt my hands, Kitty. I need some gloves."

"Wrap your skirt around your hands," Kitty said. "In time your hands will toughen up."

Sarah stuck out her bottom lip and slapped the reins across the team's broad backs. She didn't want her hands to toughen up; she didn't want callouses and blisters or freckles on her face or sunburn on her neck.

Most of all, she didn't want to spend two days with Indians.

The band led by Chief High-Backed Wolf was camped in the traditional Cheyenne way, their buffalo hide tipis in a circle with a break in the circle facing east. Three summers before, in 1840, along with other chiefs of the Cheyenne, he had made peace with their enemies to the south, the Comanche and the Kiowa. The Cheyenne were tired of the bloody clashes with the other tribes and wanted peace to insure a supply of horses from the Kiowa, who had not only the most horses but also the best. The Comanche, who preferred to fight Texans rather than other Indians, were willing to make a truce also. The Arapaho, generally peace loving, wanted nothing more than to coexist with the other tribes and avoid warfare altogether. Despite the harmony between the four tribes of the Southern Plains, the Cheyenne still had enemies, and war parties occasionally ranged north to skirmish with Pawnee and Crow.

High-Backed Wolf embodied all that a Cheyenne chief should be. He was the protector of his people, father to each one who needed him; he was dignified, fair, reserved, and generous. He was slow to anger and thoughtful in his decisions, and once his word was given, it was not broken.

He had given his word to the Warrior Woman that as long as he had Kiowa horses to trade, he would trade with her. Ten times she had visited his camp, and ten times the trade had been fair.

Sarah stopped the wagon outside the circle of tents. Within seconds, they were surrounded by barking dogs, chattering women, and children shouting with joy. Eager hands reached up for Carrie. Ben rode up and tethered his horse to the wagon. Two young Indians girls held out their arms for Hilda. Her plump hands grabbed for the deerskin doll that one of the girls waved in her face.

A Cheyenne woman with a triumphant smile took Carrie from Kitty and crooned, "*Moksiis, moksiis,*" as she lifted her above the crowd.

"It means 'pot belly'," Kitty said with a laugh. "They call lots of children that."

Sarah grimaced and shrank back. She made no attempt to leave the wagon.

Kitty was irritated. "They're not going to let you alone, Sarah. They're very friendly and curious. And kind. Don't embarrass us by being rude. We've come to do business with them."

"But I can't talk to them," Sarah protested.

Kitty swung down from the wagon. "Then use sign language. Ben and I need to pay a visit to High-Backed Wolf; he'll be expecting us. You'll have to get along the best you can."

With that instruction Kitty walked off. The Cheyenne loved children, all children, and she knew hers were in safe hands.

As always, Kitty's heart sped up a little and she felt a surge of nervousness in the pit of her stomach. It was part excitement and part anxiety, for no matter how many times she made the visit, she always feared she might forget the rules of proper behavior and somehow offend the chief. He had retreated to his tipi; the flap was open and Kitty knew that meant she and Ben could enter. Taking a last steadying breath, she followed Ben into the smoky darkness of the tipi.

Ben stepped into the tipi and stood waiting for a sign from High-Backed Wolf, who sat cross-legged at the rear. He beckoned for Ben to sit in the place of honor at his left.

Kitty entered, waiting as Ben had for High-Backed Wolf's signal to her. The chief motioned for her to take her place beside Ben, and she sank to the ground, her legs to one side. Protocol and good manners dictated that only men were allowed to sit cross-legged in the tipi.

There was a long silence. In the flickering light of the fire, High-Backed Wolf looked especially daunting. He wore a shirt and leggings of soft buckskin, fringed and beaded. Over his leggings he wore a breechclout, a soft square piece of animal skin suspended from a cord around his waist. Hanging from his neck was a silver pendant on a leather thong, traded for from Indian tribes to the south. He also wore a necklace of bear claws. The bear was an animal of importance to the Cheyenne and represented great spiritual powers, for the animal could not only heal himself but other animals as well.

The chief's hair was parted down the center and worn in two long braids to his shoulders. Owl feathers were woven into his braids, giving the chief power, he believed, to move easily about and to see in the darkness. High-Backed Wolf's coppery skin was

weathered and wrinkled by hours spent in the sun
and wind; his eyes were dark and penetrating, and
sometimes Kitty felt as though he could see into her
heart. He had high cheekbones and a prominent
nose above narrow lips.

Kitty and Ben waited for High-Backed Wolf to
begin their bartering with the smoking of the peace
pipe. The stem of his ceremonial pipe was a long
carved piece of willow decorated with feathers and
glass beads. High-Backed Wolf removed tobacco from
his pouch and packed the carved stone bowl of the
pipe. He lit the tobacco with a coal from the smoky
fire and took a deep draught, letting the smoke rise
on the air. With grave dignity, High-Backed Wolf
passed the pipe to Ben, who smoked, wrinkling his
nose against the scent, and gave the pipe to Kitty.

Kitty tried not to choke on the acrid taste of the
tobacco mixed with willow bark. She knew it was
an honor that she was included in a ceremony
usually reserved for men, and she fought back her
nausea and light-headedness. Proud that she hadn't
disgraced herself, she handed the pipe back to High-
Backed Wolf. He put the pipe aside and made the
sign for horse by putting the index finger of his right
hand across the four fingers of his left. Kitty smiled
and nodded. The bartering had begun.

Half an hour later the bartering was over, but
High-Backed Wolf was not ready to end the talking.
Only he could give permission for his guests to leave
his tipi and only when he was ready. He began to
tell a story that Kitty caught in bits and pieces. She
knew it concerned his sister, Owl Woman, and Owl
Woman's daughter, Morning Star Woman, who was
only a few years older than Sarah. Kitty remembered
her from earlier visits, a slender, pretty girl with dark,
laughing eyes.

She glanced at Ben inquisitively, wishing she had his facility for the Cheyenne spoken language. Ben said a few words to the chief, requesting his permission to translate the story for Kitty as it was spoken. The chief nodded. Quietly, pausing occasionally to listen to High-Backed Wolf's words, Ben related the tale.

After the melting of the snow, when the tribe was camped farther north, following a herd of buffalo, some of the women had gone out onto the prairie to dig for Indian turnips, a favorite spring food. They had made an outing of it, singing and laughing, not minding the hard labor of digging in the ground with their sticks for the turnips. Then their laughter had turned to terror. A strange white man had ridden into their midst, grabbed Morning Star Woman, and ridden away with her.

The women had run back to the camp as fast as they could, but only old men and young boys were at the campfires. When the braves returned from their buffalo hunt, they tried to follow the man, but the tracks had been washed away by a spring rain. Morning Star Woman was lost forever.

Owl Woman would not leave her tent, High-Backed Wolf said, she grieved so for her daughter. Ben need not interpret the rest of the story. Kitty knew how highly the Cheyenne prized a girl's purity. Young women sometimes wore chastity belts of leather or woven buffalo hair, knotted in front and drawn between their thighs, as a symbol of purity. If a girl was seduced before marriage, she was disgraced and not forgiven. No Cheyenne man would ever marry Morning Star Woman, even if she were found. She was better off dead.

Kitty's heart ached for Owl Woman and her husband Elk River, and for High-Backed Wolf, who had not been able to protect the daughter of his sister. Again and again she heard him use the word *Tsistsistas,* the name the Cheyenne called themselves, The People, and she heard the word *shame* again and again and saw him make the sign for bad, clenching his hand into a fist and then flinging open his fingers. High-Backed Wolf had lost face among the other Cheyenne bands for not protecting his kindred, and she knew he would not rest until the girl's abductors were tracked down.

Kitty wondered what would happen if the Cheyenne ever caught up with the white man who had stolen the girl. He would be killed, of course, as he deserved. But the girl . . . she was disgraced forever. What would happen to her if they brought her back?

Kitty repressed a small shudder of dread.

High-Backed Wolf, his face grave and serious, finished his story and cleaned the tobacco from his peace pipe. That was the signal that their talk had ended. Now the chief and Ben would inspect the trade goods.

Kitty followed the men into the sunlight, blinking against its glare. She asked Ben to put aside some trade beads and a blanket for Owl Woman. She wanted to do something to comfort her, but knew her gifts would do little to assuage a mother's grief at the loss of her child, or to make up for the terrible shame that Morning Star Woman's abduction had brought to the band.

Kitty had a sudden need to see her children.

She found Sarah surrounded by a group of young Cheyenne girls. "I don't know where the children are, and these . . . these . . . these Indians won't leave my hair alone."

"They've probably never seen red hair like yours," Kitty said. The anguish over Morning Star Woman's story slipped away as she looked at Sarah; Kitty couldn't help smiling.

Her sister's blue eyes were wide and frantic, her forehead damp with nervous perspiration. Four giggling girls, dressed in tubular buckskin dresses that hung below their knees and were decorated with fringes, beading, and feathers, were taking turns combing Sarah's hair with an instrument made of a porcupine tail sewn over a strong stick. Sarah gave a little squeal each time the comb was dragged through her curls.

Kitty held out her hand to Sarah. "All you have to do is get up and walk away." She pulled her sister to her feet. "You aren't a prisoner."

"I might as well be," Sarah snapped. "Where can I go? They'll follow me."

"They'll get used to you," she said dismissively. "We have good news about the horses. High-Backed Wolf will trade forty for us if he approves of our trade goods. Forty horses, Sarah! This will be a good year for us."

"When can we leave?"

Kitty chuckled softly. "What's your hurry? We didn't ride all this way just to turn around and go back. We'll stay a while."

Kitty could almost see her sister's spirits sink.

Kitty spied her children but didn't approach them. They were with two Indian women and their children under the shade of a willow tree. Hilda was playing dolls with a clutch of little girls, and Carrie was being passed from woman to woman like a doll herself. Kitty let her breath out in a sigh. All her family was safe and accounted for. Her eyes swept the horizon. It looked calm and peaceful, though Kitty knew, as did every frontier woman, that danger could hide under the most tranquil surface.

But there had never been problems at this camp; they were safe here. High-Backed Wolf brought his band to this spot twice a year to trade with the Adamsons. There was plenty of water for the horses from a small stream that fed southward into the Kaw River, and the willow trees that clung along the creek's bank gave shade and enough green limbs to keep the campfires smoky and drive away the flies and mosquitoes.

"Are you just going to leave the children there?" Sarah asked, her voice rife with accusation.

"Nothing will hurt them. They don't miss me, and the women will take care of them." Kitty held up her hand. "Listen."

Sarah cocked her head. "I don't hear anything. Except maybe a stupid dog barking."

"You don't hear children crying, do you? The Cheyenne take good care of their children and they just don't cry."

"I wish yours could learn that trick."

Kitty laughed and ruffled Sarah's hair. "It's too late now. They teach them when they're babies. If a baby cries, a mother does whatever she can to quiet him. She feeds him or dries him or holds him, but if he keeps on crying—then she hangs him out on a bush to cry it out—"

"Hangs her baby on a bush! Kitty . . . that's awful!"

"There's a reason. A crying baby might give away their position to the enemy, and the baby is in a cradle board. Like that."

She pointed to a tipi where a seated woman was braiding a rope of buffalo hide. Propped against the tipi next to her was an infant, in his soft leather pouch attached to a wooden frame. "If I ever have another baby, that's how I'm going to take care of him."

"I still think it's terrible that a mother would hang her baby out on a bush." Sarah was determined to find fault with something.

"When the baby stops crying, she goes and gets him. They tell me that babies learn very quickly that crying doesn't do them any good." Kitty looked Sarah straight in the eye. "They all have to live by the rules to survive."

Sarah cut her eyes away.

Kitty reached up and touched Sarah's cheek.

"Pouting doesn't do any good, either, Sarah. Ben and I are going to watch the braves break some of our horses, and there'll be a feast tonight. You can come with us or you can sit in the wagon in the hot sun with your lips all stuck out."

Kitty walked away, and Sarah, her shoulders stiff, followed.

The horses were grazing peacefully by the stream, feasting on the fresh spring grass. Indian braves mounted on their ponies patrolled the parameters of the herd, occasionally running at a horse that moved outside the boundaries and driving it back within the group.

Ben was standing in the shade of a tree. Kitty and Sarah joined him. "Most of the horses have been broken. Only a few are left. Sun Road is the best the Cheyenne have."

Ben leaned closer to Kitty. "There's no reason to be here, Kitty. You should be with Owl Woman."

"I want to see the horses," she said. "When we sell them, I need to know as much as possible about each one."

Ben lowered his voice. "It's man's work, Kitty. You

know that. Do you see any other women around here?"

Kitty didn't bother to look. "You say that every year, Ben. Yes, I know for the Cheyenne it's man's work, but we're not Indians." She glanced up at him in amusement. "Have the braves been teasing you again? Saying you can't control your woman?"

Ben's mouth drew down in resignation. "Well, that's the price I pay for being married to you, I guess."

Kitty's eyes danced. "And worth every minute, right?"

"I didn't say that, you wicked woman." But his gaze was warm.

"High-Backed Wolf knows I wouldn't show disrespect for the ways of the tribe," Kitty said, "and I think he respects my ways."

Kitty was well acquainted with the Cheyenne's way of life. There was strict division of labor. Women gathered and cooked vegetables and the meat that the men brought to the campfire. They were responsible for tanning the buffalo hides, and sewing blankets and clothing. The women stitched together the tipis made of twelve or more buffalo hides and were in charge of lowering and raising the shelters each time the band moved. The men were hunters, makers of weapons, wagers of war, trainers of horses.

"Well now," Ben drawled, "I don't know. There's a lot to be said for the Cheyenne way of doing things."

"You know you don't mean that."

"If I did, I sure married the wrong woman."

Kitty laughed and linked her arm through his. She had been reared by her adopted mother to believe that women were as strong and smart as the men they married, which, in truth, wasn't all that different from the way Cheyenne women were raised.

Kitty knew that the Cheyenne women, despite their specified roles, exerted a strong influence on their men. Wives were the final authority, the voice of reason, and if Calf Woman, High-Backed Wolf's wife, was unhappy with the trade, it wouldn't take place.

Kitty had forgotten about Sarah, standing behind them. "Let's leave now," Sarah said. "I hate it here. You and Ben are fighting, and it's hot and dusty. Please can't we go?"

Kitty was close to exasperation. "Honestly, Sarah! We are not fighting, and we are *not* going home. Will you stop whining?"

Then she saw Sarah's face and her heart softened. The child looked upset and frightened and very out of place. Kitty left Ben to put an arm around her sister's waist and pull her close. With her other arm she reached for Ben so that the three of them were linked together. She tried to lighten the mood. "Maybe at the feast tonight you can do the Omaha dance, Ben. You can throw me away."

Ben's eyes twinkled. "Don't think it hasn't crossed my mind once or twice."

Sarah swallowed hard and made an effort to appear interested. "What's that?"

"The Cheyenne have a ceremony," Kitty explained, "where a man dances with a stick in his hand, and then he throws the stick in the air and cries out that the stick is his wife and he's throwing her away. It's the Cheyenne way of ending a marriage."

"I don't think it's very funny."

"You don't think Ben dancing around an Indian fire would be funny? I can see him now—"

Ben raised an eyebrow. "It works both ways, Kitty. If you were a Cheyenne woman, all you'd have to do is move back to your family's house. 'Course, since your ma's in Illinois that might be a little hard."

"But I'd get to keep my share of the horses," Kitty said. "Cheyenne women do."

"Stop it," Sarah said. "I don't care if you are teasing. It's not right to talk about things like that."

Kitty squeezed Sarah's waist. "Just husband and wife talk," she said. "You'll see when you grow up and get married."

Sarah's eyes darkened. "When I get married," she said in a low voice, "I won't be living in a log cabin and trading with Indians."

But Kitty and Ben weren't listening to her. They were concentrating on the horses and taking care of the business that had brought them to the Cheyenne.

The feast was over—at least as far as Sarah was concerned. She lay in the smoky tipi, listening to the tribe playing music and singing around a huge campfire. High-Backed Wolf had been more than pleased with the trade goods, and the feasting had been generous.

There had been pots of stewed buffalo and deer meat, the gravy thickened with the ground corn meal that the Adamsons had brought. Some of the Indians had sweetened the whole mess with molasses. Sarah had almost gagged at that.

They'd eaten boiled Indian turnips, which Sarah had found bitter, and some kind of soup with boiled milkweed buds. Sarah had hated that, too. It almost made Billy's Kansa soup seem appetizing.

During the meal, the dogs had fought and snapped over scraps, and the children, including Hilda, had galloped wildly on stick horses among the adults seated around the fire. The meal had been noisy and confusing, and Sarah had never been sure of what was in her food bowl. When Ben had mentioned that the Cheyenne had a fondness for roasted puppy, she had stopped eating.

Her stomach growled as she tried to sleep. Carrie and Hilda lay on pallets near her; Ben and Kitty hadn't yet come to bed. She doubted they'd join the children in the guest tipi that High-Backed Wolf had provided. Sarah had seen the look on Ben's face as he watched Kitty in the firelight.

Sarah pulled her blanket over her head to blot out the noise of the singing, the drums, and the rattles, and finally fell asleep.

In the middle of the night she awoke gasping for breath, a scream lodged in her throat.

The wolf was getting closer. And there was nothing she could do to stop it.

Chapter Six

Jim's ankle was not broken, though for all the good it would be to him for the next few days it might as well be. The red-bearded man, McClellan, caught his horse, and after they hoisted him out of the pit with a rope, he was able to hobble to it and mount with help. But that was about all he could do.

He kept seeing spots in front of his eyes and had trouble staying in his saddle. They rode a couple of hundred yards, then somebody said it was getting late and why didn't they just make camp?

There were all kinds of people on the prairie, Jim knew that. There were men who'd give a stranger the shirt off his back, and there were men who'd cut a stranger's throat for the same shirt. Jim knew a wise man measured his trust with a dose of caution, but he was almighty grateful to the three of them, whoever they were.

He wolfed down two plates of beans without drawing breath, and it was only then, with the edge off his appetite and the good hot food starting to stiffen up his muscles, that he had a chance to take a good look at his rescuers. And a chance to start feeling like a danged fool.

One of them was about his age, but even he sported a mustache; the other two were older, obviously seasoned men of the prairie. They hadn't lost their rifles or let their horses go lame or fallen into a pit. They knew what they were doing out here; this land would never eat them alive.

Rafferty came back from checking Jim's horse. "Ain't nothing but a little stone bruise." He squatted down beside the fire and helped himself to a plate of beans. "You'll want to let him rest up a couple of days, but he'll be good as new."

"I've been walking him," Jim said. He looked down at his leg, stretched out stiffly before him, the ankle so swollen now that there wasn't a chance in hell of ever getting his boot back on. "If I hadn't been," he added glumly, "I wouldn't have fallen in that pit."

Rafferty and McClellan exchanged a look, and then McClellan said boisterously, "Hell, son, you ain't done nothin' new. Put your plate out here. Have another mouthful."

Jim knew it wasn't good manners, but he held out his plate again. As close as he had come to dying, he supposed he could be forgiven a little gluttony.

McClellan filled Jim's plate high and added another heaping ladle to his own plate.

"Yep," he continued, pushing a forkful of beans into his mouth, "I reckon about the worst that ever happened was to ol' Possum Jones. You remember me tellin' you about Possum, don't you Rafferty?"

Rafferty ate intently, giving no sign he had heard. Leo fixed himself a plate and settled down on the ground next to the storyteller to eat. Bean juice splattered on McClellan's beard as he lifted another forkful and went on. "Now, you think you was dumb, son, for falling in, what'd you think about a fella that jumped in? Now that's *dumb*.

"But let me tell you something, boy." He shook his fork at Jim soberly. "This prairie'll do things to you, trick your mind, make you see things and do things you'd sure wish you hadn't. And that's exactly what happened to ol' Possum. Folks said it was the sun that got to him, but I say it was the prairie, pure and simple, although I will allow it was almighty hot that day, and we'd been riding since sunup when Possum starting yelling his head off about the swimming hole up ahead. Now it wasn't nothing but the worst kind of luck, because if some critter hadn't broke through the grass cover on that trap, he never would've even seen it. But he spotted it, and he pure whipped his horse into a froth running for it, rode right over the edge."

Rafferty kept eating. Jim and Leo had slowed down considerably, listening to the tale. McClellan shook his head sadly.

"Boy, you don't know how lucky you was. Because that ain't even the worst of it. By the time we got there, them Injuns had done come out of the grass, lit a fire in that pit, dressed poor ol' Possum out, and had him roasting on a spit over that fire like a jackrabbit. Him and his horse too."

McClellan shoveled down another forkful of beans. "Et him up that night for supper with popping corn."

The last bite Jim had swallowed stuck like a lump of clay in his throat. He stared at the red-bearded man, feeling cold and sweaty inside, and so did Leo—for a moment.

Then a sheepish grin crept across Leo's face. "Aw, hell, McClellan. You're joshing again."

McClellan washed down his last bite with a swig of coffee. "Son," he said mildly, "you'd best start listening to your elders. I'm tellin' you, there's man-roasting Injuns out there, maybe laying in wait for us right now, watching from the grass."

Leo guffawed and filled his mouth with beans, but Jim noticed he cast an uneasy glance over his shoulder, at the tall grass spreading to the horizon. Jim wasn't too easy in his mind himself until his saw a twinkle of dry mirth in Rafferty's eyes. Then he grinned and relaxed. He dug in his fork again.

"You headed anyplace in particular, son," said Rafferty, "or are you just wandering?"

Jim swallowed and nodded. "I've mostly been wandering here lately, but I've got a sister and brother-in-law not far from Fort Leavenworth. With the shape my horse is in I'm figuring I'd do best to head straight there. They trade horses," he explained.

Jim knew he didn't imagine a slight stiffening among the three when he mentioned the fort, and he didn't like what it seemed to imply. This was not the first time he had noticed the identical dusty blues the three men wore, and if he looked closely, it wasn't hard to see where the rank insignia had been torn off McClellan's uniform. He wanted to think there were other explanations besides the obvious one, and that was made a little easier when Rafferty said casually, "Their names wouldn't happen to be Adamson, would they?"

"Yeah, that's right." Jim felt an eagerness rising in him and was surprised at how good it felt to hear even so much as the name of a family member. Kitty, Sarah, images of home. He could almost hear their voices. "You know them?"

Rafferty focused on his plate, scraping up juices. "Know of them," he said briefly. "Good folks. Know their horseflesh."

He plucked up a clump of grass and began to scrub his plate with it. He nodded back toward the string of horses. "You treat that one of yours right and he'll get you there. You ain't but what? Four, five days away."

Jim didn't much like the sound of that. He was tired of solitary wandering, and had counted on the safety of numbers for the rest of his journey.

"You're more than welcome to ride along with me," he said. He gave what he hoped was a nonchalant wave of his fork that extended the invitation to all of them. "I know it ain't mannerly of me to eat up your grub when I don't have anything to bring to the pot, and I sure would be glad of the chance to pay you back with one of my sister's home-cooked meals, considering what you done for me, and all."

A look went around the group that was almost palpable. Then Rafferty said, "Thank you kindly, son, but we're riding south. If you expect to meet up with your sister, you'll be riding west, won't you?"

Jim thought, perhaps irrationally, that that proved their innocence. If a man was trying to desert from the army, he would flee west, not south.

"Got family down south, do you?" he said.

But nobody seemed to want to talk about that much, and the mumblings were uncomfortable until McClellan said, "You got any idea how to find this sister of yours?"

Jim was a little embarrassed to admit he did not. McClellan took a stick from the fire and etched a map on the ground, while the other two spread out their bedrolls. The sun was setting, and dawn would come early.

Jim sat up and drank the last of the coffee. He was tired, but his leg hurt too badly for him to sleep. He wasn't looking forward to the morning, when he'd be left here alone, a cripple with a lame horse, wondering how to keep himself alive until he got to Kitty's. Whoever these men were and whatever they'd done to get here, Jim would be mighty sorry to see them ride off.

He was half-inclined to ride with them. East. Home.

Leo's voice startled him. "What is that, anyway?"

Jim looked at him. The other boy was stretched out in his blanket, using his saddle for a pillow, watching Jim in the light of the setting sun. Only it wasn't Jim he was looking at. It was Jim's chest.

It took him a moment to figure it out, then he absently touched the pendant he wore around his neck. "It's just something that's been in my family for a long time. It came over from Scotland with my folks a lot of years ago."

"Looks like one of them Injun geegaws," Leo commented, but he'd already lost interest. He rolled over and closed his eyes.

After a while Jim hobbled into his own blanket and willed himself to go to sleep. He wondered if his companions would try to steal the pendant during the night. He wondered if they would be interested in trading food or maybe even a rifle for it.

Eventually, he too fell into an exhausted sleep.

Marcus picked up the trail of the three men about midafternoon. Immediately he ordered his detail to fan out—in the opposite direction. He arranged a rendezvous point and rode off on his own.

At sundown he spotted the smoke of their campfire. From that point on, all he had to do was wait.

Under the cover of full dark he approached the camp. He left his horse some distance away lest it give a warning sign and crept in near silence toward the glowing embers of the campfire. He felt nothing in particular about what he was going to do. His senses were operating at peak efficiency; his body was alert and responsive. He felt neither fear nor remorse. He had a duty to perform and he would execute it cleanly, efficiently, and without regret.

Three men slept in the glow of the dying fire. He recognized the private's blond hair and McClellan's red beard. The third would be Rafferty, the sergeant, who was responsible for the action of his men. Marcus walked up to him silently and, without hesitation, fired a bullet through the sleeping man's temples.

The horses were tied in a stand of cottonwood a few yards away and the sound of the bullet caused them to squeal and snort. At the same instant McClellan bolted upright and fumbled for his rifle, while the boy, inexperienced and less alert, pushed himself to a half-sitting position with a querulous, groggy sound.

Marcus was prepared. His rifle was loaded and aimed at McClellan even as he put the pistol shot through Rafferty's head; the blast that tore McClellan's head from his shoulders was almost simultaneous with the first. The private, paralyzed with horror, never even thought to reach for his weapon. With casual contempt Marcus turned his pistol on him, and shot him between the eyes.

It was carefully planned and flawlessly executed, as any good battle plan should be, and from beginning to end it took less than ten seconds. The only thing Marcus had not counted on was that the noise of his own fire would conceal the approach of an intruder. The rider was upon him before he knew he was being watched. He calmly reloaded his rifle and turned toward the newcomer, drawing aim.

Jim had moved away from the fire to relieve himself.

For weeks, months after the massacre he would be haunted by the nightmare demon of *What if . . .* What if he hadn't chosen that particular moment to leave the camp? What if he'd returned a little later? What if he'd had two good legs instead of one?

But his ankle hurt like the very devil, which had kept him dozing in and out of sleep, and when he finally got up it took him a long time to move off behind the string of horses. He had just started back when the first shot came.

He didn't feel the pain in his ankle as he stumbled forward, heart racing; for a pistol shot at this time of night could mean nothing good, and it was followed almost immediately by a rifle blast. Jim caught himself against the mane of his own mount, who was pawing and shuffling nervously, and he watched in horror as a uniformed army officer leveled his pistol at Leo and shot the young man in the head.

In a flash Jim was transported back in time: hot and crowded in a small church that smelled like new wood and gentle perspiration, squirming on the hard pew and trying to smother a yawn as the preacher droned on. And then the air was split with gunfire, people screaming, children running, blood flowering on a woman's dress, his mother trying to push him down on the floor and his pa—one moment standing, the next flung backward with blood spurting from his throat. Over and over again, his pa's eyes open and fixed, blood exploding; his pa's face, still and dead, blood splattering . . .

Another sound drew him out of his stupefaction and back to the present. Not his pa, but a boy named Leo Jones, and not far from him the bloody mass of what had once been a friendly, red-bearded face, and Rafferty, dead and still; and the soldier now reloading, now aiming his rifle at the sound of racing hoofbeats.

Jim couldn't move, didn't even think of moving as the second soldier skidded into the camp and dismounted not three feet from where Jim stood, huddled behind his lame horse. The soldier never once glanced in Jim's direction.

Marcus lowered his rifle slightly as Tompkins, white-faced in the firelight, swung off his horse. He was so shaken he forgot to salute.

"Captain Lyndsay! Sir!" he barked.

His eyes were big with shock and disbelief. Marcus did not have to wonder how much he had seen.

Marcus said crisply, "You had orders to rendezvous at sunset."

Almost instinctively, Tompkins straightened his shoulders. "Yes, sir. We were worried when you didn't return, sir. I was sent to scout for sign, and saw the campfire. Sir."

Marcus nodded casually toward the bodies. "These are our men. They were shot trying to escape. We'll arrange a burial detail in the morning."

Tompkins didn't move. His eyes were an agony of horror and denial. He struggled to speak and it looked for a moment as though he would lose that struggle. Then he said in an odd, choked tone, "Sir. That's not what I saw, sir—"

Marcus fired the rifle into Tompkins's midsection. The last thing he saw as the blast flung his sergeant backwards was that same stunned look of stupid disbelief.

And then Marcus saw something that startled him.

A shadow took form and lunged toward Tompkins's horse. It had actually grabbed the reins and prepared to mount before Marcus recognized it as a man.

Not a man, a boy. And the boy was injured, because as he swung one foot into the stirrup, the other leg collapsed beneath him, returning to Marcus that second's advantage that he had lost to surprise. He lifted the rifle to his shoulder. The boy's head turned to look at him. Instinctively Marcus squeezed the trigger.

And, of course, the rifle was empty.

For a single endless moment the two men stared at each other, one expecting to die, the other expecting to kill. Reality was half a breath ahead of perception, and while Marcus waited for his mistake to register on his consciousness, every feature of his opponent's appearance was etched into his brain. One foot was bootless. His shirt was out, galluses down. Around his neck he wore an unusual iron ornament whose simple design was immediately imprinted on Marcus's brain. The red hair, the sprinkle of freckles across the bridge of his nose, the look in his young eyes—Marcus thought he would never forget that look. Fear, yes, as he gazed down the barrel of death, but beyond that, loathing. And beyond that, fury and defiance. Later Marcus would decide it was that look more than anything that cost him the fatal moment's hesitation.

As though the world had been only temporarily suspended in its orbit, everything snapped suddenly back into motion again. Marcus flung aside the rifle and reached for his pistol. By the time he had it in hand, the boy had thrown himself into the saddle and was wheeling the horse around. Marcus fired and the horse reared. But the rider maintained his seat and, incredibly, the horse came down running.

Marcus fired into the dark again, and yet again, but the hoofbeats didn't slow.

Chapter Seven

Sheldon Gerrard had given up. Once, he'd been one of the wealthiest men in St. Louis. He'd owned a fine brick house on a cobblestoned and tree-lined street. He'd had plans and dreams about establishing a colony in Oregon and of cashing in on the great wealth of the Orient.

And now it seemed his life had come full circle.

He'd started out in the 1820s like so many others, trapping and trading beaver pelts on the Missouri. Only he'd been smarter than the others. He'd bought pelts from the trappers at two dollars and taken them to St. Louis himself where he'd sold them for four. Pretty soon he didn't even bother to go upriver. He had agents for that—to buy the pelts and bring them downriver, where he negotiated the sales of rich beaver fur to the eastern United States and to Europe for the greedy makers of top hats. In the mid '30s, when interest in beaver hats waned, he turned his attention to Oregon. He wanted an empire in that newly settled land; he was ambitious and power-hungry and had no scruples about how he obtained his goals.

With his own money he outfitted a wagon train,

paying for the wagons, the oxen, the supplies. And he hired the best guide he could find: Boothe Carlyle. Sheldon and the others set out with high hopes and the finest equipment that money could buy. Only they didn't count on God or fate or maybe just nature to stop them. An early snowstorm trapped them; many died, and others who survived were never the same again. Sheldon lost his leg, crushed by a wagon and amputated by Boothe Carlyle.

A large part of his money gone, Sheldon went back to St. Louis and drifted for five long years. His one attempt at taking hold of life again didn't spring from ambition but from revenge. He hired Oliver Sherrod, a one-time friend of Boothe Carlyle's, to sabotage a wagon train of missionaries Carlyle was leading across Indian territory in 1837. There had been no profit in it; Gerrard just wanted Boothe Carlyle to suffer and know the bitter taste of failure as he knew it. But that attempt failed also. Sherrod had a last-minute surge of conscience and saved Carlyle and the rest of the group.

Gerrard couldn't even succeed at revenge, and after that he cared about nothing. His capital was depleted; little by little he sold off his belongings until finally his house was gone. By then it didn't matter to him; he'd discovered the comfort of liquor. First it was fine brandy and then, when his money was gone, he drank whatever he could get his hands on.

After his house was lost to those to whom he owed money, he got on a riverboat and went up the Missouri. Back where he'd started twenty years before. Full circle. He was in his middle forties, but he felt like an old, old man. He got off at a place called Bellevue, miles up the Missouri where the Platte joined the big river.

Even in his alcoholic haze, Sheldon had to laugh at the name. The view was hardly beautiful. There was the muddy Missouri and atop some dun-colored bluffs a few shacks and stores that made up a so-called trading post.

But in Bellevue he found just what he wanted.

Sheldon stumbled ashore in the fall of 1841, not caring whether he lived or died. The first place he headed was a run-down shack built of logs where a hand-lettered sign proclaimed SALOON.

Rene LaFitte owned the place. "Monsieur, welcome to Bellevue. Lovely, isn't she?"

LaFitte laughed, revealing a mouthful of rotted teeth. He was old, Sheldon realized. Really old, maybe in his seventies. His skin was like leather, deeply creased and lined, and later Sheldon decided it was pickled, tanned by the large amounts of the swill that he sampled and served in his saloon. His clothes were the color of dirt and smoke, and he smelled like a wild animal. His hair, or what was left of it, was worn in a long white pigtail down his back.

He poured Sheldon a drink. Sheldon took a long draught and shuddered.

Rene laughed again. "Strong, no? Well, strong drink for strong men. Where you bound for, monsieur?"

"Nowhere," Sheldon said shortly.

"Nowhere, anywhere. What does it matter, eh? We all die in the end." Rene poured a tumbler of whiskey and downed it easily.

"Who do you sell this whiskey to?" Sheldon asked, wondering why anyone but someone like him, who was desperate, would frequent the saloon.

"Indians. Traders. Trappers. Anyone who wants to buy. And anyone who wants to forget. A little of Rene's brew and you will forget very quickly."

It was just what Sheldon Gerrard wanted.

Winter turned to spring. Sheldon stayed. He paid Rene what he had left of his money and slept on a hard mattress on the floor of the saloon. It was a long cruel winter, and Sheldon drank enough so he didn't feel the cold or the winds. By spring his money was gone, but it didn't matter. He and Rene had become friends of a sort. Not the kind of friends who told each other their life stories, but at least friends who didn't knife each other in their sleep. In a place like Bellevue that was all a man could hope for.

Sheldon knew Rene was a French Canadian; he knew he'd been trapping and trading in the far north reaches of the Missouri for a long, long time. He didn't know anything else and didn't care.

That summer Rene taught him how to make the filthy brew that he sold as whiskey. It was a potent mixture of alcohol, chewing tobacco, Jamaican ginger, red pepper, and black molasses, mixed with water and boiled in a big kettle over an open fire.

On a bright September day in 1842, Rene went out to stir up a batch of whiskey. Three hours later, when Sheldon realized the old man hadn't reappeared, he grabbed his crutches and went out to the still behind the saloon. There he found Rene face down on the ground, lying in a pool of molasses. Dead.

No one else in Bellevue seemed to care. It was a transient kind of place, where people rarely asked your name and were so intent on their own survival they took little note of death. Sheldon couldn't bury Rene by himself. His one leg made it hard for him to balance and wield a shovel. So he just left the old man where he was until two crewmen off a riverboat came into the saloon. Sheldon gave them free drinks for digging a grave.

The next day he made a new sign: Saloon. Sheldon Gerrard, Prop.

That saloon was what Captain Dakins was thinking about as he tied up at Bellevue landing. It was early yet, but by the time he got passengers and cargo unloaded and the boat refitted for the rest of the journey, the saloon keeper would have slept off last night's excesses and be pouring again. And Dakins was working up a mighty thirst already.

"Bellevue. Everybody off. Move along." His voice cut brusquely through the mist and fog of early morning. The sun was not yet up, and a chill wind blew off the river. Meg stood by the rail and looked up the bluffs at Bellevue. The town didn't appear inviting, just another small trading post huddled along the banks of the Missouri River. Her fingers wrapped around the gold coin in her reticule. She was wracked with indecision.

Lionel appeared by her side. "You're gettin' off here, ain't you, Miz Louis. Guess your husband'll be real glad to see you."

Meg nodded and formed yet another lie in her mind. "He might even be surprised," she responded. Still she hesitated at the railing, watching the other passengers and traders disembark.

"We won't be here long," Lionel warned. "Got to keep movin' up the river."

Meg nodded, and Lionel moved away. She didn't have to get off; she could give Captain Dakins the coin and stay on the *Katherine K.*, travel upriver and down again to St. Louis. And from St. Louis she could go back to Cairo. Back to her mother, her home, her family. Meg usually wasn't indecisive. Usually, she acted hastily, precipitously, impulsively, and that's why, she told herself, she was in the trouble she was in.

She looked for Dakins. He was standing on the bluff, overseeing the off-loading of the traders' goods. The coin was hard and cold in her hand. She didn't know what she was going to do.

She felt a man at her shoulder, his thigh and groin pushed insinuatingly against her hip. Vincent Matoon. "Getting off here, Miz Louis? Bet your husband can't wait to see you."

"I'm eager to see him," she snapped.

"Yep, I'm glad to get here, too. Got my wagons waiting to be loaded. Taking those furriners with me. You don't know how valuable a blacksmith is on the trail, even one who don't speak English."

"I can imagine. Now if you excuse me, I have to speak to the captain." She'd made up her mind. She'd tell Dakins her mythical husband had vanished. Run off. Died. It didn't matter; she'd tell another lie and then she'd get back on the *Katherine K.* and start the long journey home.

Meg pushed her away across the gangplank, past men heaving and grunting as they unloaded the heavy supplies for the traders. Slipping and sliding on the dry sand, she clambered up the bluff and looked around for Dakins. He'd vanished. She looked down the street of the straggly little town—a few shacks, barns, and lean-tos. Not much of a place. She was glad she'd decided to get back on the boat. There was nothing for her in a place like this.

The sun was an hour away from rising, and there was a strange eerie glow on the river as dawn grazed the fog and mist. She glanced back down the bluff. Vincent Matoon was striding across the gangplank giving orders to the husky blacksmith who followed him. Meg headed down the town's rutted and dusty street, moving away from Matoon and toward Dakins, she hoped.

The light that shone through a greasy window beckoned her. The place was no more than a shack, but perhaps Dakins had business there. Meg pushed open the door. The room was empty; an oil lantern sputtered on the table, giving off an acrid scent that mingled with that of stale whiskey and stagnant air. She wrinkled her nose in disgust. She hated the smell of whiskey or ale. It reminded her of Caleb.

"Captain Dakins?" she called softly. Silence answered. Her eyes swept the room contemptuously. There was a pitiful makeshift bar of planks laid across some barrels, three scarred tables, and half a dozen rickety chairs. Behind the bar were a few bottles of a dark liquid that Meg imagined to be whiskey. What kind of man, she wondered, would choose to make a living from a place like this?

She turned to leave when the door swung violently open and clattered against the wall. Vincent Matoon's form filled the door. Meg's heart began to pound, and she felt a frisson of fear slide along her spine.

He stood blocking her way. "Meeting your husband, Miz Louis?"

"Yes, yes, I am. He just stepped out for a moment. He'll be back shortly." She hated the way Matoon was looking at her, as if he knew she was lying. She hated the sneering smirk on his lips that said he knew better than she what she wanted.

"I'd like to meet the fellow that's good enough for you." He sauntered in and took a chair near the door. There was no way Meg could get past him without coming within arm's reach. He leaned back in the chair and stretched out his legs. "How about getting me a shot of whiskey, Miz Louis? And pour one for yourself and your husband, too. We'll wait for him together. That is, if you have a husband."

"I do; he doesn't drink, and I'm not a barmaid."
She stepped toward him. "Let me pass."

He slouched indolently in the chair, his legs
blocking her way. "Not until you get me a little
drink. That's all. Just one. Surely your wifely ways have
taught you how to take care of a man's needs."

Again there was that mocking grin. Meg wanted
to slap the look off his face, but instead she took a
long, deep breath and thought. If she poured him a
drink, that might distract him and give her time to
rush around him. Or if he made a move for her, she
could throw it in his face and run out the door.

"All right," she said, trying to keep the shakiness
out of her voice. "No harm in pouring you a drink."
She moved behind the bar and made a pretense of
finding the right whiskey bottle and a clean glass.
The latter was impossible. She turned her back on
Matoon and used her skirt to wipe the smudges off
a dirty tumbler. Before she turned, she reached into
her reticule and took out the carving knife. It gave
her courage just to hold it. She took it in her left
hand, hiding it in the folds of her skirt as she poured
the whiskey with her right.

Praying that her trembling wasn't noticeable, Meg
walked toward Matoon. She held her head high; if
she had to kill him to get away, she would. She
knew she had the will; she didn't know if she had
the strength.

He made the first move, surging out of the chair
before she reached him, grabbing for her with his
big hands. Meg screamed and threw the whiskey in
his face.

"You bitch," he shouted. "I ought to beat your face
in for that, but I won't. I'm going to do what I've
wanted since the first time I saw you."

He was fast and strong, and he had his hands on her shoulders before she could react. Meg struggled to use the knife, but he pinned her arms and spread-eagled her across one of the tables. She kicked and bucked, fighting with all she had. She heard some-one screaming and realized the terrorized sounds were coming from her own throat. His face was close, his mouth hovering over hers. The feel of him—his scent, his touch—made her want to gag in revulsion. But instead she raised her head and bit down on his chin with all her strength.

He let her go momentarily, spewing curses. She raised her left hand; the knife gleamed wickedly in the lamplight. She knew she had one chance. "Please, God," she whispered. She drew back her hand and aimed for his heart; he lunged toward her and her knife grazed his shoulder.

His body hit her with a terrifying thud, and they fell together to the floor. "I'm going to rape you, you bitch, and then I'm going to kill you. Cut you apart with your own knife. Scream your head off. Nobody will hear."

Sheldon Gerrard was sleeping the sleep of the innocent and the drunk. He was dreaming about the cold and the snow, a dream he had often, but something was different this time. He could actually hear the screams of the wagon train party dying in the snow. Or was it the echo of his own screams when Boothe Carlyle cut off his leg? He wanted the screams to stop; he wanted them to go away.

The screams didn't stop.

Slowly Sheldon opened his eyes. He was lying on his pallet in the small room behind the bar. He'd pas-sed out about midnight as usual, leaving his patrons to stagger home whenever they chose. He pressed a hand against his pounding head. He had to stop the noise, he had to stop the screaming. Groggily, he reached for his crutch and raised himself on his one good leg. By the time he reached the doorway into the saloon, he realized the screams weren't in his head. They were real. A man and a woman lay struggling on the floor. The awful sounds were coming from her.

He acted instinctively. "Stop. Let her go." He hobbled toward the thrashing figures. "Let her go, I said."

The man raised his head and looked Sheldon dead in the eye. "The whore is mine. Go to hell, peg leg."

Sheldon felt an emotion he hadn't experienced in years, a mixture of righteous indignation and anger. Without another thought he raised his crutch high over his head and made a long, swooping strike toward his target. The man's head exploded in a mass of bone and blood. Sheldon tried to stop his own forward momentum and grabbed for the edge of the table, but it slid away from him and toppled over. The lantern crashed to the ground, and its flame hungrily gobbled up the whiskey that Meg had spilled. Sheldon fell heavily to the floor, his head striking one of the legs of the table.

Meg struggled to free herself from the heavy body that lay across her. Matoon's blood was trickling down on her face and hair. Trying to keep from gagging on her own bile, she crouched beside him on the floor. She had no doubt that he was dead, and she wasn't sorry. Then she smelled the smoke. The broken lantern, the spilled whiskey, the wooden chairs and tables—the place would go up like a tinderbox. Meg staggered to her feet; she'd escaped her husband and Vincent Matoon. As sure as God was in his heaven, she wasn't going to be burned to death in a saloon fire.

She quickly moved beside the body of the man who'd saved her. "Hey, mister. We have to get out of here. Hey, mister."

Sheldon lay immobile.

"Damn it, mister, we have to move. Now." She rolled him over, pushing and shoving the dead weight of his body. The greedy flames were lapping at the flimsy walls; smoke filled the air. Meg knew she had only a few moments. If she couldn't wake this man, then she'd have to leave him. She wasn't going to burn with him.

She slapped his face, once, twice, three times. Harder each time. "Wake up, damn you!" she screamed. "We have to get out of here." Her mouth and eyes were filled with smoke, and she could hear the crackle of burning wood.

He opened one eye. "Can't walk," he said.

"If you can't walk, then you'll crawl, do you hear me?" Meg slapped him again. In the distance she heard two sounds. The first was that of the *Katherine K.*'s whistle; the boat was pulling away from the landing. The second were voices coming toward the saloon, shouting, "Fire! Fire!"

"Crawl," she shouted in Sheldon's ear. "Do you hear me, crawl!"

Smoke blinded their eyes, and flames danced wildly around them. The roof was now aflame and at any moment, Meg knew, burning debris could hurtle onto them. She rolled him to his stomach, grabbed his shirt, and pulled him to his knees. "Crawl," she ordered once more.

He looked at her blankly, uncomprehendingly, and then like a crab he began to scuttle across the floor toward light and air. Behind him, on her hands and knees, Meg followed her savior into the dawn.

*   *   *

The fire was out. Nothing remained of the saloon but smoking ruins. Vincent Matoon's body had been found, so badly burned that his head wounds weren't noticeable unless someone took the time to examine the body closely. No one did. Folks in Bellevue took death in their stride just as they did everything else. Their interest was turned on the living now, toward a young red-haired woman standing by the wagons assembled on Bellevue's one street.

She was talking to the foreigners, and the other traders hovered nearby in groups of two or three, blatantly eavesdropping.

"You're traveling with me now," she said, using her index finger to point at her chest. "Kincaid. That's me. I'm your new . . ." She struggled for the right words. "I'm your boss now. Boss? Understand?"

A look of comprehension lit the blacksmith's face. "Boss," he repeated.

Meg nodded. He pointed to himself. "Henryk." He pointed to his wife. "Anna."

"Anna, Henryk. Good. Good." Meg shook their hands. How could she explain to them what she was going to do when the idea had only come into her head minutes before? She'd seen the wagons lining up, heard the men talking of Matoon and how there was no one to drive his wagon, listened to them discuss how they'd divide his goods and what they'd do about the foreigners.

The answer came to Meg as clearly and cleanly as the answer to a prayer. There was no indecision or hesitation this time. She knew what she had to do.

Anna and Henryk were watching her warily, but not in an unfriendly way, she decided. He was powerfully built with a head of curling dark hair and a fierce-looking mustache and beard. His eyes were as dark as a midnight sky. Anna was strongly built, too, with a full bosom and wide hips. Her hair was wispy and faintly blond, her eyes pale blue; she was sunburned and windblown, and she looked exhausted and scared.

Meg felt a sudden burst of compassion for these people; they were as desperate as she to survive, for why else would they have undertaken this long journey into a land that was so strange and hostile to them?

She pointed at Henryk. "From Russia?" she asked. "Russia?" she repeated to Anna.

"No, no." Henryk shook his head angrily. "No Russia. Poland. Henryk Wydowski."

"Poland." Meg had no idea where Poland was, or Russia for that matter. She knew they were somewhere in Europe; she tried to remember the map that had hung in the one-room schoolhouse in Cairo and couldn't. All she knew was that Poland was very far away, and that Henryk and Anna were somehow her responsibility now.

"Poland," she said again, nodding her head. "Good."

Anna and Henryk nodded wisely, too.

Meg pointed to one of Matoon's wagons. "You drive."

"I drive," he said. Then he pointed to the second wagon and raised his eyebrows.

Meg understood. "I'll drive that one," she said.

One of the men who'd been listening approached her, a belligerent look on his round, clean-shaven face that let Meg know without his speaking that he was the enemy.

"Donnelly's the name, ma'am. Wagon master for this here group. What did I hear you telling these folks?"

"How do you do, Mr. Donnelly." Meg pushed her hair out of her face and held her head high. She knew she cut a ridiculous figure, her dress torn and dirty, her face smudged with soot and smoke, her hair billowing wildly around her head, her dress splattered with streaks of Matoon's dried blood. She lied about that to the people who'd helped her after the fire. She told them she'd cut herself on the broken lantern. That lie came easily, and so would the next and the next. She had told so many lies now that there was no way of stopping.

"What's this I heard you telling those foreigners? You say you're their boss? They were indentured to Matoon. We can't let no woman take over his wagons and his goods, ma'am."

"Well, of course not, Mr. Donnelly." She'd expected that and she was ready; she'd endured so much these past weeks that nothing or no one could stand in her way now, certainly not a short little Irishman. "My husband and I bought both wagons from Mr. Matoon a short time before his unfortunate demise, and of course we bought the indenture papers also."

Donnelly's eyes narrowed in disbelief. "Matoon sold out to you? Nah, I don't believe it."

Meg didn't waver for a moment. "It's true, but sadly Mr. Matoon isn't here to verify the sale, and even more sadly all the papers and the cash that exchanged hands burned in the fire. You just have my word—and my husband's—against—" she forced herself to laugh lightly, "against that of a dead man."

"Why would Matoon do a damn fool thing like that?"

"He said something about getting a fair price and going right back to St. Louis to resupply. He'd get two trips in this summer, not one."

Donnelly rubbed his chin nervously. "Well, Matoon

was a go-getter, but he didn't say nothing to me about it."

"I think it was a spur of the moment decision." Meg smiled tightly at Donnelly. "And now if you'll excuse me, I need to find my husband. We don't want to hold up the wagons." Six wagons were lined up, drivers on the seats, looking anxious and restive as the sun climbed higher in the sky.

"Well, I don't know—" Donnelly took off his hat and scratched his bald head.

Meg knew she'd won. A surer man would have claimed the wagon himself. Donnelly had waited too long, thrown off by the fact that Meg wasn't alone. She had a husband, someone to stand up for her and secure her position on the train. Meg smiled innocently at Donnelly. "Now if you want to go ahead, that's fine. Of course, the only blacksmith on the wagon train is in my employ—I'd hate to be out in the wilderness without help if a mule throws a shoe or an axle breaks." Thank God, she thought, for Lionel and his stories, although in the midst of telling such lies she felt guilty for even thinking that God would hear her.

Donnelly checked the sun. "We got fifteen minutes, no more." The suspicious look came back in his eyes. "Where's your husband? Don't look to me like you got one, and if you don't"—he turned aside and spit a stream of tobacco juice into the dirt— "ain't no way you're going on this trek without your man. It just ain't allowed."

"I'm going to find him right now." Meg turned back to Henryk and Anna, and positioned one of them in each wagon. She'd seen how the other traders had treated them on the boat, as if they were half-human. Anna and Henryk owed no loyalty to them; she would earn their trust and they could have their freedom as soon as they reached Fort Laramie.

She strode across the street toward the still smoldering saloon. She saw the man who'd saved her groveling in the hot ashes. It made her sick to see him, crawling on the ground like an animal. He was hopeless, but it didn't matter. He was a man—of sorts—and she needed him. Not because she was weak, but because she was strong.

She had vowed never to make herself subservient to a man again, never to be taken in by pretty words and promises or offers of security. But this was 1843 and once she made her decision to steal Matoon's wagons, she knew she needed the protection of marriage and a husband—not a mythical one, but a flesh and blood man. The man who'd killed Matoon was the only likely candidate around. He ought to be as anxious to get out of town as she was. He had as much to run from as she did. It seemed a fair deal to her; neither of them had anything in Bellevue.

He saw her shadow over him and looked up.

"What in the name of heaven are you doing?" she asked.

"Looking for something." He said it calmly and continued to push through the ashes with a stick.

"I have a proposition for you."

He ignored her.

"Aren't you interested?" she persisted.

"I'm not interested in anything but what I'm doing now."

"Too bad, mister, because my proposition could mean a great deal of money for you."

Sheldon reached for a rough plank he'd been using as a crutch and laboriously pulled himself to his feet. "Lady, I don't know who you are or where you came from, but you are nothing but bad luck for me. Last night I had a saloon and a place to sleep. Then you show up, and I have nothing."

Meg bit her lips. He was as disheveled as she, dirty, tired, with rivulets of sweat leaving tracks on his sooty face. She almost started laughing, thinking about the two of them forming a partnership, but she controlled her hysteria.

"I know this seems strange, but I think we can help each other, just for a while. A month or two. No longer. Until those wagons get to Fort Laramie."

Sheldon glanced at the wagons, uninterested.

"Matoon—the dead man—had two wagons filled with goods that we can sell on the Oregon Trail. I've claimed them for us."

"For us?" Sheldon's mouth fell open in amazement.

Meg took a deep breath. "I've told the wagon master, Donnelly, that you're my husband and that we bought the goods from Matoon before he died." The words came out with a rush.

Sheldon didn't smile, nor did he laugh. Instead he sank back to the ashes and resumed his slow examination of the ruins.

Meg knelt beside him. She felt feverish and light-headed and determined to make him listen to her. "For God's sake, man, have you nothing to say?"

He looked at her, his eyes blank and dead. "Nothing except you're not only bad luck, you're a thief to boot, and crazier than I am."

"No, I'm not, mister." She grabbed his arm. "Not crazy anyway. I'm just more desperate than you. Now you listen to me. Those wagons are ours for the taking—"

"You take them," he interrupted.

"I would if I could, but I'm a woman alone in the middle of nowhere, and even though I've learned that most men are worthless and cause nothing but pain, I need one now. I need a husband."

For a moment something flickered in his eyes.

Meg made a spitting sound and dropped his arm. "Oh, not for that. I've had enough of that to last me forever. I need a man to be my husband until we get to Laramie. To make these men think I'm a respectable lady who's married to a man who could actually get Matoon to sell him the wagons."

"You have some nerve for a woman," he said grudgingly.

"I come by it naturally," she said. "It runs in the family. You'll do it?"

"No," he answered. "I'm staying right here. I don't care about Fort Laramie or money or whatever's in that wagon."

Meg leaned closer and whispered in his ear. "How do you feel about being hanged by the neck until you're dead?"

"What are—"

"Because if you don't get up on that one good leg of yours right now and get in that wagon with me, I'm telling the good folks of Bellevue that you killed Matoon outright. In cold blood and, mister, I've told so many lies lately that it will roll off my tongue as sweet as honey."

"Dying means nothing to me, lady."

Meg took his measure, eyes narrowed. "There's dying and then there's dying, isn't there? Being in Bellevue is one kind of death, I guess, and drinking that rotgut liquor is another. That's death in life and something you chose. But having a lynch mob put a rope around your neck and hang you up like a pig at killing time—now that's another kind of dying. Your body just hanging on the gallows while the vultures pick it clean."

Meg wasn't sure where the words or the ideas came from, but the images were powerful for her, and by the look on the man's face, she knew he was listening, really listening.

She lowered her voice. "If you come with me, just for a while, you can choose the place you want to die. They got whiskey in Fort Laramie, too."

He drew a deep, shaky breath. Meg noticed his hands were trembling. "Looks like I'm between a rock and a hard place."

"It's not a difficult decision," Meg said, getting to her feet. "And, mister, if you really wanted to die, all you had to do was crawl back in that fire. You didn't do that. You may say you want to die, but you don't. Not yet."

His look was one of hate. "Damn you, woman."

Meg knew she'd won; she'd gotten him to feel. He looked mean and angry and dangerous. The way she felt.

"Hand me my crutch." Awkwardly he got to his feet. She didn't help him. He liked that about her. She was the wildest-looking woman he'd ever seen, her red hair swirled out in Medusa-like locks around her face, her blue eyes bright with desperation. He took one last look around the ruins and shrugged. "Hell, I'd just as soon drink myself to death in Fort Laramie as here."

Together they started toward the wagons. Suddenly Sheldon bent down, using the plank for balance, and plucked something shiny out of the ashes and held it in his hand.

"Is that what you were looking for?"

"It's all I have left now." He opened his hand and showed her a coin gleaming gold in the sun.

Meg's face paled under the layer of smoke and dirt. She couldn't speak; instead she scrabbled in her reticule and pulled out a gold coin, identical to the one he'd scooped out of the ashes.

"Tell me where you got that coin," she demanded.

"Years ago, in Pennsylvania. Some trader found it along the Ohio and I bought it. I've never seen another like it. Where did you get yours?"

Her voice was hoarse. "From my mother. She got it from her granny, who brought the coins from the Old Country. There were nine or ten of them—my mother used one over twenty years ago to pay her way down the Ohio. There was a boat wreck. Maybe her coin—"

"I'll be damned and double-damned," Sheldon said. "I'd been hoping for years I'd find another one. What did you say your mother's name was?"

"My mother is Katherine Carlyle. I'm Meg Kincaid."

"You any relation to Boothe Carlyle?" He felt as though he couldn't draw a breath. His question sounded far away, as if someone else had asked it. He knew the answer, of course. The coin, the girl. It was as if some great net had been flung out, and he was helplessly being drawn to the center of a deep black hole, his future and his past connected to the gold coin he'd cherished over the years.

"My uncle. Do you know Boothe? Have you seen him?"

Sheldon smiled, a bittersweet grimace that turned down his mouth. "Oh, yes, I know your uncle well. Everything I am I owe to him."

Meg heard the bitterness in his voice, and the pain.

He looked back at her. "My name is Sheldon Gerrard," he said softly.

Meg took a step back. Her fingers clutched

spasmodically around the two gold coins. Sheldon Gerrard. She knew the name; she knew the story. He was the enemy, the devil incarnate, the evil one. And of all the men in the world, he was the one who had saved her life. He was the one she had asked to give her a future.

The laughter that she had held down earlier could no longer be controlled, and it burst forth, peal after peal, hysterically rising toward the sky.

Sheldon didn't laugh. He took Meg's arm and led her across the ashes toward the wagons, while the traders looked at the pair in stunned silence. He helped her into the wagon seat and managed to climb in himself. There was nothing else he could do, he thought. The hand of fate had found him at last, and he couldn't run any further.

Chapter Eight

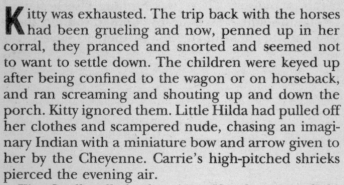

Kitty was exhausted. The trip back with the horses had been grueling and now, penned up in her corral, they pranced and snorted and seemed not to want to settle down. The children were keyed up after being confined to the wagon or on horseback, and ran screaming and shouting up and down the porch. Kitty ignored them. Little Hilda had pulled off her clothes and scampered nude, chasing an imaginary Indian with a miniature bow and arrow given to her by the Cheyenne. Carrie's high-pitched shrieks pierced the evening air.

Kitty finally called to her sister. "Sarah, can you help me with these children? We need to bathe them."

Sarah's irritable voice came from inside the house. "I'm washing myself, Kitty. I have dust and dirt in my ears and in my hair—"

Kitty bit back a sharp retort. Sometimes she thought her sister was more trouble than she'd ever be worth.

Just then the dogs started barking. "Someone's coming," Kitty called out. "Maybe it's Jim!"

That was enough to calm the children momentarily and bring Sarah out of the house, her long red hair streaming water. Both women started down the path toward the road. Kitty knew she should have snatched up a gun; it was foolish to go rushing toward an unknown horseman without a weapon, but she was sure this was her brother. The dogs ranged ahead of her, barking deeply and fiercely.

The first sight of the man who rode into view stopped both Sarah and Kitty in their tracks. He was tall, dressed in a cotton shirt and trousers, wearing a large-brimmed straw hat. His skin was the color of rich dark coffee.

Sarah grabbed Kitty's arm. "My Lord, it's a Nigra."

The two women stared. To their knowledge there were no black men in Indian territory. Slavery was practiced in Missouri, and occasionally on their trips to Westport or Fort Leavenworth, the family might run across Missouri settlers with slaves. But to have a black man appear on the Adamson farm was enough to take their breath away.

"Evenin' ma'am." He tipped his hat.

"Good evening," Kitty managed.

He stopped his horse, a big roan, Kitty noted instantly.

"You Miz Adamson?"

"Yes, I am. I'm Kitty Adamson." The dogs were still barking furiously, running at the horse, which skittered nervously and rolled its eyes. Kitty called them off and after slashing at them with a stick she found on the ground, got them under control.

They lolled at her feet, tongues hanging out, but their eyes were still watchful of the intruder.

The tall black man got down from his horse. "My name is Vertie. I have a letter for you. From my master, Mr. Charles Gallier." There was pride in the man's voice. "He owns a farm farther north in the hills."

Kitty vaguely remembered Ben talking about another family that had moved in. She reached for the letter. "It looks as though your horse could use some water and you might like some refreshments yourself."

Kitty didn't open the letter until the man had watered his horse at the trough near the porch. Then she ordered Sarah, "Go fetch Mr. Vertie something to drink. Spring water or maybe coffee."

"Just water," Vertie said.

"Then water, Sarah." Kitty gestured to the porch. "Sit down, Mr. Vertie."

"Just Vertie, ma'am, and I'll stand."

Puzzled, Kitty looked at him. Why would a man who'd obviously ridden a long way and had the look of exhaustion on his face refuse to sit down? Then she remembered. He was a slave, and perhaps slaves weren't allowed to sit while their masters stood. The whole idea irritated her. "Oh, sit down, Vertie, while I read this letter."

Gratefully he sank to the steps of the porch and even more gratefully drank the cup of water that Sarah brought. Sarah hung back near the door, watching curiously. Kitty's children were hardly as circumspect. They had stopped shrieking the moment the dogs announced a visitor and now like little animals crept close to the large form seated on the porch. Vertie smiled at them and that broke the ice.

Hilda ran toward Vertie, touched his sleeve, and then raced away. Carrie was braver. She crawled up to him and pulled herself up on his shoulder and then tentatively ran her fingers across his face.

"Look, Mama," Hilda called out. "He's got black

on him and it doesn't come off."

Kitty hid her embarrassment in sharp words. "Carrie! Stay away. Leave Mr. Vertie alone."

Vertie smiled. "She don't bother me none, Miz Adamson. She's a cute little thing. I have a boy about the same age."

Hilda crept close again and began to play a kind of tag around the man. Since he didn't seem to mind, Kitty turned her attention to the letter. Just then Ben appeared from behind the house. "I heard the dogs . . ."

Kitty waved the letter at Ben. "This is Vertie, Ben. He's . . . well, he works for the Galliers up north in the hills."

Vertie was on his feet now; Ben shook his hand. Vertie seemed uncomfortable. "Welcome to our farm. We take it you'll be spending the night."

"Oh no, sah. I got to git back. Mr. Charles be expectin' me. I need to take your answer, sah."

"Then I guess we need to know the question." Ben went up the steps and stood by Kitty.

"Mr. Gallier and his wife have smallpox vaccine, Ben! They say they can inoculate the children for us. All we have to do is let them know when we can go to their farm. Isn't that wonderful? Do you know them?"

Ben took the letter and read it quickly. "No, I don't know them. I heard of them at Fort Leavenworth. Southerners. Slave owners. You know how I feel about slavery, Kitty."

"And I feel the same way, Ben, but this is a generous offer. One we should think about. An inoculation for the pox—"

"We can go to the fort and ask the doctor there—"

"He's an army doctor. He has no responsibility for us."

"No, Kitty," Ben said. "We aren't going to be beholden to slave owners."

Kitty's mouth set in a stubborn line. She loved Ben because of his high moral standards. She knew he was a good man, the best she'd ever met. But she also knew that to survive sometimes even the most righteous had to bend.

She spoke softly so that the children wouldn't hear her. "I know how you feel, Ben, and I respect that. But I also know what smallpox can do. It can kill our babies, Ben, and all the righteousness in the world couldn't bring back our children. So if you won't go, then I will. I can drive the wagon and take Hilda and Carrie and Sarah. It's not that far and I can do it. Maybe Billy can ride with me."

Ben's jaw tightened. "I don't want to argue, Kitty."

"I have to do this, Ben. I have to take care of my babies, and if the devil himself had the vaccine, I'd ask him for it. I'd beg him for it," she said defiantly.

Ben shook his head in defeat. "I wish you'd think about this for a minute."

"I have." She crossed to Vertie. "Tell Mr. Gallier that we're grateful for his offer and we will come in three days' time. You'll need to tell us the quickest trail through the hills."

Ben turned to go into the house. "Sarah, get those children and get them in bed. They're running around like heathens." Then immediately sorry for his sharp words, he stooped down and held open his arms. "Come on, little ones. Papa will bathe you tonight."

Over their heads he looked at Kitty and in her eyes saw her smile.

Jim rode the entire first night without remembering any part of the trip. He'd almost killed the poor horse, and at that breakneck speed in the blind dark it was a wonder either one of them had come out of it as well as they had.

Sunup found him slumped in the saddle while his weary mount grazed. His face was wet and it took him a moment to realize the moisture was from tears. It took him even longer to remember why he was crying.

A ten-year-old boy, watching his pa die. Seeing that stricken look of profoundest grief on his ma's face and knowing there was nothing he could do to comfort her, knowing there was something he *should* have done . . . The anger, the helplessness, the loss. The certainty that if he had been a little braver, a little stronger, faster, smarter, or better, he could have saved his pa. He could have stopped it.

His sister Kitty had thrown herself on the killer. It wasn't talked about much in the family, but the unspoken story was that she had fired the weapon that put an end to the madman. She had done something. She had stopped it. But Jim just stood there and watched stupidly while his father fell dead.

At ten years old he was the man of the family, and he had spent a lifetime trying to make it up to his mother and the children, knowing he'd never be half the man Byrd Kincaid had been, but trying, in his own clumsy fashion, to fill his shoes. It had gnawed at him all those years, trying his best and knowing his best would never be enough. Finally he'd just walked away.

Last night another madman had ridden in. And Jim had stood by in helplessness and shock while the night was bathed in blood, and then he'd run away. He should have stopped it. He should at least have tried. But he had done nothing.

With its own instinct for survival, the horse had

taken its rider to water. Jim slid off and washed his face in the stream, allowing a little of the water to trickle into his swollen throat. That was when he realized he was not being followed.

That simple truth washed through him like a slowly cresting wave, dragging exhaustion in its wake. He tied up the horse without bothering to unsaddle it and lay down on the ground in the shadow of a scrawny tree. He was asleep almost immediately.

The noonday sun, hot on his face, woke him. It was then, and only then, that he was able to take stock of the situation.

He had a horse now, good army stock that had already proven his stamina. There was a rifle in the scabbard and ammunition. The soldier had apparently expected to be on patrol a while, for he carried a good supply of emergency rations—cornmeal, hardtack, and coffee.

That soldier was dead now, shot to death by his own commanding officer. And Jim had stood by and watched it happen.

He was missing one boot and his hat, and even the slightest pressure on his injured ankle caused excruciating agony to flare in his leg. But in almost every way he was better off than he had been at this time yesterday.

Last night he had stood by and watched four men being murdered in cold blood. How could he be better off?

Captain Lyndsay. He would never forget that name or that narrow, cold face or those eyes like chips of blue ice. Without a flicker of remorse he had shot three men in their sleep, and blown his own subordinate in half without so much as a whisper of warning. Jim felt bile rise at the memory.

An army officer had murdered four men, and Jim

was the only witness. What was he supposed to do now?

Unbidden, Jim saw before his mind's eye the map Rafferty had drawn in the ground. Five days, he'd said. Five days away from family, from safety, from Sarah.

Rafferty, quiet and strong. McClellan, with his boisterous laugh and wild stories. Leo, too young to die. Jim owed them his life. But what choice did he have?

Sarah, he thought, *I'm coming. I'm coming to get you and then we're going home, both of us. Home . . .*

Chapter Nine

S arah was so excited she could hardly sit still in the back of the wagon. They'd left the farm long before sunrise and now, near noon, it seemed as though they would never arrive at their destination. The trip was hard on the children, and it wasn't made easier on any of them by the fact that Kitty and Ben were still arguing. Ben was angry, angrier than Sarah had ever seen him, and Kitty's mouth had a tight look to it.

The children seemed to have picked up some of the tension. Carrie cried almost nonstop for the first ten miles and then fell into an exhausted sleep, her head nestled in Sarah's lap. Hilda chattered nonstop, and Sarah listened with half an ear. What she was really listening to were snatches of conversation from the front of the wagon about the Galliers.

"Southerners . . ."

"Slave owners . . ."

"Too fine for the likes of us . . ."

"A Christian thing to do . . ."

Sarah didn't care if they were Christian or not.

Just the thought of meeting another family, of seeing their house and entering their world, was infinitely exciting to her. She'd tried to pretend it didn't matter that much, but she'd begged Kitty to let her wear her best dress, a pale blue muslin, and she brushed her hair until it gleamed and tied it back from her face with a pink bow. The Galliers were from the South, they had slaves, they probably lived in a mansion. Maybe they had children, maybe a girl her age. Someone to be her best friend.

Sarah shut her eyes and gave way to the rolling and rocking of the wagon. In a place halfway between waking and sleep, she imagined herself in a lovely new dress, white with a full skirt, her hair pinned up, her arms and neck adorned with shiny jewelry. She was dancing with someone who was tall and handsome. She couldn't quite see his face, but she could almost hear the music.

"I think we're almost there." The tension in Kitty's voice roused Sarah, and she sat up and smoothed down the wild bits of hair that had escaped the bow.

The Gallier house sat at the edge of the prairie, sheltered in the shadow of the hills. "Oh," Sarah said, feeling let down. It wasn't a mansion. It was simply a house.

"Oh," Kitty repeated with envy. "A stone house. Look at it, Ben. Isn't it wonderful?"

Sarah looked again.

The house was two stories tall, made of pale, gray limestone with a high gabled roof of shingles. There were eight windows across the front, four up and four down, and two huge stone chimneys on either end. The rectangular front porch was supported by six white columns. Bushes and flowers bloomed along the curved drive that led to the porch. It wasn't a mansion, but it was certainly a more commanding house than any Sarah had seen before in Cairo or in Kansas Territory.

Ben pulled the horses to a stop and began to help Kitty and the children out. Carrie, just awakened, was dazed and half-asleep, but Hilda was wide awake and talking. The family stood uneasily by their wagon, not sure what to do next. Sarah climbed out of the wagon and stood beside them.

"Well, just go knock on the door, Kitty," Ben ordered. "Tell them we're here." Kitty was hesitant. "It's your idea," he reminded her.

Before she took a step down the gravel path of crushed stones, the front door opened and a woman hurried down the path toward them.

"Welcome, Mr. and Mrs. Adamson. I'm Emilie Gallier, and my husband and I are so pleased that you could visit us."

Sarah felt another twinge of disappointment. She'd expected Emilie Gallier to be young, beautiful, and fashionable; instead, she was old, almost as old as Sarah's mother, and, if not fat, certainly plump. She wasn't very tall either. She was neither exciting nor sophisticated.

Emilie Gallier chatted easily, making them feel welcome. "What a long journey you've had. Shall we have something cool to drink? Do you like lemonade? We received lemons from New Orleans only this week. Such a long journey, but what a fine taste."

"Something to drink would be nice," Kitty managed.

"I need to see to the horses," Ben said.

"One of the slaves will do that," Emilie said. "Our stable boy's very good with horses."

"I need to see to my own horses," Ben said stubbornly.

"As you wish, Mr. Adamson. Just follow the drive

around behind the house. You'll see the barn. There is a trough for water . . ."

But Ben had already begun to lead the horses and wagon away; Sarah blushed with embarrassment. Ben was being rude, but if Emilie Gallier noticed she gave no sign. "And now these poor children—they must be so tired. Come, little one." She held out her hand to Hilda. "Let's have something good to eat and drink."

She turned her attention to Sarah. Emilie's face was round, her mouth full. Her eyes were a deep dark brown, so dark that it was hard to see her pupils. Her brown hair, streaked with silver, was pulled away from her face and worn in wings over her ears and then caught in a bun in back. She wore a dress of pale lavender; Sarah thought the material might be satin, but she wasn't sure. There was a fichu of white lace at Emilie's neck, fastened with a cameo set in a pale pink stone and circled with gold. A ring of pearls and diamonds glittered on one of her fingers.

"You're Sarah, aren't you?" Her voice was low and soft, with a drawling kind of accent that Sarah had never heard before. "I heard there was a young woman visiting the Adamsons."

"Yes, ma'am, I'm Sarah Kincaid."

"What a pretty girl you are. And your hair—*mon Dieu*, half the women I know would kill for hair like that. The color of burnished copper."

Sarah had always taken her red hair for granted. It was a family trait, one she shared with all her sisters and brothers except Kitty. She couldn't imagine that anyone would kill for hair like hers . . . but it sounded very flattering.

"Now come in," Emilie ordered. "Let's get out of the sun. It's bad for our complexions."

Like chickens following the mother hen, Kitty and

Sarah, each carrying a child, filed down the path behind Emilie. She opened the door and stepped inside. Sarah drew a long breath. She felt as though she'd stepped into paradise.

"So you like my house?" Emilie Gallier smiled at the look of awe on Sarah's face.

"Yes, ma'am."

"Then I'll be honored to take you and Mrs. Adamson on a tour. But first we must take care of these children. Dorcas, please."

Appearing as if by magic, a black servant stepped from the shadows.

"I think the little ones might need something to eat and drink now. Feed them in my office."

Carrie was fascinated by the black face that bent near her, just as she'd been intrigued by Vertie on his visit.

"Come on, li'l missy. Come with Dorcas." Carrie held out her arms eagerly; Hilda was less sure and clung to her mother's skirt, but when Dorcas whispered, "Our barn cat just had kittens, missy. You like kitties?" Hilda giggled with delight and let Dorcas lead her away.

Emilie touched Kitty's arm. "Don't worry, Mrs. Adamson. Dorcas took care of me when I was little. She knows everything about children. They'll be safe. My husband and I have no children of our own, and Dorcas misses having little ones around."

"I guess she's a slave," Kitty said slowly.

"All our servants are slaves," Emilie said evenly. "And now would you like lemonade or to see the house?"

"The house, please—" Sarah broke off, blushing. She hadn't meant to be so forward.

"The house, of course," Emilie said with a smile.

"I'm sure it's not much different from your own. Life is very—well, simple here in the hills."

Sarah bit back her reply. *Simple* wasn't the word she'd use. The Gallier house was the most elegantly furnished she'd ever seen.

Emilie led them through the house. "This is our parlor. All of the furniture was brought from Louisiana with us. *Mon Dieu*, what a trip. Up the Mississippi by steamboat to St. Louis and then up the Missouri on another boat, and then by wagon and caravan from Weston Landing. So much was damaged . . ."

Sarah thought everything was perfect, from the heavy draperies at the windows to the pale carpet on the floor. There was a tilt-top table between the windows, a sofa and two high-backed chairs covered in cream-colored fabric shot with threads of gold. Side chairs and small tables, cut-glass vases filled with flowers, a miniature tea set of blue and white crowded the treasure-filled room.

Sarah drank in everything not only with her eyes but also with her other senses. She smelled the scent of flowers and underlying that, a potpourri of spices. Her fingers traced the pattern of the curtains. Her eyes sought out the loveliness of the room and dwelled on silver candlesticks and dainty porcelain figurines, a hearth rug embroidered with petit point roses, and a picture in an ornate frame.

"Oh, how pretty." She stood in front of the fireplace and looked up at the watercolor. "The house looks like a palace!"

Emilie laughed delightedly. "That's my family home on the Mississippi River above New Orleans. We call it Deveraux House."

Sarah stared at the painting and wondered what

it must be like to live in such a place. The white
house had a high pitched roof and a wide veranda
running around the second floor. There were ten
huge columns supporting the roof of the veranda.
The lawn was verdant and green, and a huge magnolia tree grew beside the house.

"I know you must miss it," Kitty said.

"Sometimes." Emilie kept her tone light.

Kitty asked the question that Sarah had been too
shy to speak. "Why did . . . I mean it seems odd that
you would move here into the wilderness."

For a moment Sarah thought that Emilie might
be offended, but she wasn't. She smiled. "It is odd,
isn't it? I think so myself. I'm here simply because
of Charles, my husband. He's a very remarkable man
and he has chosen to live here—at least for a while."

"Is he a farmer?" Kitty asked carefully.

"We farm," Emilie said vaguely. "But my husband is
also a scientist and philosopher. And a scholar. And
a horticulturist of some renown."

Sarah wasn't sure what a horticulturist was and was
too embarrassed to ask. Then Emilie explained.

"He's experimenting with different kinds of crops
and plants. Fruit trees, too. And grapes. He must
show you his arbor, but first the rest of the house.
That is if you are not too bored?"

Bored? Sarah was less bored than she had been in
months. They saw the dining room with its walnut
drop-leaf table, which Emilie explained had been
so much easier to transport than their big heavy
mahogany table. "We had to leave so much behind,"
Emilie said sadly. The Gallier table and its eight
dainty chairs looked nothing like the walnut table
that Billy and Ben had built.

She led them into Charles's library with its built-
in bookshelves filled with leather-bound volumes.

"Charles brought all his books," Emilie said. "So many heavy boxes."

Sarah stared. She'd never seen so many books in her life. Emile caught the look. "Do you like to read?"

"I love to," Sarah lied.

"Then we shall lend you books. My office is in the room next door. I do my accounts at my desk and take care of problems with the slaves there. We have only twenty, you know, but still there is much to keep track of."

"Twenty seems like quite a lot," Kitty said.

"In Louisiana my father owned three hundred slaves to work the sugar fields. And Charles's family owns as many. His family's plantation was upriver from ours. His brother lives there now since Charles has wandered so far afield. Now just a bit more, upstairs if you wish, and then we'll have our dinner."

Sarah and Kitty followed Emilie up the wide staircase. "Our bedroom is here."

Sarah thought the room seemed crowded with its massive four-poster bed hung with draperies and mosquito netting. There was a huge walnut wardrobe and a tall maple chest of drawers with shiny brass keyholes and ornate carving on top. There were several religious pictures on the wall, Christ hung on the cross and another of a man whose body was riddled with arrows and dripped blood. Sarah wondered why someone would hang a picture like that in her bedroom. On the bedside table was a Bible and a cross attached to a necklace of beads.

Emilie took them to another set of rooms, not quite as elegantly furnished but every bit as grand. "These will be your rooms while you're here," she said. "I knew you'd want your children close by. I really hoped you might see your way clear to stay several days with us."

A little overwhelmed, Kitty murmured, "You're too kind. But my husband thinks we need to leave after the children are inoculated."

"Your business to tend to, of course. The horses. You see," Emilie said with a wave of her plump hand, "I know all about you, our closest neighbors. Well, we'll hunt up our missing husbands and tell them that it's time to eat."

"The children—" Kitty began.

"Now don't worry about the little ones. Dorcas will take care of them, and I think it is so much more pleasant to eat without the children around. Isn't that so?"

Sarah could not have agreed more. Then a thought hit her. What if Emilie thought she was one of the children? A stricken look passed across her face that Emilie didn't miss.

"Not you, *cherie*. You'll eat with us in the dining room. You are a *jeune fille*. A young woman. Do you know French?"

"No, ma'am, I don't."

"I grew up speaking French, and I would love to teach you. My mother was born in France and came to Louisiana when she was a little girl. I think it is really the mark of a civilized woman to speak French."

"Yes ma'am," Sarah said, following Emilie down the stairs. How could she have thought Emilie Gallier old and uninteresting? Without a doubt she was the most fascinating person Sarah had ever met, and she felt herself glowing under the attention. Emilie was talking to as if she were an adult, a sophisticated adult who might speak French and live in a world peopled by families like the Galliers. This was the best day of her life.

The table had been set for five; even though it was midday, candles were lit and the silver and china gleamed in its light. Kitty was glad that her mother had always impressed the importance of good manners on the Kincaid children. She watched proudly as Sarah unfolded her linen napkin and placed it in her lap. Kitty smiled across the table at her.

Charles Gallier sat at the head of the table. He was in his late forties, Kitty judged, tall and whipcord thin. His faded blond hair was thinning rapidly and worn combed back from his high forehead. His eyes were pale blue and looked calmly out at the world.

He had slipped a black frock coat on over an embroidered vest and white shirt, and Kitty felt a little embarrassed that she and Ben were dressed so simply. Ben was wearing an open shirt, no cravat, and his sleeves were rolled up. Kitty tried to remember that she and Ben were dressed the way everyone dressed in Kansas Territory; the Galliers were the exception.

Charles gave the blessing, thanking God not only for the food they were about to receive but also for the opportunity to share with neighbors. He then reached for a cut-glass decanter in front of him. "May I pour a glass of wine for you, Mrs. Adamson?"

Kitty shook her head.

"It's a nice wine, a favorite of ours—"

"Kitty and I don't take spirits," Ben interrupted. "It's against our religion."

Kitty frowned at Ben. A simple "no thank you" would have served, but Ben was determined to be difficult, she saw, and to make her uncomfortable too. She was equally determined that he wouldn't succeed.

Sarah, who'd been watching the interplay, spoke up. "I've never had wine. Perhaps I should try some."

Emilie laughed gaily. "I think we should ask your sister and brother-in-law what they think."

"No, thank you," Kitty said firmly. "Sarah doesn't drink wine."

Unperturbed, Charles sipped from his glass. "My wife might have told you that I'm growing grapes here, or at least trying to do so. Perhaps one day I'll be pressing my own wine."

Emilie laughed lightly. "My husband is full of dreams. Charles coddles his plants like children."

Kitty wondered if she were the only one to notice a trace of sadness in Emilie's voice. Obviously this was a home without children; Emilie must get lonely, Kitty realized.

Quiet-footed slaves, a man and a woman, served their soup. "Vertie!" Kitty looked up and smiled. It was the man who'd brought the Gallier's letter to their farm.

"Ma'am." He ladled the soup into her bowl and passed on, eyes lowered.

"Vertie has been with us for many years," Emilie said.

Kitty saw Ben open his mouth and she knew that he was going to make a remark about slavery. Kitty didn't want to get into an argument, not when they were sharing the hospitality of the Gallier's table, and so she spoke first. "We're so grateful that you offered to inoculate Carrie and Hilda. I worry about the pox."

"It's a terrible disease," Charles said, "and I've seen what it can do if left unchecked. We owe a great debt to Dr. Edward Jenner and his work in the last century."

Kitty had never heard of Jenner, but she assumed

he was the doctor who had discovered the vaccine. "I don't understand about the vaccine," she said, "but I know it works."

"When I inoculate your children, I can explain the process—not something that one talks about over meals."

Kitty was embarrassed, as if she'd raised an unpleasant specter of death at the table, but Charles didn't seem offended. "One of my goals is to inoculate as many people as I can, settlers and Indians alike. I've heard that in '37, more than ten thousand Indians died of the pox, brought up the Missouri, I believe, on a riverboat by some traders."

Ben nodded, and Kitty was relieved he was joining in the conversation. Up to now his face had been closed and judgmental. "We were with the Pawnee the summer of '37 out in the plains. At a mission," he added. "The missionaries had some vaccine and we did what we could—but many of the Pawnee died."

"As well as Mandan, Blackfoot, and Crow. I read that only a handful of Mandan were left—the whole tribe wiped out. And still it's been difficult to get the Indians to accept the vaccine; they don't like white man's medicine. Lewis and Clark had a mandate from President Jefferson to try back in 1804. We haven't come very far in forty years."

"Are you a doctor?" Sarah asked.

"Oh, no." Charles shook his head and laughed. "I'm not a physician, though I did study medicine at Harvard College for a brief while."

"My husband is interested in too many things to settle on just one," Emilie added. She regarded her husband fondly.

"So you were missionaries," Charles said to Ben. "I sometimes go to the Kansa school and mission on the northern boundary of the Flint Hills. The Kansa are a much misunderstood tribe. People in Westport and other towns consider them beggars; they don't understand the basic decency of the people. They are the most hospitable tribe that I have ever met. They always share whatever they have. They can't understand why, when they ask whites for food, they're turned away and spit upon. If a white man asked a Kansa for food, it would be immediately forthcoming. I'm writing a small treatise on the Kansa; I fear that if more settlers move in, their ways will be lost forever."

"Do you really think more people will move into the hills?" Kitty asked. "Everyone seems to be passing through on the way to somewhere else."

"Eventually," Charles answered. "But right now they want the promised land—California, Oregon. Six hundred acres to every man, and a hundred and sixty to his wife and each child. That's what President Tyler has promised is waiting for them in Oregon. The little trickle we've seen crossing the Flint Hills will be a torrent this year, Mrs. Adamson. I hear that a thousand settlers will be taking the Oregon Trail this month. They're already congregating in Independence. Eventually more people will settle here in the hills, too. It's just a matter of time."

A thousand people, Kitty thought. More than lived in Cairo; more than at the fort. It was hard to imagine so many people going west.

Vertie and a woman slave cleared away the soup bowls and brought out fresh plates, followed by platters of food. Kitty felt her mouth water and her stomach growl. The meal looked wonderful. There were black-eyed peas cooked with slices of bacon, sweet potato pies, and hot flaky biscuits. The butter was molded in the shape of a flower and served in a pressed glass dish. Little bowls of honey and blackberry jam were passed by the female slave.

"It's too early in the year for our fresh vegetables," Emilie apologized, "so these are from our root cellar, stored over from the fall. You must come back when we have fresh squash and beans. And do you know okra? Probably not. A vegetable from our part of the country. We'll make you a special stew with okra if you come back this summer. That is if we can grow it this far north. Another experiment!"

The slaves reappeared carrying platters of smoked ham and baked chicken. Kitty remembered that she hadn't seen any signs of cooking in the house and mentioned that to Emilie.

"Our kitchen is across the back courtyard. Perhaps not a wise arrangement for the Flint Hills, but one that we bring from home. In the summer in Louisiana, the heat is so oppressive that our kitchens are separate; it keeps our houses much cooler."

"It must be difficult for the slaves," Ben said.

Kitty noticed the look that flashed between Charles and Emilie Gallier and held her breath. Charles defused the comment gently. "It is," he said, "and we hoped the summers would be cooler in Kansas, but we've not found it to be true. Shorter but not cooler."

"It must be very different for you," Kitty said. "Not like Louisiana."

"We've lived in many places, Mrs. Adamson. I'm afraid I'm somewhat of a wanderer and I have been lucky enough to have a wife who would travel with me these past twenty or so years. We lived in Boston for a while, in London for a year, in our nation's capital, Washington, D.C. We settled in Missouri for a while, but there were too many people."

"Too many?" Sarah blurted.

"More than a quarter of a million settlers have

poured into Missouri since it became a state. I needed room to breathe and to experiment."

Kitty's curiosity couldn't be controlled. "Your wife said you farm."

"Experimental farming. We're trying different kinds of crops to see what will flourish here. We have stands of corn and wheat—small parcels, of course—and a few groves of apple, plum, and peach trees."

"The trees might do all right," Ben said grudgingly, "but as for planting . . . grass is the only thing that grows well in these hills."

"You may well be right, Mr. Adamson. So we have a few head of cattle and sheep of different breeds, just to see which thrives. I'm writing a report for some friends in Washington who are interested in bringing settlers into the territory." Charles paused as if taking their measure and Kitty wondered if he'd say more. He went on, "You know of Colonel John C. Fremont?"

"Yes, we do," Kitty answered excitedly. "My uncle, Boothe Carlyle, was a scout for Colonel Fremont in '42 when he led the expedition to map the Rockies."

"Then your uncle must be a fine explorer, for only the best went with Fremont. I must remember that name. I knew Kit Carson was with Fremont—"

"Kitty's uncle was too," Ben said defensively.

Again there was Charles's gentle response. "A fascinating expedition. They mapped what's now called the Oregon Trail, across the Rockies through South Pass, and then back along the Platte River."

Kitty's mind wandered a little as Charles went on to describe Fremont's trip. She was sure Emilie had heard the story a hundred times and marveled at the interest that still showed in her face.

Charles was telling of his involvement with Fremont through the Colonel's father-in-law, Senator Thomas

Hart Benton of Missouri, who wanted the western lands permanently settled. Benton had pushed a thirty-thousand-dollar appropriation through Congress to be used by Fremont on his expedition, and now Benton was supporting the printing of Fremont's report of the trip. It was a two-hundred-page treatise on where to find the best camping, grass, and food on the way west, and Gallier said that Congress had approved a printing of a hundred thousand copies for those eager to learn about the way west. The report was sure to lure more settlers across the Mississippi.

Charles Gallier had become friends with Senator Benton in Washington, D.C., an acquaintance forged by the many interests they shared. When the senator learned that the Galliers were interested in moving out of Missouri, he helped to arrange for special permission from the soldiers at the fort for the couple to settle in Kansas Territory. In return, Benton wanted to keep abreast of Charles's experiments. Benton felt that Americans needed to learn as much as possible about how to survive in this new land, and Gallier's observations would make life easier for the settlers that would follow.

"I'm interested in establishing larger grape arbors," Charles went on, talking about his experimental farming. "When Francisco Coronado explored this land—probably not far from where our homesteads are—he wrote of the sweetness of the wild grapes. And that was three hundred years ago." Charles smiled benignly. "I'm amazed by the ignorance of some of our fellow Americans, who believe they were the first to come here when the French and Spanish were in the hills in the sixteenth century. But such is the conceit of Americans to think we are the first."

Charles sipped his glass of wine. "You must excuse me, I talk too much about myself, as my wife often reminds me. What about this uncle of yours? Does he have wondrous tales to tell of his travels with Fremont? I would be honored to talk to the man myself."

Kitty shrugged. "Uncle Boothe hasn't returned home yet. He left the expedition somewhere in the Rockies last autumn. We heard he was wintering with the Nez Percé Indians, but we know nothing for sure." She wondered if the story sounded strange to the Galliers so she added, "Uncle Boothe has always been a wanderer."

"An American original," Charles said. "Bravo. One of those intrepid types who hunted and trapped beaver up the Missouri, no doubt."

"Yes," Kitty answered, "and my father Byrd Kincaid was like that, too. He saw a lot of the West before he and Mama settled down in Cairo."

"Then I applaud your father too and envy him his adventures." Charles smiled at Kitty, and she decided that, slave owner or not, he was a very nice man and she liked him.

"He's dead now. He was killed in '37, the year I came west," she explained.

"Do you have other family?" Emilie asked. "I don't mean to be personal, but I do enjoy finding out about our visitors. They are so few."

"I love to talk about my family, Miz Gallier," Kitty said. "My mother is still at home in Cairo. She and my father both were from Kentucky."

"Southerners, also," Charles commented.

"Yes, sir. My mother still runs the farm; my brother Luke and my sister Amity are still there. They're pretty young. Meg is married and living in St. Louis, and Sarah, of course, is with us for a while . . ."

"A great help, I'm sure." Emilie smiled at Sarah, who managed to look angelic while stuffing a biscuit in her mouth.

"Most of the time," Kitty replied. "Then there's my brother James. Jim we call him. He's got the family wanderlust like my pa and Uncle Boothe. He's supposed to be on his way to our farm . . . In fact, he's overdue. We needed him to help with the horses—" Kitty broke off in mid-sentence. She'd been asked to talk about her family, not hang out the dirty laundry. She had good manners, and she wanted the Galliers to know it.

But Emilie Gallier simply smiled and rang a little silver bell to call the servants.

It was near sundown when Jim spotted the little house nestled amid the trees, and by that time he was so weary and so heartsore he was almost incapable of feeling relief. He absently took note of the neat row of crops behind the log house, the split-rail corrals, and the horses munching clumps of grass within. Strong, good-looking horses. He could see Kitty's hand in that. It was just as he'd pictured it: quiet, orderly. Home.

Or maybe it was too quiet. No smoke came from the chimney. No children played in the yard. No man worked the crops. No woman stirred a wash kettle. The place looked deserted.

As he rode into the yard, a pack of big brindle dogs came bounding around the side of the house, barking furiously. No one came to the door. No one rode up to see what all the noise was about. Dread went cold in Jim's stomach. Had something happened to Ben and Kitty? Disease? Attack? And Sarah . . . Dear God, had he come all this way only to find his family dead?

He dismounted before the front door, ignoring the dogs that surged around him. "Kitty!" he called. "Ben!"

He let the reins trail and limped toward the house, heart pounding.

"Sarah? Anybody home?"

He pushed open the door and hobbled inside.

Sitting in a cane chair before the fireplace was an Indian with a rifle pointed at Jim's chest.

Chapter Ten

Over and over Jim kept thinking what a fool he was. He could have been shot. He could have walked in on a pack of bandits or a tribe of Indians bent on raping his sisters and ransacking the house, and there wouldn't have been a damn thing he could have done about it. How many more mistakes could he make before one proved fatal?

One less, he resolved grimly. Because he was learning. This land was an unforgiving teacher, but it was a teacher nonetheless and he was learning what it took to survive. He would not be so incautious again.

Billy had recognized him immediately by the red hair, and possibly, Jim thought, though Billy didn't say, by the idiotic way in which he came stumbling into a stranger's house unprepared for what he would find. They were now sitting at the wooden table inside, eating big bowls of Kansa soup.

"You missing a boot," Billy said.

He had a flat, expressionless way of speaking that left a man wondering what he was really thinking. Hunched over the bowl of soup with the wooden spoon held in his hand like a shovel, he made the comment as though it were something he had just noticed.

Jim said tiredly, "It's a long story."

Billy did not look up. "You in bad trouble?"

Jim sighed and pushed the bowl away. "Yeah. I guess you could say that."

And haltingly, not knowing why he did, Jim told him the tale of the midnight massacre. He couldn't even tell whether Billy was listening, but it felt good to tell it. Just to get the words out.

"I don't know what to do now," he finished heavily. "I guess I should go to the fort and tell them what I saw, but what if they don't believe me? That officer tried to kill me." He dropped his head to his hands, overcome with a fatigue so great that it actually seemed to thicken the air, making it hard to breathe.

Billy scraped the remains from Jim's bowl into his own. "Mister and missus back tomorrow, day after," he said. That was his only comment on the story.

Jim pushed up from the table with an effort. "I'm tired. I just want to sleep in a real bed for about four days."

Billy looked at him sternly. "You go wash in the creek. Miss Sarah, she have my hide you get her clean sheets dirty."

For a moment Jim just stared at the Indian. Then he smiled. Sarah. That sounded like her.

As tired as he was, he went down to the creek to wash.

After breakfast the next morning Ben was anxious to be on his way. He cleared his throat and looked at his wife. "Kitty and I thank you for your hospitality, but it's a long ride back to the farm, and the children came for their smallpox inoculation."

Charles and Emilie looked disappointed. "I'm so sorry you have to leave so soon; you really should think of spending another night," Emilie said. "I feel I hardly know you."

"I hear you trade with the Cheyenne," Charles added. "They are a tribe that interests me and I'd like to write a treatise on them. I'd hoped we could talk."

"I would love to tell you about the Cheyenne. They've been good friends." Kitty knew Ben was anxious to leave, but she was determined not to be rude.

Charles was thoughtful. "Then we must make plans for you to visit again, and I'd like to see your horse ranch. Vertie says you have some fine animals."

"We do," Ben said with finality, pushing back his chair, but Charles wasn't finished.

"You know those Indian horses of yours are almost pure Spanish blood. Horses of conquistadors. Andalusian horses, the finest in the world. Just look at some of your horses sometimes, Mrs. Adamson. You'll see the blood of Arabian and Barbary forbearers in those horses. They're still pure, here on the plains, not yet mixed with stock brought over from England to the East Coast." He leaned forward, interested. "Have you ever thought about breeding your stock? Choosing the best of the males and females . . ."

Kitty's face lit up. "I'd love to. Ben and I talk about it, but we never have time."

"Nor would we know what we were doing," Ben said bluntly.

"I could help you," Charles offered. "I know a little about breeding. It's something that I've studied. I have some sheep here that I'm experimenting with."

"Horses and sheep are different," Ben said. "It's just something Kitty and I talk about. It probably won't happen; at least not for a long time." He stood up. "Kitty, we should find the children."

Sighing, she stood up and put down her napkin. "All your meals were wonderful, Mrs. Gallier. We're very appreciative. I hope that you'll come to our home soon. Both of you. I'd love to talk to you about our horses, Mr. Gallier."

He nodded graciously.

"Now come and let's find your babes. I'll bet they're playing with the kittens." Emilie took Kitty's arm. "We keep bees, too, and have the sweetest honey. I want to send some home with you. Come Sarah, *cherie*. I will put you in charge."

The women left the room, and Ben turned to follow.

"Just a moment, Mr. Adamson. I feel we should talk. It will take a while to organize the children. We have time."

Ben suddenly felt trapped. He didn't want to talk to Charles Gallier. In some ways he had the feeling the man could read his mind.

"I know you're uncomfortable here. I imagine you're an abolitionist and the fact that we own slaves is upsetting to you."

Ben nodded. "Neither my wife nor I believe in slavery. We think it a sin, an abomination against God. I didn't want to come here—"

"But your wife insisted for the sake of the children," Charles said softly.

"We can't visit again," Ben said simply. "What you are doing here is not right."

"Even if I showed you the cabins I've built for my slaves, even if I told you how they are taught to read and write, I doubt you'd change your mind. My wife and I conduct church services for our slaves each Sunday and they receive the best of medical care from us. We are Christian people, Mr. Adamson, and have a love for all of God's children."

"Then show your love and let the slaves go free."

Charles shook his head in dismay. "That is not possible, sir. Where would they go? What could they do? Would it not be cruel to send them back to Africa, to a land they've never seen? Why, all my slaves were born in America. They know nothing of Africa. Starvation and illness abound there as well as Africa's own version of slavery. Slavery is not an American invention."

"They could stay here," Ben argued. "There's no need to send them back to Africa."

"My slaves are not ready for freedom, Mr. Adamson. They are like children in many ways, accustomed to being taken care of. How would they support themselves?"

"They can farm and work just like the rest of us."

"Indeed you are an idealist. I like that in a man; some have called me a dreamer, too, but not on this issue. History is on my side. Great societies like those of Greece and Rome rose on the backs of slavery and reached their flower. Slavery is necessary for this country to survive."

"The civilizations of Greece and Rome fell," Ben said.

Ben thought he read respect in Charles's eyes. "I would enjoy talking further with you, Mr. Adamson. There is room for two points of view on every topic."

"Not on this one," Ben answered. "I will never change my mind. No man should be another's slave. Our country was founded on the idea that all men are equal."

"Our Mr. Jefferson owned slaves," Charles said.

Ben felt frustrated and inept in the argument. He knew what he believed; there was no doubt in his mind that Charles Gallier was wrong. Owning slaves was a sin and those who supported the practice were sinners. Yet Gallier purported to be a Christian.

Ben heard the voices of his children. "My family is back. I hope we can get on with the inoculation. And, sir, whatever our differences, I am appreciative of what you are doing for my children." Ben said the words grudgingly, but he knew they must be said.

"In this wilderness, we must all be friends, even family to one another. Come now, they're waiting for us in my wife's office."

"I work on the books here," Emilie was saying, pointing to a pile of ledgers on a small cherrywood desk. "And I dispense medicines here for the slaves." There was a cabinet in the corner with a myriad of tiny drawers. Kitty quickly glanced at some of the labels: pennyroyal, mustard seeds, blackberry root, juniper berry, rose hips, peppermint. Some of the same remedies she had in her cabinet at home.

"Charles keeps his vaccine here, too. This is a fresh batch that has just come from a physician in St. Louis. Charles is going to take it to the Kansa mission."

Charles opened a small drawer in the cabinet and took out a well-wrapped packet. He unwound the cloth, which covered two pieces of glass pressed together. In between the glass plates were a number of threads.

"Look here, Mrs. Adamson. You wanted to know about the vaccine and how it's prepared. I can show you. When a case of cowpox, or kinepox as some call it, develops and the ensuing pustules are at their peak, a piece of thread is run through the matter that escapes from the sores. Then these threads are carefully protected—"

"The vaccination is for the cowpox disease, not smallpox?" Kitty asked.

"Jenner and others learned that material taken from the smallpox sores often caused a virulent reaction, but lymph taken from the sores of cowpox disease caused no serious reaction for those inoculated and more importantly prevented the recipients from contracting smallpox."

"It's like magic," Sarah said.

"Indeed it is. Now who will be first?"

Carrie nestled in her father's arms, tired from the day's activities. Hilda was more suspicious and peered around her mother's skirt. It was as if she knew something important and unpleasant might take place.

"I will," Sarah said. "I'm not afraid." She looked at Emilie for support and received a wide smile.

"Ah, how brave you are, setting an example for the little ones. I have already prepared the knives."

Sarah blanched visibly.

"I sterilized the tips of three very sharp knives. My husband will scratch your skin, just enough to draw blood."

Sarah bravely rolled up the sleeve of her dress. She was determined to be brave in front of Emilie.

Charles's hands were as gentle as his voice. "After I break the skin, I'll lay a treated thread across the scratches and bind your arm. Remove the bandage and the thread tomorrow. Shortly a pustule will erupt and become crusted over. You may feel feverish and a little sick for a few days, but that will pass. When the crust falls off the sore, you will have a small scar on your arm, and I guarantee, Mademoiselle Sarah, that it will not affect your loveliness."

Sarah was so fascinated by Charles's instruction and compliments that she hardly felt the scratches. Hilda, who was next, was not a willing patient. She kicked and screamed out, "No knives, Mama. No knives." It took both Ben and Kitty to hold her. Her screams frightened Carrie, who also kicked and bucked as her arm was scratched and the thread and bandage applied. Hilda only cried more, sobbing, "No knives for the baby, Mama. Please."

When the inoculations were complete, Kitty felt as though she'd been through a cyclone. The children's faces were red from their tears and they clung pitifully to her skirts. She looked at Charles with a little laugh. "Is it worth it, Mr. Gallier?"

"My dear woman, you wouldn't ask that question if you'd ever seen a smallpox victim. It is a terrible disease. Chills, fever, delirium, coma perhaps. A virulent rash inside the mouth and throat, followed by pox sores. Pox sores on the whole body, the extremities, the face. Sometimes the victim's face is swollen beyond recognition—and if one survives, there can be horrible scarring. And blindness. No, a few moment's tears are a small price."

"I know that," Kitty answered. "And I'm grateful for what you've done."

Emilie bent down to talk to Hilda. "Would a new kitten help you feel better? I know all little girls love kitties."

"No, thank you," Ben said. "A gift like that's far too rare."

"Not for us." Emilie laughed. "My favorite cat traveled west with us. In a basket on my lap. And as soon as we arrived . . . she gave birth to kittens. And now those kittens have grown and had more babies. *Mon dieu*, we are up to our knees with cats. Please take one."

"Well . . ." Kitty said slowly.

Hilda was hanging on to her mother's skirts. "Please, Mama, please."

"We've been needing a barn cat," Kitty said.

Hilda knew she'd won. "I want a yellow one, Mama."

"There's a half-grown male from our cat's last litter," Emilie said. "He fights with the other toms so I think he needs a new home. Come, Hilda, we'll get a basket for him."

Ben looked at Kitty over the children's heads. Kitty knew he was angry with her. They'd been at cross-purposes the whole day. But Ben wasn't always right about things. The Galliers were kind, even if they did own slaves. There were lots of worse things, Kitty decided. She knew he was angry at her about the cat, too, but what difference did one more animal make? She dreaded the ride home. It would be long and tedious, and she knew that Ben would have a lot to say.

They said their goodbyes and were on their way with very little fuss. Sarah waved from the wagon until the stone house was out of sight.

Emilie watched, too, until the little wagon was barely a speck on the horizon, and still she lingered, enjoying the shade of the front porch, thinking about the visit. She and Charles had lived in many places and done many things, but there had always been people nearby. This was the loneliest that Emilie had even been, and although she was a woman of many interests, she missed the companionship of others, especially women. How lonely it was to be a settler on the prairie.

But now she had met the Adamsons. Emilie was a sharp judge of character, much better than her husband. She could usually sum up a man's character rapidly and correctly. Ben Adamson, she concluded, was a good man, a sound man, but he was unbendable. He would break if the pressure became too much for him unless he learned to bend like the willow tree.

His wife—oh, Emilie really liked Kitty Adamson. She could tell the girl had been well brought up. Her manners were fine and she spoke well, too. There was something a bit fey about Kitty, as if she didn't quite fit into society. She could see why a woman like Kitty would be happy out in the prairie. And Kitty Adamson was a pragmatist, too, like most women, Emilie realized. She would do what she had to do for her children and her family. Despite their differences, Emilie believed that she and Kitty could become friends.

But Sarah. She was like a blank canvas waiting for the hand of the artist. So eager to learn, so eager to raise herself from her station. Sarah was a jewel, a rare find, and Emilie vowed that despite Ben's protestations, she was going to help the girl in any way that she could. Just as Charles had his interests, Sarah Kincaid would become her great project.

Jim slept for fourteen hours and awoke feeling safe for the first time in what seemed like a decade. He found his appetite again and put away two bowls of the warmed-over gruel Billy called soup. He found a shirt and a pair of Ben's pants that almost fit him—Jim was the taller man by far—and donned them while he put his own clothes to soak in the big washpot out back. Billy found him a pair of soft deerskin boots that he could get on without causing too much pain to his still-healing ankle, and for which Jim was profoundly grateful.

He scrubbed up the dishes they had used last night and this morning, and helped Billy feed the stock. He chopped firewood and brought in a load. It felt almighty good to be doing those things. Small things, normal things. The things of home.

He worked in an easy rhythm beside the silent Indian, and he thought, *Today they'll be home.* Sarah, Kitty. Surely they'd come today.

He hadn't seen Kitty since she'd left home six years ago, but she would always be his older sister. He missed her. And even though Ben had been away at school those last few years before he came home to get married, he had always been like another brother in the Kincaid household. It would be good to see him again.

And Sarah. It was funny how in big families there often were such pairings off, favorite siblings, special relationships. He didn't know why that should be. Meg was actually closer to his age, but she was always the bossy older sister with whom he had never gotten along. Luke was his little brother, and Jim loved him, but it was Sarah he missed. Sarah he was sorriest to see leave home, Sarah he worried about, and Sarah he would be gladdest to see.

"Do you know," he said thoughtfully to Billy when they paused in the heat of the day for a drink from the water barrel, "my ma always said that once she got to Cairo, her feet were planted there and nothing could make her move another step. I never understood that. Thought it was crazy talk. But now . . ." His voice was almost lost in the weight of rumination. "I can see it. I wonder if the Flint Hills ain't as far west as I was meant to go, too. Or maybe even that's too far."

It took a moment for him to realize Billy was holding out the dipper to him. Jim brought himself back to the present, and filled the dipper with cool, mossy-tasting water from the barrel.

Billy said flatly, "Riders coming."

Jim looked up quickly, spilling the water in his excitement. "It's them! They're back!"

Billy shook his head. "No wagon. Riders."

Jim frowned into the sun as he scanned the landscape. "Where? I don't see anything."

Billy was silent for a moment. Then he lifted his arm. "There."

Jim felt the life drain out of him as he followed the direction of Billy's gaze and saw the line of blue-uniformed riders appear atop the hill.

Sarah sat in the back of the wagon with the children, the sleeping yellow tom kitten on her lap. Hilda and Carrie, wrapped in blankets, slept too now that the sun had dipped low in the sky.

Sarah could hear Kitty and Ben in the front, still arguing about the Galliers.

"There's nothing wrong with taking a kitten, Ben. We need a good ratter, and besides, the children love him."

"We've accepted enough from those people, Kitty. I don't want us beholden to them in any way at all. A cat's unheard of out here on the plains. It's a valuable gift."

"They gave it out of the kindness of their hearts. Not to bind us to them in some way. I think Charles and Emilie Gallier are fine Christian people."

"If they were true Christians, they wouldn't own slaves. They *own* those people, Kitty. Can't you see that?"

"I understand what slavery is, Ben, and I don't like it any more than you do, but it's their lives. They seem like kind people and it's not our business to interfere—"

"A man has to stand up for what's right."

"You're stubborn, Ben. And always have to be right."

"Then I'm no different from you, Kitty." After a moment of quiet, he went on. "They're Papists, too. Did you see the crosses and rosary?"

"They're still Christians," Kitty said. "You can't argue with that."

Ben gave a loud grunt of disgust and was quiet.

Sarah reached under the blanket and felt the book that Emilie had loaned her. They'd slipped off quietly for a moment to the library and Emilie had urged, "Take a book, *ma petite*. Choose any one at all."

"But what if I can't return it?" Sarah wondered. "I'm not sure when we'll be back."

Emilie put her hands on Sarah's cheeks. "We'll see each other, Sarah. I know that, so don't worry. Now choose."

Sarah reached out blindly and picked a leather-bound volume. "*Greek and Roman Myths,*" she read.

"Perfect!" Emilie said. "There will be so much for us to discuss. Won't that be fun, Sarah?"

"Yes, it will," she said, meaning it with all her heart.

Riding in the wagon, jostled by the bumps, Sarah caressed the soft leather book. She knew that today had changed her life; she knew that after meeting Emilie Gallier she would never be the same. She wasn't sure how it would happen, but it would. She didn't care if the Galliers owned slaves or if they were Papists, whatever that meant. Emilie Gallier liked her and wanted to be her friend, and that was enough.

Sarah looked up at the huge expanse of blue sky and for once was content.

Chapter Eleven

Over the days that had passed since the shooting, Marcus had plenty of time to review the battle, assess his strategy, pinpoint his weaknesses, and analyze his mistakes. In such a way were great military minds formed, flawless campaigns executed. A mistake that was never repeated was not a mistake at all, for it was a wise man indeed who practiced his failures on small battlefields.

As Marcus saw it, the outcome could have been changed in only two ways. The first was obvious and an error for which he would have severely disciplined even the rawest recruit. He had been startled by the appearance of the red-haired boy and had instinctively lifted his rifle which only had two shots, when he should have reached for his pistol instead. That was unforgivable. But it would never happen again.

And he had been less than accurate in his tracking and observation skills. He should have picked up the four horses, but he'd found his way to the camp by way of the fire, not ground tracks, and he had approached opposite the string of horses. He had learned something. Next time he would be more astute. He would take nothing for granted. Every day he was improving.

It was unfortunate about Tompkins, but there was no way he could have prevented that or predicted it. The man had essentially disobeyed orders, and there was no room for that kind of renegade thinking under Marcus Lyndsay's command.

They had buried his body with those of the deserters, for the distance was too great to transport him back to the fort. Though it galled Marcus to bury him with honors, he had no reasonable explanation for not doing so. As far as the army and the world at large were concerned, Tompkins had been killed by the same red-haired outlaw who had robbed and killed the three deserters. That was the report he intended to make to Colonel Kearney when he and his men reached the fort.

But the fort was two days away. His men were tired and dispirited and his horses in need of a rest. They all could use a hot meal, and though it was said that saucy Mrs. Adamson was an indifferent cook, she'd never been known to turn a hungry man away from her table.

He paused atop the small rise that overlooked the Adamson farm, and he could feel the rising spirits of the men who followed him. Families were few and far between in this part of the country, and it always did the men good to be reminded what they were defending the outpost for. So that pretty young women like Mrs. Adamson and her flame-haired sister could sleep safely at night, and tow-headed young ones could grow up strong and free. Yes, it was good to be reminded.

He lifted his arm as though calling the men to battle, kept it poised there for a moment, then dropped it forward. He led the riders down the hill.

Marcus had had occasion to stop by the Adamson farm once or twice before on routine patrols. He was familiar with the spread and with its occupants in a vague way, though he took no personal interest in either; Kansas Territory and all its concerns were merely a stepping stone in his master plan, and of hardly enough significance to be counted in the wider picture.

It was immediately apparent that the Adamsons were not at home. His patrol was greeted by a barrage of dogs but no pretty blond-haired woman, no excited children. He was disappointed on behalf of the men, for that meant no home-cooked meal, no chance for the idle socializing they enjoyed and sometimes needed. He, of course, was indifferent to the quality of his food and company, but recognized the need for such in others.

A thin stream of smoke came from the chimney, and in a moment the explanation for it stepped around the side of the house. The Adamsons' hired man shoved his hands into the baggy pockets of his trousers and regarded the soldiers sullenly.

Marcus turned to his second-in-command. "Have the men water their horses at the stream."

As the patrol moved off at a walking pace, Marcus dismounted. "I was hoping to speak with your employer," he told Billy. "When do you expect him back?"

Billy said nothing.

Marcus had noticed on the way in that the corrals were filled with new stock, so he knew the Adamsons' absence had nothing to do with trading the horses.

"I hope there's no trouble."

Still no reply.

Marcus turned impatiently to his second, who had dismounted and stood respectfully a few feet behind him. "Does this Indian speak English?"

"Yes, sir. That's Billy Threefingers. He used to help out the quartermaster with the horses at the fort."

Marcus just smiled as he turned back to the Indian. "Well, Mr. Threefingers. Not that anything you have to say would be of interest to me, but it's reassuring to know I'm not wasting my breath. We'll avail ourselves of some of your fine spring water and then be on our way. But first I think I'll have a look at what kind of stock the army will be negotiating with your employer for this year."

He tossed his reins to Minnows and walked toward the corral.

Marcus was not interested in horse trading, nor did he know very much about how it was done. But it would make good conversation at the officer's mess to have previewed the new offerings, and it wouldn't hurt his standing with his commanding officer to take the initiative in a matter like this.

Besides, it was good to spend a quiet moment, looking over peaceful rolling landscape and healthy, spirited horseflesh, arranging one's thoughts. And then something caught his eye.

He climbed between the rails and moved across the corral. Some of the more skittish horses scattered at his approach. Others ignored him. He reached the bay gelding and caught its mane, bending down to examine its hooves, then moving to the opposite side to look at its flank. He called for Minnows.

"Check the barn," he commanded quietly. "You're looking for an army saddle and gear. And ask the Indian where this horse came from."

Less than five minutes later Minnows reported back. "There's an army saddle in the barn," he said.

"Billy—the Indian—says the horse just wandered up. Sir . . ." He looked a little confused. "That is an army horse, isn't it?"

Marcus's jaw hardened. "Not just any army horse," he said. "Tompkins's horse."

He bent to climb between the rails again, exiting the corral. He straightened up, brushing the dust off the cuffs of his coat. He looked straight ahead, toward the horizon.

His orders were swift and precise. "Search the premises, from springhouse to storm cellar. Leave no stone unturned."

Minnows looked astonished. "But, sir . . ."

Marcus knew precisely what he was thinking. They had no authorization for such a search. The Adamsons were good citizens and their relationship with the fort made them valuable to the territory, not the kind of folks one wanted to offend. But on such frailties did mighty campaigns crumble, and Marcus had no time to waste on niceties.

"That was not a request, soldier," he said coldly.

Minnows snapped to smartly, saluted, and turned on his heel to gather a detail.

It seemed to Jim he had been buried alive forever, drowning in his own hot sweat, his chest crushed beneath what felt like a wagon load of corn, suffocating with every breath he took. His mind was racing like a terrified rabbit fleeing from the hounds. How had they tracked him here? He could have sworn he wasn't being followed. How could he have been so stupid as to lead this killer right to his sister's home? How long would it take them to find him? How much longer could he survive here?

The air was thick with chaff and he tried to take shallow breaths, but he could feel it filling up his lungs. Pretty soon he wouldn't be able to breathe at all. He could feel panic stirring inside him and he wanted to push his way out of the corn crib, clawing and kicking, to run into the yard gulping in breaths. The only thing that kept him still was a fear even greater than that of dying of suffocation here in the corncrib, and that was the fear of what would happen to him if the madman found him . . . what would happen to them all.

He could hear them moving across the yard, shouting back and forth to each other. The outhouse, the springhouse, the smokehouse, twenty feet away . . .

"All clear, sir!"

"Nothing here, sir!"

"Move on."

Jim heard the doors to the barn creak open, striding footsteps burst in.

"Little, Barton, check the lofts."

One by one the doors to the three stalls were opened and searched.

"Empty, sir."

"Take a pitchfork to the feed bales."

Jim couldn't remember the last time he took a breath. His lungs were burning, bursting, but he was afraid if he breathed someone would hear him— he'd choke or sneeze or cough. His face itched. His muscles tingled and began to cramp from the effort of holding one position. If only he could move his leg, stretch his arm . . . His eyes watered from the irritation of dust and chaff, and the moisture that trickled from them mixed with sweat and dust and tickled unbearably. He wanted to scratch. He wanted to stretch. He wanted to cough.

And then the door to the corncrib opened and he forgot about scratching, he forgot about coughing, he forgot to breathe. Light flooded the small enclosure and he was certain the uniformed soldier could see him just as easily as Jim could see the soldier.

This time of year the supply of dried corn that was used to supplement the stock's winter diet was almost exhausted. What was left was piled against the rear of the bin, halfway to the ceiling. In crawling underneath the corn Jim had disarranged a good bit of it, and now he started to worry how much of himself he'd left visible through the top layers. The way the soldier was examining the floor, he wondered if he had left footprints in the dust, or had dropped something that would give away his position.

He knew, of course, that he had not. Billy had made sure of that before he'd closed the door. All he had to do was stay still and not breathe for a moment longer and he'd be in the clear. The soldier wouldn't come in, he wouldn't search the corn. In a moment he'd close the door and go away.

But Jim did not know what it was like to be under the command of a fanatic.

The soldier glanced over his shoulder as though debating whether to enter or not, as though not quite certain how far his orders went, then apparently decided it was better to be safe than sorry. He stepped up into the corncrib and crossed the dusty floor. He started poking the stacked-up corn purposefully with the stock of his rifle.

Jim could only listen helplessly as the sound of the rifle butt came closer and closer, scattering corn as it moved. He couldn't get out of the way, he couldn't burrow deeper; anything he did would only bring exposure sooner, and in another moment he would be exposed anyway; there was nothing he could do.

Suddenly the soldier stopped, frozen with the rifle

in mid-thrust. At first Jim didn't understand, but then he heard it too and his blood turned to ice.

There was no sound quite like the rattle of a snake. Nothing could be mistaken for it and it couldn't be taken for anything else. Jim heard it and the sweat on his face popped out cold; his fingers convulsed into fists before he could stop them. The movement caused the corn around him to shift fractionally and the soldier's eyes swung to the movement even as he leapt backward, turning his rifle barrel forward and aiming at the stack of corn.

The rattle came again, louder, angrier, sustained this time. From the sound of it the snake was five feet long at least, coiled and ready to strike from wherever it was. It was hidden in the corn somewhere, threatened by the presence of the men, but whether it was poised to strike the soldier or Jim, he couldn't tell.

Jim fought to keep his muscles immobile when everything inside him shouted *Run*! If he moved now he was a dead man, whether from the blast of a rifle or the strike of a snake.

Another second, maybe two, and it was the soldier who broke and ran. He stumbled and almost fell in his hurry to get out the door, and in a moment Jim heard his voice, tight and breathless.

"Empty, sir!"

The rattle had stopped, but it was an ominous silence. Jim dared not move lest he divert the snake's attention to him. He braced himself to feel the heavy body of the snake crawling over his leg, his hand, his face. Would he be able to stay still then?

Then another figure appeared at the door. Billy Threefingers gave a casual shake of the rattlesnake's tail that he wore on a leather thong around his neck, then tucked it inside his shirt. Not a flicker of expression crossed his face as he closed the door.

Alone in the darkness, Jim took the first breath he had drawn in what felt like an hour.

Marcus trusted no one but himself to search the house, not because he thought the renegade was hiding there, but because he thought there might be some crucial piece of evidence inside that only he could read. And he was right.

The clothes soaking in the tub out back, the one battered boot without a mate—those could, if one were pressed, be explained away. But the iron cross lying on the mantelpiece—that was what he was looking for. That was what he needed.

Marcus Lyndsay did not believe in coincidence. A whole family away from home in the middle of their busy season, with corrals full of newly acquired horses that were costing them in feed every day they delayed getting them to the fort. A dead man's horse that just happened to wander into that same family's corral—from a distance of four days away. And now this distinctive iron cross, last seen on the chest of the red-haired boy.

He heard the wagon drive up, the barking of the dogs, the querulous voices of children. He turned idly toward the window and watched Adamson help his wife down from the wagon box, concern and confusion marking both their faces. The young girl clambered over the back, a baby in her arms. Her bonnet hung from its strings on her back, her flame-colored hair spilling over her shoulders.

He studied her thoughtfully.

"Captain," Ben Adamson said coldly behind him, "what is going on here?"

Marcus turned with a polite nod. "Mr. Adamson, forgive me. This is irregular, I know. The fact is we are on the trail of a killer, and we have reason to believe he may have taken refuge here."

The anger in Ben's eyes was replaced with shock, then anxiety. His wife, who had appeared beside him in time to hear the last part, echoed, "A killer? Here? Captain, surely you're mistaken!"

Ben put a protective arm around his wife's shoulders.

"I hope so, Mrs. Adamson. But you understand, for your safety as well as the sake of the law, I couldn't delay the search until you returned. I trust you won't find anything out of order; I instructed the men specifically in that matter."

"Kitty?"

The red-haired sister appeared behind them, her voice timid with alarm.

"Sarah," Kitty said sharply, "where are the girls? Bring them here, now!"

"They're here, Kitty. But—"

"Is it safe?" Kitty demanded of Marcus. "Have you checked the house?"

"The house is clear, madam." He gave a small polite bow. "Come in, please. I am sorry for frightening you, but it couldn't be helped."

"I'll get my rifle," Ben said, and turned back toward the wagon, his face grim.

Marcus held up a staying hand. "Not necessary, Mr. Adamson. My men will function better without any civilian help. May I ask if you saw signs of anything unusual on the road?"

"No, nothing." Ben glanced at Kitty and she agreed there had been nothing.

"What direction were you traveling from?"

Kitty told him about the visit to the Galliers and their overnight stay while Sarah did her best to quiet the whiny children.

Nothing like this would ever happen to Emilie Gallier, Sarah thought, and she tried to bolster her spirits with that reassurance while she quickly diapered the baby. But the anxious little bird that fluttered around inside her, hopping from bush to bush, refused to be stilled. Coming home to find your house surrounded by soldiers in search of a murderer was only another one of those unpleasant little surprises the frontier held, one of those things Kitty insisted she would enjoying telling her children about one day. Sarah did not see anything amusing about it.

She didn't like the soldier who was talking to Ben. He made her very uneasy, as though he were watching her out of the corner of his eye when he thought she wasn't looking. Besides, desperate fugitive or not, what right did he have to walk right into their house? She began to wonder if there ever had been a killer on the loose, though what reason the soldier would have to lie she couldn't imagine. She wished he would just go away.

She put the baby down in her cradle and pacified Hilda with one of the dried plums Emilie had slipped into her pocket just before they left. She *had* intended to save it for herself, but she wanted to hear what the soldier was saying and it was impossible with the children fussing.

"Your hired man said the horse just wandered up, but I think you'll agree that seems unlikely."

Kitty frowned, looking annoyed. "It seems even more unlikely that he would lie about it. You can't possibly be suggesting Billy would *harbor* this murderer."

"Probably not, ma'am," the soldier replied smoothly, "but you know how these people are. Sometimes they lie for reasons you and I can't begin to fathom."

Kitty's expression grew frosty. She was more than annoyed now. "Actually, Captain Lyndsay, I *don't* know how these people are. Perhaps you'd like to tell me."

Ben laid a restraining hand on his wife's arm. "You say this man shot three in their sleep? And another one who tried to stop him?"

"That's right. The first three were deserters who apparently hooked up with the wrong sort." He made a gesture with his hand that seemed to suggest they had gotten no better than they deserved. "Tompkins and I were tracking the deserters and heard the shots. Tompkins was somewhat faster than I was, more's the pity. He was a good man. He was shot in cold blood as he tried to apprehend the felon. Of course, I returned fire, but he was too far away, and it was dark."

"Odd," Ben said thoughtfully. "That he should steal your man's horse when he must have known how easily it could be tracked. Surely, after committing such a heinous crime, he had his own horse ready to mount."

Perhaps no one but Sarah saw that momentary lapse in the soldier's smooth mask. It was very quick—so quick, in fact, that she barely had a glimpse of what lay behind it. But what she saw frightened her.

"Who can fathom the workings of such a mind, Mr. Adamson?" he asked.

And then, to Sarah's great consternation, the soldier turned to her. He smiled in a way that made her feel slightly nauseated, although she could not say exactly why. It was really a very nice smile.

"I don't believe we've ever been formally introduced on my previous visits, miss. I'm Captain Marcus Lyndsay."

Sarah had to swallow to get her voice. "Sarah Kincaid."

He bowed from the waist and took her fingers in his cool, slim ones, raising her hand to his lips in a gracious formal gesture. And that was when Sarah saw the ring he wore on his hand, and she knew what was wrong with him.

It was a big, heavy thing made of onyx and silver, with some kind of fancy crest emblazoned on it. Worked into the crest and raised slightly above the rest was the head of a wolf.

Something gripped her spine like cold talons, and ice water spread through her veins. He spoke, but his words were like a buzzing in her ear. He released her fingers and straightened, smiling.

"I've often remarked on the difference in coloring between your sister and yourself, Mrs. Adamson," he said pleasantly. "One would hardly know you're related."

Kitty's tone was suspicious. "I was adopted."

"Ah, of course." He nodded solemnly, as though the matter was of great fascination to him. "So it's the Kincaids who have wonderful Titian coloring. Or is Miss Sarah the only Kincaid?"

Kitty looked as though she were puzzling over the word "Titian," and Ben stepped in. "It's quite a large family, and they all look alike. I'd say Sarah most closely resembles her brother Jim though, wouldn't you, Kitty? When they were younger they were often taken for twins."

Sarah wanted to scream. That smooth smile never wavered, and the soldier didn't take his eyes off Sarah. "And are you the only one who has made it this far west, young lady?"

"Actually," Kitty said a trifle impatiently, "all the Kincaids are wanderers. Our brother Jim is due here any day now."

There was a flicker in his eyes. No one could have seen but Sarah, and it looked like satisfaction. Panic rose inside her, like a giant black bird beating its wings against her rib cage. She wanted him to go away. Why wouldn't he go away?

Like an answer to her prayer, a second officer appeared at the open door. "Sir," he said, "I'm sorry to interrupt. We've searched every outbuilding and attachment. I even sent my men into the hills looking for caves. We didn't find a sign, sir."

The smile left Captain Lyndsay's face and his eyes went hard. He was silent and when next he spoke it was obvious the words were not the ones he wanted to say.

"Very well, Minnows. Have the men mount up."

He turned to Ben. "It seems we were too late. I suspect he took one of your fresh horses to make his escape. Perhaps we can still pick up the trail."

Ben's arm tightened around Kitty's shoulders as Lyndsay brushed past them. "Good luck, Captain. I hope you catch him."

Lyndsay paused to look at Ben, his eyes cold. "I'll catch him," he said. "I promise you that."

He was gone, and Sarah felt weakness drain through her. She turned toward the fireplace, bracing her hand on the mantel, breathing deeply.

Kitty said, "Well, that was a thoroughly delightful thing to come home to after the trip we've had. Ben, you don't think that killer could still be here, do you? That they might have missed him?"

"I don't know." Ben's voice was thoughtful. "There was something a little off about the whole story, if you want my opinion. But I'll feel a lot better after I've had a look around myself."

"Kitty," Sarah said hoarsely.

She turned around, her face white, her fingers trembling. The Celtic cross lay in the palm of her hand.

When Jim first walked into the house, escorted by a wary and watchful Billy, Sarah flung herself upon him and hugged him until she thought her arms would break. He returned her embrace with a force that threatened to crack her ribs, then opened his arms to Kitty, and to Ben. Sarah thought that was the happiest, most intense moment of her life.

Two hours later, she knew it was the bleakest.

They sat around the kitchen table with the doors and windows closed and the curtains drawn, talking in hushed tones that were more than once tinged with horror. Jim sat across from Sarah, his hands wrapped around a cup of coffee, looking gaunt and drawn, his eyes still dark with shock.

For a while Kitty had bustled around, fussing over his injured ankle and the scratches he had gotten in the corncrib, frying up apples and bacon for his supper, keeping her hands—and Sarah's—busy while they tried to pretend nothing was wrong.

No one was pretending anymore. They were waiting for dark.

Kitty worked quietly at the pantry, packing his provisions. Now she was tired, her face showing the strain of wrestling back distress. "This all seems so *wrong*," she said. "Maybe we should at least try to go to the fort, to tell Colonel Kearney . . ."

Ben shook his head slowly. "Jim is right; they wouldn't believe him. It would be his word against a respected officer's, and I'll tell you God's truth, if I didn't know Jim Kincaid I wouldn't believe him."

"But if he starts running now—"

"He's got to," Sarah interrupted sharply. Her voice

was so tight it was on the verge of breaking, but even that did not accurately reflect the state of her nerves.

"You've got to get away from that man," she told Jim desperately and reached for his hand. "He means to kill you, Jim. You've got to get away from him, as far and as fast as you can."

She wanted to say more, she wanted to say it louder and harder; she wanted to scream the urgency of it. She wanted to tell him about the wolf, but she didn't know where to start.

Jim closed his fingers around hers, squeezing gently. His smile was sad. "I sure meant this visit to be different, Pigtails," he said. "Pretty big disappointment for a big brother, huh?"

She couldn't speak. Her throat was filled with sawdust and tears, and all she could do was squeeze his fingers back, hard.

"I still can't believe it." Kitty's voice was hushed. "The man stood right here in our *house*..."

Her voice caught and she turned away quickly, resuming her packing with short jerky movements. Ben got up quietly from the table and went to her, resting his hand on her shoulder for a moment.

Jim pulled his hand away from Sarah's and dragged his fingers over his face, into his hair. "God," he whispered, "I meant for *everything* to be so different."

Sarah managed to smile then, weakly, for his sake. "Me, too," she said.

There was a sound at the door, and it struck them all like a gunshot. But before they could react beyond the stiffening of muscles and the flash of fear, the door opened quietly and Billy stepped in.

Kitty released an audible breath, her hand pressed to her breast. "They're gone?"

Billy nodded curtly. "Di'n' leave no spies. Scout

for tracks a while, but di'n' look serious to me. High-tailed back to the fort, big hurry-like."

Kitty looked at Ben with the dawning of a new fear in her eyes. "Ben, you don't suppose—they couldn't have *known* Jim was hiding here, could they? They couldn't be planning to come back with—with more men or something?"

Ben looked worried. "It's possible. That Lyndsay knew something he wasn't telling us, I'd swear to that."

"But if he knew Jim was here," Sarah said hoarse-ly, "he would have arrested him. He wouldn't have ridden off."

Ben shook his head slowly. "He knew he'd have to go through me—and both you women—to get to Jim. Killing four soldiers out on the prairie is one thing, but shooting down settlers in plain view of his own men . . . I don't suppose even he was willing to take that chance."

He looked at Jim. "This Lyndsay is a dangerous man," he said soberly. "I'll go to Colonel Kearney, and I'll tell him what you've told me. But I want you to be long gone out of the territory by then."

Jim pushed up from the table, nodding. "And I'd best be going."

Sarah's throat convulsed on an involuntary cry. "But—it's not safe yet! It's still light out, you could be seen . . ."

Jim looked at her tenderly. "And the soldiers could be back. Tonight, tomorrow morning . . . No, I have to leave now, while we know they're not watching the house."

Sarah felt her heart rip in two in her chest, but she knew he was right.

"Just head for Fort Bridger," Ben said. "You'll be safe there. Boothe will be by there sooner or later, and until he comes, Jim Bridger will take care of Boothe's kin like you were his own."

Kitty said briskly, "Billy, you go saddle up that roan for my brother. And put an extra blanket on."

She tied the string around the big parcel and came over to Jim, thrusting it into his hands. Her eyes were bright with tears, but her smile was brave. "I sure was hoping you'd stay longer."

Jim glanced affectionately over at the girls, Carrie asleep in the cradle and Hilda sprawled out on the floor on a quilt beside her with her thumb stuck in her mouth. "They're beauties," he said. "You raise 'em up right, you hear?"

Kitty nodded and touched his face and then had to turn away.

Jim shifted the bundle under his arm and turned to Sarah. They looked at each other for a long time, but there weren't enough words for what needed to be said between them.

Then Sarah stood and walked over to him. She stood on tiptoe to drop the pendant over his head.

"You take care, Jim Kincaid," she said thickly. "And—and watch out for wolves."

He embraced her fiercely. "I'll be back, Pigtails, so you mind yourself. And . . ." His own voice seemed to thicken for a moment. "Tell Ma I love her, will you?"

"I will," Sarah whispered.

He kissed her forehead, ruffled her hair, and made her smile at him. Then he turned away before the pain finished crossing his face, and moved toward the door. He didn't look back.

No one went to the window to watch him ride away. No one could bear to.

Chapter Twelve

Meg sat in the shade of the wagon and ate her midday meal. The valley of the Platte stretched endless and unbroken before her, flat and featureless. The river, like a twisting brown snake, writhed slowly east toward the Missouri two hundred and fifty miles away. She chewed on the fresh crusty bread that Anna had baked and wished she were back in St. Louis. Or in Cairo. Again her impulsiveness had gotten her into a situation that wasn't easy to get out of. No matter how many times she lectured herself that stealing Matoon's wagons was the only way out of Bellevue, she harbored the fear that she'd made the worst mistake of her life.

She and Sheldon rarely spoke, and when they did, it was usually to argue. The fact that he was the enemy of her Uncle Boothe hardly seemed to matter now; what was important was surviving day to day, harnessing the mules each morning before sunup, climbing aboard the wagon and traveling as many miles as possible before the noon break. The mules were watered, a meal eaten, and then in the blazing heat of the sun the journey resumed until sundown.

Who Sheldon Gerrard was or had been was of little concern to Meg. He kept the other men away from her, he talked to Donnelly about the business deals they'd make in Fort Laramie, and most importantly, he usually ignored her.

Meg was lonely, and she tried to make friends with Anna and Henryk, but their English was so poor that her attempts at conversation failed. Most of the time she sat in the wagon beside Sheldon, staring out at the barren valley of the Platte River, and wondered what was going to happen to her.

Meg moved deeper into the shade of the wagon and tore off another piece of bread. Sheldon was maneuvering along the line of wagons toward her. Henryk had made a new crutch for him, and Anna had washed his clothes. Without a two days' growth of stubble on his cheeks, he looked almost presentable, like a man who should own two wagons filled with goods. As he got closer she noted that he was scowling.

Meg held out a piece of bread. "It's fresh; Anna just baked it."

He shook his head angrily. "Bread isn't what I want."

"You are in a foul mood. Of course that's nothing unusual." Even though Sheldon Gerrard was at least twenty-five years older than she, Meg showed no deference toward him. He was just a man to be dealt with and, she hoped, disposed of in due time.

He eased down beside her, using the side of the wagon to give himself leverage. He wiped his face and squinted up at the sun. "Damn, it's hot in this godforsaken place."

Meg ignored his complaint. There was nothing she could do about the heat. "What's got you riled up today, Mr. Gerrard? The heat, the flies, the gnats, or the company?"

"Whiskey, Miss Meg, or the lack of it. Donnelly tells me there's no more aboard this wagon train."

"At the rate you've been drinking it, no wonder. You've been lucky," she said coldly, "that Donnelly would take your IOUs for it."

"He knows he'll be paid."

"I'm glad it's gone," she said bluntly.

"I don't see how it's any of your business, Miss Meg. I drink alone, I drink in private. Why should it matter to you?"

"I don't like whiskey of any kind, you know that. I've told you about Caleb. And I don't like to see you lying drunk like a dead man. It's disgusting."

"I only drink at night, and then it's for the pain."

She made a contemptuous sound. "Your leg's been gone for almost ten years. The only pain is in your head."

"Were you always such a hard woman?"

Meg was surprised at the question and ignored it. "Here, take some bread; it's wonderful." She tore a hunk off from the loaf and handed it to him.

"Answer my question. Were you always such a hard and blunt woman? I'm interested."

"When I was growing up, my sister Kitty used to say that I was spoiled and stuck-up, but never hard. I wanted to be a singer. I was lost in daydreaming. Can you imagine that? I wanted to sing on one of those big boats that steamed up and down the Mississippi. I imagined myself in wonderful clothes, laces and satins . . ."

Her face was sad and wistful, and Gerrard realized how young and vulnerable she was for all her tough exterior. She was young enough to be his daughter. For the first time, he felt compassion for her, an emotion long suppressed. "We all had our dreams, Miss Meg," he said softly.

"And each time we lose a dream, we become a little harder, a little tougher, I guess, and we learn that the world isn't made for dreamers. It's made for survivors, and I intend to survive. Somehow."

"With me or without me?" He asked it jokingly.

"Our 'marriage' can be instantly dissolved in Fort Laramie after we sell the supplies."

"What about them?" He jerked his head toward the other wagon.

"Anna and Henryk? I don't know."

"They think a lot of you, Miss Meg."

"How would you know that?" she asked sharply. "You hardly ever talk to them."

"Can't. Don't know that Polish tongue of theirs."

"Neither do I, but I try, and they're attempting to learn English. Do you know what it's like for them?" she asked in a burst of passion. "To be thousands of miles from home with no one to turn to, not to speak the language, to have people look at you as if . . . as if you aren't even human? Matoon treated them like animals."

Sheldon looked across the trackless waste of the Platte Valley and said quietly, "I was wrong, Miss Meg, you're not as hard as I thought. You know what it's like to be cast out."

They sat quietly, side by side in the shade of the wagon for a long time. Meg finally broke the silence. "We are two of a kind, I guess, Mr. Gerrard. Maybe our partnership isn't so strange after all."

"People like you and me, coming together in the middle of nowhere, those coins . . . Something like that can't just be an accident. It almost makes you believe in patterns, purpose."

Meg looked surprised. "That's a thoughtful thing to hear you say."

"I think sometimes." His tone was dry. "And then, more likely than not, I drink. This is what I've been thinking lately, Miss Meg."

She waited.

"When all of us traders get to Fort Laramie and start selling our supplies, none of us is going to get what the goods are really worth."

"Since these two wagon loads of supplies cost us nothing, everything we make is profit," she argued. "We'll come out better than anyone else."

"We'll be competing with the rest of this crew; the storekeepers who buy from us have to keep their prices to us low so they can resell at a profit to the overlanders. That's where the money is, Miss Meg, selling to those fools on the wagon trains."

"And how do you propose we do that, Mr. Gerrard? Sell out of the back of our wagons like tinkers?"

"Don't be turning your nose up at that, Miss Meg. There's nothing wrong with honest commerce."

"My family were farmers and trappers, not merchants."

"Maybe it's time for that to change."

"You have an idea of some kind, don't you?" Meg pushed her damp hair back from her face and looked speculatively at Sheldon. "Is it something that can make us more money?"

He laughed out loud at that, and the sound surprised even him. How long had it been since he'd really laughed in pleasure? "You are a greedy one, Miss Meg."

"Tell me," she insisted. "When your mind isn't befuddled by liquor, I know you're as smart as any man in the West. Or at least I heard that about you."

Sheldon felt an unexpected twinge of pride. "In

my time I was one of the best at making money."
And losing it, he thought to himself. He went on,
"After we cross the North Platte in a week or so, the
land starts tilting uphill and then it drops down real
sharp to a place called Ash Hollow."

"Ash Hollow," she repeated. "It sounds lovely."

"Those that have seen it say it is. Donnelly says it
has trees and a stream and shelter from the wind.
There's a meadow west of the place where overlanders graze their stock. It's one of the nicer stopping
places on the way west. The only problem is that to
get to it, the wagons have to go down a sharp grade.
Almost forty-five degrees." He showed her the steep
angle with his hand.

"Most of the overlanders don't have an idea in
Hades how to handle that grade. Wagons end up
at the bottom, without wheels or axles. Some of 'em
broken to pieces. They need supplies when they get
to the bottom of that hollow and a good blacksmith
to make repairs."

"Why hasn't anyone set up a trading post there?"

"Because most people are in an all-fire hurry to
get to Oregon or California, come hell or high water.
They do the best they can, repair or abandon their
wagons, start out on foot or muleback determined to
make their fortunes. But I'm beginning to think that
the real money's to be made on the trail, not at the
end of it."

"You think we should set up a post at Ash Hollow?"
Meg asked thoughtfully.

Sheldon shrugged. "We have a blacksmith on hand;
his wife can make the best bread west of the Mississippi. We have a wagon load of wheels and harness
and spare wagon parts. We can probably scavenge for
what's been left behind, and we can sell it all for any
price we decide."

Meg tried to think of reasons why it wouldn't work. She knew that desperate people on the trail would pay any price to keep on going. "We wouldn't have a place to live or a store or—"

"We've been sleeping in the wagons; we've been cooking over an open fire, and we've done all right."

"And after we sell the supplies? Then what?"

"Whatever you want, Miss Meg. We pay off Anna and Henryk, divide the money, and go our separate ways. Except we'll be richer than we thought."

Meg got up from the ground and brushed the dry red soil from her skirt. "I think your idea bears looking into, Mr. Gerrard. But if we set up a trading post at Ash Hollow, I have one demand. No whiskey on the premises."

He started to protest, but she cut him off. "It's not forever. By the end of the summer, we'll be done. You can take your profits and go back to Bellevue or on to Fort Laramie and drink yourself senseless. Doesn't that give you something to look forward to?"

He smiled. "It does indeed, Miss Meg. A winter of drunken oblivion will make a summer of hard work and abstinence worthwhile."

Colonel Stephen Kearney looked across his desk at his quartermaster. The sergeant's red, fleshy face was creased with concern. "You can't do it, sir. They're my best suppliers of horseflesh. If you cut me off from the Adamsons, I ain't gonna have nothing decent this fall for the men to ride."

"I understand your situation, Sergeant Moore, but I'm under pressure from Washington." He pointed to the stack of papers on his desk. "Inquiries and reports about the Kincaid affair. Four of my men shot down like animals by some mad dog killer. Not given a chance. Damn it to hell." Kearney brought his fist down hard on his desk.

"But the Adamsons didn't do the shootin', sir. It was just hard luck that Kincaid rode into their place to hide out."

"It wasn't luck, Sergeant. It was planned. The Adamson woman's his sister. Your horse traders lied and hid him, and they made a mockery of the U.S. Army and of justice. There is no way we can continue to support them while they stick knives in our backs. The subject is closed, Sergeant. Look for your horses elsewhere."

The quartermaster made one last desperate attempt. "There ain't no place I can get that many good horses by this autumn, sir. You know the trouble I used to have. I need—"

Kearney rose from his desk and leaned forward, his weight resting on his hands. His face was red with anger, and his eyes flashed dangerously. "No more discussion, Sergeant. We will not be buying horses from the Adamsons. Now send my aide in. On your way out," he added pointedly.

The aide, a young lieutenant fresh from West Point and forewarned by the sergeant about Kearney's mood, stepped inside the colonel's office. "Sir?" he asked nervously.

"Where the hell is Captain Lyndsay? I sent for him fifteen minutes ago. I want him here now."

"He rode out, sir," the young man said softly, dropping his head as if in anticipation of his colonel's reaction.

"Rode out? Where the hell did he ride out to? I haven't finished with him."

"He said, sir, that he had permission to pursue this Kincaid fellow. He said since he could identify the criminal it was only logical that he pursue. He said—"

"Dammit to hell!" Kearney bellowed. "He was given no such permission."

"He said—" the lieutenant began.

"Dismissed," Kearney said curtly.

"Yes, sir." His aide scurried from the office.

Kearney was furious. What the hell was Lyndsay up to? It was true that he and the captain had discussed a plan for bringing Jim Kincaid to justice. They had learned that Kincaid's uncle, Boothe Carlyle, had once worked for the army as a scout for Fremont, and was possibly still somewhere up along the divide. It seemed logical that Kincaid would hightail it to the Rockies to hide out with his uncle.

Lyndsay had wanted to pursue on his own, arguing that a detail of men would alert Kincaid to the chase and drive him deeper underground. One man could travel fast and not raise suspicions.

Lyndsay's plan had merit, Kearney agreed, but there was something about Captain Marcus Hunt Lyndsay that set the colonel on edge. Kearney still had more questions about the deaths of the deserters and Tompkins. Kearney had been in the army a long time. He knew men, and he had a suspicion there was something about Lyndsay that didn't ring true, and so he'd hesitated about sending the captain after Kincaid.

For all his brilliance and experience Kearney had come up with no better plan. Lyndsay knew the culprit; there was bad blood between them and that sometimes was enough to keep a pursuer going when an ordinary man would give up. Kearney knew with certainty that Lyndsay wouldn't give up. Kearney had been planning to interview Lyndsay again and agree to the assignment. With certain restrictions, of course. He couldn't allow Lyndsay to travel alone. This time Kearney wanted witnesses.

But the young buck had taken it on his own to bring Kincaid to justice. Kearney ground his teeth in anger. He wanted Kincaid alive. He wanted to know why he'd slaughtered the soldiers like animals. He wanted to know the reasons behind the massacre. He wanted a trial, and he wanted to see Jim Kincaid hang.

If Lyndsay got hold of Kincaid, he'd probably kill him on the spot. Now Kearney had two problems. Bringing in Kincaid and tracking down Lyndsay. And realistically he knew he didn't have any men capable of doing either.

Chapter Thirteen

Boothe Carlyle could smell autumn in the air even now at the end of August. The trees hadn't yet begun to turn, and the sky was still a brilliant blue. The sun shone warmly on his back; there were no external signs yet that the season was changing. It was just something he knew inside. Autumn was fast coming.

He'd known two weeks ago it was time to leave Jim Bridger's trading post and head on toward Kansas Territory and his family, but Old Gabe had talked him into staying just one more week . . . and then one more. Boothe had given in to his old friend, out of loyalty and something else—a quiet certainty that once he left the fort he'd never see Gabe or the fort again. Instinctively he knew that this was his last summer with his mountain companion, and it was good to talk of the old days, trapping up the Missouri, forging through unmarked territory, living off the land like the Indians. Days that would never come again.

So he'd stayed.

And his staying had brought him a piece of news that still churned around in his mind like a twig in a whirlpool. Some late-traveling settlers on the Oregon Trail had stopped at Fort Jim Bridger and told of a new trading post they'd stopped at a few weeks east. It was something to talk about because it was run by a red-headed woman whose name was Kincaid, whose temper was as fiery as her hair. She had a partner, a one-legged man called Gerrard, and the two of them struck a bargain that was tighter than a tick on a hound's back.

Boothe felt as if he'd been kicked in the stomach by a pack mule when he heard the news. He'd refused to believe it, almost started a fight with the pasty-faced fellow from Missouri who'd told the story. A Kincaid with Gerrard? Gabe had calmed him down and questioned the traveler more thoroughly. The woman was his niece, Meg Kincaid, there was no doubt of that, Boothe learned, and the one-legged man was Sheldon Gerrard.

God only knew how the two of them had hooked up; no, Boothe had corrected, shaking his head. The devil knew. His niece with Gerrard? Last he'd heard Meg had been married and living in St. Louis. Gerrard had been there, too. What cruel act of fate had brought them together? Didn't Meg know enough about Gerrard to stay away?

That news had been the deciding factor in Boothe's decision to leave. The Kincaid-Gerrard trading post, he learned, was to the east of Fort Laramie, at a place called Ash Hollow. Boothe knew it well. It was a good place for a post, plenty of water and even some trees for shelter, a welcome sight after the barren plains of the Platte River valley the wagon trains crossed. But what in the name of the good Lord was Meg Kincaid doing running a trading post with a man like Sheldon Gerrard?

There was only one way to find out.

He'd packed up his horse the next day, said his farewells to his old friend with a catch in his throat, and at sunrise headed east into the rising sun. Boothe made good time and had the trail to himself. Except for the unwary fools from Missouri who'd brought him the news about Meg, there were no wagons and no travelers on the trail. It was too late in the season; snowfall was only a few weeks away.

Boothe knew only too well what could happen to a wagon train bogged down in snow. He'd tried to exorcise the ghost of his own failed expedition, trapped by the snow in '35, but it still haunted him, and his subsequent successes had done little to appease his conscience. Losing a wagon train was something a man couldn't forget even if he wanted to.

Although the Oregon Trail that day in late August was devoid of travelers, their recent passing could be seen in the refuse and mementos they'd left behind. Nothing had changed, Boothe realized, since the days he'd lead wagon trains over the mountains and across the prairies. Settlers started out, wagons loaded to the rooftops with stoves and trunks, rocking chairs, benches, anvils, spades, axes, crowbars, corner cupboards, sets of china, rolled up carpets, and linen chests.

Travel across the flatlands was hard enough for the oxen and mules pulling the overladen wagons, but when the wagon train hit the hills and headed into the mountains, no amount of cajoling, whipping, or praying could get the animals to do the impossible; they were a hell of a lot smarter than the humans who urged them on, and so the settlers started dumping their prized possessions, the things they once vowed they couldn't live without.

Overlanders learned very quickly that survival was what it was all about; staying alive and getting across the mountains seemed a lot more important than hauling a brand new iron cooking stove or a trunk filled with fancy duds out west.

Boothe ignored most of the debris; he had no use for it. But one of the leavings caught his eye. He reined in his big horse and swung down.

"Well, I'll be damned," he said softly. "A bookcase."

Some overlander, discouraged by the steep upgrade and tired of urging on his exhausted team, had unloaded an entire bookcase filled with leather-bound volumes, slightly moldy now from the rain that had fallen a day or two earlier. Boothe couldn't remember when he'd last seen a decent book. There hadn't been any when he'd been fighting his way through the Rockies with John C. Fremont or when he'd spent the winter with the Nez Percé, and old Jim Bridger was lucky to have a newspaper on the premises.

Boothe pulled out one of the books. A volume of Shakespeare.

He heard a whinny nearby and raised his head to see a horse tethered at the side of the road. Boothe should have paid more attention, but he was distracted by the book in his hand. He opened it and flipped through the pages. He remembered his gran, Fiona, that indomitable Scotswoman who'd instilled the love of books and reading in him and in his sister Katherine.

His fingers traced the fine leather bindings. How his niece Kitty and her husband would love to have a set of books like this. Many a long winter night would go by so much faster with someone sitting by the fire reading aloud in the flickering light. Nostalgia wrapped around him like a comforting cloak and made him careless.

It was foolish to think he could take the whole set with him, but maybe one or two of the books, tucked in his shirt or in his saddle bags . . .

"Drop it, mister. Them leavings is mine, and they ain't nobody else's. If I have to kill ye for 'em, I will."

Boothe didn't consider drawing his own gun. He'd heard the click of a rifle bolt being drawn back, and he knew the man behind him was serious. Slowly Boothe rose to his feet, arms over his head, and turned to face his accuser.

"No sudden moves now. This here firin' piece is loaded for bear and I'm ready to use it."

"I can see that," Boothe said evenly. He studied the man holding the gun on him. He was well past middle age, short, no more than five feet six, dressed in buckskin trousers and a faded blue striped shirt. Instead of the usual broad-brimmed hat favored by westerners, Boothe's adversary wore a red knit stocking cap from which flowed a river of scraggly white hair. His beard was white, too, coming halfway down his chest. His face was tanned, and under grayish-white eyebrows, the man's eyes were a bright, startling blue, canny and wily and, Boothe judged, a little mad.

"This here's my property." He gestured with his head to the scattered detritus lying along the trail. "I staked claim to it, and I'm damn well gonna have it."

"It's all yours," Boothe said. "I was just looking at the books. Thinking I might take one or two to my niece."

"Well, think agin, mister. I ain't about to break up that set. All of it is mine. First come, first serve. Possession is nine-tenths of the law."

Boothe shrugged. "Then it's yours." He wasn't about to get into a battle with a crazy old coot over abandoned books. A set of Shakespeare was a mighty fine thing, but it wasn't worth dying over. "But I have a question, Mr. . . . ."

"Name's Andrew. Andrew MacVane, but most folks call me Mac." MacVane didn't lower the gun an inch, and Boothe noted the older man's hands were steady as a rock. "And I ain't got use for no questions."

"I think I'll ask it anyway. What the hell do you want with all this?"

"I been a trader all my life, son. From the East Coast to Texas and up here to the Rockies. A man never knows what might be valuable, and a long hard winter's a-comin'. I can feel it in my old bones. Never can tell what will help a man get through."

Amusement flickered within Boothe, though he kept his expression grave. "No, I guess you can't. Now that we've agreed the spoils of the trail are yours, do you mind if I put my hands down?"

MacVane pointed the gun at the ground with surprising abruptness. "Please yourself, son. I can get the mark of a man pretty damn quick, and you seem all right to me. You got a name?"

"Carlyle. Boothe Carlyle."

"Carlyle, eh?" The old man's face lit up. "Sounds like a fellow Scotsman."

"You'd be right about that. Both my grandmother and grandfather came from the Old Country. Settled in Kentucky."

"Kentucky, eh? One place I never been. Come over myself in '17. I was a young man then lookin' for adventure and a quick way to make a profit. No doubt about that. Never tried to hide it. No, never have. Profit is a strong goal for a young man."

Boothe realized that any physical danger from MacVane was past, and he knew that the garrulous old scavenger was about ready to launch into a story.

There was nothing to do but sit back and enjoy it. Boothe sank down on an abandoned iron stove beside the trail, took off his hat, waved away a few circling gnats, and settled in to listen.

MacVane leaned against the butt of his rifle, one leg bent, his eyes narrowed in the sunlight. "I started out in New York City. Met and married my first wife there. A lovely young woman, she was. She died of childbirth, her an' the babe, too, which was a blessing I'll warrant. So I just decided to haul off and head for New Orleans. That was the place to be. Did some tradin' down there, met a woman. Oh, yes, a pretty woman. Creole. French speaking. Just as pretty as you please." He savored the memory. "Oh, pretty as a flower. Her papa owned a little store and when he died I took over. You would be surprised at how much business a sharp trader could do with those Frenchy bastards. But the problem was, my wife wanted a husband who'd stay at home, and I was still a young man with a lot of roamin' to do."

He leaned a little forward toward Boothe. "Now a woman, she don't understand about a man's need to roam, but there's no denyin' it when it comes on you. You look like a man who's found that true, son." He gave Boothe a conspiratorial wink.

"Occasionally," Boothe replied mildly.

"So in '35 I decided to go fight with Sam Houston against the Mexicans. Why not? I asked myself. I was still a young man; I could still fight. I'm as tough as a little banty rooster." MacVane puffed out his scrawny chest.

"I was with Houston myself," Boothe said, wondering if the Scotsman had ever made it as far as the Mississippi River in '35, much less to Texas.

MacVane was unimpressed. "Were you now?"

"What did your wife think about you taking off?"

"Not a hell of a lot," MacVane answered with a chortle. "She called me every name in the book and then some, but I didn't care. She had the store; she had the children—"

"Children?"

"Lord, yes. I'm a powerful manly man, Mr. Boothe Carlyle, as skinny as I may be. I had five sons off my wife in New Orleans and two more in Texas—"

"Then I guess you stayed in Texas after the fighting was done?" Boothe was trying to steer MacVane's life story toward its conclusion.

"Oh, yes, tried to settle down there. Met me a little Mexican gal. Cute as a button. 'Bout sixteen years old. So I married up with her under Texas law, but after a few years I got the wanderlust again so I started tradin' with the Indians. Kiowa. Comanche. Cheyenne. They like those bright shiny beads, you know, for their fancy work, and they like blankets and pots and pans. Some of this stuff I'm findin' on the trail I'll be tradin' next spring with the Shoshone and the Crow. A man's got to take his luck where he finds it."

Boothe stood up, knowing that to end the story he would have to walk away from it. "Well, good luck to you, MacVane. I'd invite you to throw your camp in with mine, but I've got some traveling to do before I lose the daylight. It can be a mighty lonesome thing wandering these high trails by yourself, and it was good to meet a fellow Scotsman."

MacVane just grinned. "A smart man never travels by his lonesome if he can help it. Me, I got myself a new woman. A little Cheyenne girl. Now she's a sweet one and sharp as a tack. Not a half bad little cook, either."

Boothe tried to hold back his own grin. Andrew MacVane was an amazing man, that was for sure, but for all his stories, Boothe didn't see much to admire in him except that he'd managed to survive without some woman putting a knife in his back or a bullet in his head.

Now MacVane looked at the sky. "You ain't got many hours of daylight left. I reckon you'd do best to come on back with me and have some of that Injun stew the woman's stirrin' up. My guess you'll find what you come after there too. Why don't you help me load these goods on my travois over there. Won't take long." He pointed to his horse grazing by the side of the trail. Two long poles covered by a blanket were lashed onto the sorrel.

Boothe could hardly refuse either the invitation or the request. Naturally he was curious about MacVane's Cheyenne woman, and a female-cooked meal would be welcome. And it was the unwritten law of the trail that folks helped folks out, strangers or not. And in MacVane's case, Boothe mused, crazy or not. But he reckoned the old man was crazy like a fox. He'd gotten Boothe to give up the books and to agree to help him load up.

It was the last part of MacVane's statement that intrigued Boothe the most, as it was no doubt meant to do.

Together the two men began to place the items that fitted on the travois. "What makes you think I came after anything?" Boothe said.

MacVane grunted a little as he overturned a travel trunk, spilling out the contents. "It's right apparent to me. Just thought I'd save you some trouble, is all. Forget the cookstove. Too damn heavy to mess with. But these clothes——" He poked through the scattered clothes on the ground, selecting several ladies' dresses. "My little Star would think mighty high of these. Yep, she would."

He glanced at Boothe. "Ain't no secret, is it? You're trackin' that boy. I got him back at camp. Hell, he ain't no use to me. You can have him."

Now Boothe was intrigued. He didn't like the idea of lingering this high with a snow coming on that could delay his reaching Meg until spring, but this MacVane character definitely could stand some investigating. Just how many people did he have back at that camp of his anyway? And what made him think Boothe might be interested in one of them? Did any of them know what they were letting themselves in for if they decided to winter here?

"I don't think she can pull any more," Boothe said of the patient horse. "You're gonna have to walk this horse back."

"Easy to do. We're no more than a few miles from here. I'm a tough old bird. Hell, I've walked almost across this whole country. Walkin's nothing to me. Understand that, son. Walkin' ain't nothing to me," he repeated emphatically. "What about you?"

"I've walked a few miles in my day, too." Boothe thought about his days trapping up the Missouri.

"That's good. We'll put a few trade goods right on that big horse of yours and you can walk back to my camp with me. Meet little Star Woman. Have a decent meal. And don't you forgit to tell the army you've got Andrew MacVane to thank for leadin' you to your quarry, too. Of course, ain't none of that gonna happen unless I get some help with these here goods. My back's about broke."

Boothe grinned. He didn't have the first idea what connection Andrew thought he had with the army and wasn't entirely sure he wanted to know, but he was curious to see what kind of woman would hook up with Andrew MacVane. Of course, if she was a

Cheyenne girl as Andrew claimed, she wouldn't have many choices.

The Cheyenne were among the most moral of the Indian tribes; the chastity of their women was vigorously protected. This Star Woman knew she couldn't return to her tribe without bringing disgrace on her whole family—not just her parents, but uncles, aunts, and cousins. He felt sorry for her—and curious.

"You drive a hard bargain, MacVane." Boothe started loading up his own horse.

MacVane took his time joining him. "That's a strange lookin' animal. I noticed him the minute I saw him. Kind of pokey-dotted, ain't he? First time I saw a horse like that. Where'd he come from?" The questions poured out almost nonstop.

Boothe's horse was big and powerful, with a pure white coat marked by a heavy splattering of dark brown spots, some the size of a man's hand, some no larger than a penny.

Boothe rubbed his hand along the horse's neck. "I got him up in Oregon Country. There's a tribe of Indians up there called the Palouse, and they breed these horses. Some folks are starting to call 'em Appaloosas now. Whatever he's called, Mercury's a fine horse."

"Palouse, eh? Well, he's a big 'un, I'll say that. Looks like he can carry this here butter churn. Strap it up there, son. Star Woman just might take it in her head to make me some butter."

"You have a cow back at your camp?"

"Hell, no, but I might find one! Those overlanders been letting their stock go, too. Who knows, we might run up on a damn cow. You jest can't tell, young man. You know, that's what's the matter with you young folks. You got no imagination about the future. Why, anything can happen. Bet you had no idea you'd run into Andrew MacVane and be enjoying a decent meal tonight and about the best damn conversation this side of the Mississippi."

"No idea at all," Boothe said dryly. "All right, Mac, we're packed up. Let's head out before that little wife of yours decides you ain't worth waiting for and lights out on her own."

"Hell, ain't much chance of that," he returned cheerfully. "That gal's crazy about me, don't you know." He picked up the reins of his horse. "Not that she's exactly a wife in the legal sense of the word, of course. More of a companion, you'd say. Her folks didn't exactly like my runnin' off with her so we ain't had benefit of clergy to bless our union. Don't mean I don't take good care of her, though. Come on, camp's this way."

Boothe fell in behind Andrew and his laden travois, thinking of the many white men who'd come west and married Indian women without benefit of clergy or commitment. How many children had been born of that union? he wondered. Boothe's heart was heavy with sadness and remorse for all the women abandoned by their sometime husbands and for their children, half-breeds, fitting in neither the white man's world nor the Indian's.

It was not a legacy to be proud of.

"Not much farther," MacVane called over his shoulder, and picked up the thread of a conversation Boothe had almost forgotten. "Now this boy, I ain't saying he's fit to travel yet—snake bite got him and he's been out of his head nigh on to three days now—but Star'll fix him up. Them Injuns know what kind of plants to use to take that poison right out. I reckon my little Star's saved his hide."

"What makes you think I've got any interest in this boy?" Boothe had to ask.

MacVane gave him an irritated look. "I ain't no idiot, am I? First he's here, then you're here, him claimin' the army's on his tail and you lookin' to be an army scout if ever I saw one." His look turned shrewd. "Don't reckon there's a reward out on him, is there?"

"Don't reckon so."

MacVane looked disappointed. "Well, he hadn't said very much, at least not to me, but nursin's a woman's job, now ain't it?"

"I guess it's the job of whoever can do it best," Boothe said mildly.

"Well, that's Star. I'll tell you, son, she's the best female I've ever lived with. But you'll see that for yourself."

MacVane's camp was in a clearing surrounded by evergreens. Above towered the Rockies, ragged and forbidding and already topped with snow. A small stream trickled between rocky outcroppings; near the edge of the clearing MacVane had put up his shelter—a lean-to of fir limbs, their needles dry and bristly, covered by greasy blankets. It didn't hold much promise as far as winter shelters went, but surely MacVane would be seeking something more permanent before first snow.

A slender young woman was kneeling by a fire. When the men entered the clearing, she rose and came toward them. MacVane's first words were, "Boothe Carlyle, this here's my woman, Star. He'll be staying to supper with us."

She was no more than sixteen, Boothe judged; her skin was smooth, the color of a new penny. Her eyes were wide apart and slightly slanted, and her nose was fine and aquiline. Her lips were full and wide. He could see the proud blood of the Cheyenne in her. Her English was accented but easy to follow.

The look she gave him was cautious and wary, but not frightened. Her dark eyes said that she'd seen much and endured more, and still wasn't afraid.

"Welcome, Boothe Carlyle, to our camp. I am called Morning Star Woman."

"You honor me by having me, Morning Star Woman." Boothe used her full name, as was customary among the Cheyenne.

She smiled and Boothe felt rewarded. She wore doeskin moccasins, but her dress was of calico, too short and loose for her, made to fit around the waist with a strip of rawhide. Over it she wore a man's flannel shirt, its folds hiding most of her figure. Obviously, MacVane had already brought home castoffs from the trail, including clothes for the girl. Blankets, cookpots, and other items were piled to one side of the clearing.

"I got a fine mess of stuff today," MacVane said. "Gonna unload it now. You give us a hand, Star. Some mighty pretty dresses for you."

She moved to help the men unload. Her voice was low. "I don't care about the dresses."

"The hell you don't. Ain't a woman born who don't like pretty clothes. Sometimes Star just says things like that to get my goat, son. But she's appreciative. I know she is."

Star didn't respond. Instead she efficiently organized the new stores. Boothe wondered how MacVane thought he'd transport his collection over the Rockies, but he decided not to ask. The old scavenger would have an answer, no matter how hare-brained, and in reality it wasn't any of Boothe's business. He was here for dinner. That was all.

Star went back to the fire, hunkered down, and stirred something simmering in the pot.

"She trapped a rabbit this morning," MacVane said

with pride. "So rabbit stew tonight. You like rabbit stew, son?"

"I've been known to eat my fill in the past," Boothe said easily. He reached in his saddlebag and pulled out a small package. "This here's coffee that I got up at Jim Bridger's fort. I'd be happy if you'd share it with me."

"Now that's mighty neighborly, son. Star, boil us up some coffee."

Boothe studied Morning Star Woman as she went about her tasks. She was deliberate in her movements, none wasted. There was nothing servile or frightened about her; more and more he was intrigued with why she was with MacVane. Surely she didn't love the old man. He looked at MacVane. He looked at the girl. Yet she didn't seem a prisoner, as if she were held against her will.

"How's our invalid doing this afternoon, Star?" MacVane asked. "Any better?"

Star seemed to brighten at the question. Her face appeared to glow with pleasure, though it might have been, Boothe thought, from the reflection of the fire. "He is better. He had some broth, and the fever is broken. We even talked a while."

"You know his name now?" MacVane asked. Before she could answer, he went on. "Fella was so delirious when we found him, didn't even know his own name. You never heard such babbling as he was doin'. Talkin' about killin' and shootin' and the U.S. Army. Now my guess'd be that youngster ain't never been in no army, but you'd be the one to tell about that, wouldn't you, Carlyle?"

Boothe nodded, not paying much attention. What had caught his eye was the glint of something metallic that he'd glimpsed beneath Star's shirt as she moved. She stood up and came toward him, holding out a tin cup of coffee, and the folds of the shirt opened, giving him full view of what she wore about her neck. Boothe's heart stopped beating.

He was on his feet before his heartbeat could catch up with him, lunging so suddenly that Star cried out and spilled the coffee. He grabbed the pendant around her neck.

"Where did you get this?" he demanded hoarsely.

"What the bloody hell!" MacVane was on him, tearing at his arms. "This is the way you repay a man's hospitality—"

Boothe shook him off like an annoying insect. "*Where?*" he demanded of Star. He tried to keep his voice quiet so as not to frighten her, but intensity blazed in his eyes. "Where did you get it?"

Star raised her chin defiantly. There was fear in her eyes, but pride outweighed it. "I did not steal. Jim gave it to me. I keep it only until he is better."

"Jim." Boothe repeated the word in a half-whisper, staring at her. Then he released his grip on the pendant abruptly and spun around.

MacVane strode toward Boothe, shaking his finger. "Now if you're saying we stole that cross from that young man, that's a lie. We take what's abandoned, but by all that's holy, Andrew L. MacVane has never stole from no man."

Boothe crossed the clearing toward the tent in four long strides and pushed open the flap.

Chapter Fourteen

The interior of the shelter was dark and musty, smelling of sweat and sickness and the faint sharp tang of an herbal poultice. He had to bend over to avoid brushing his head against the stick roof, and it took a moment for his eyes to adjust to the dimness. He saw the figure wrapped in blankets and dropped down on his knees beside him.

Even in the poor light the shock of red hair was clearly visible, lying lankly across the white forehead of a young man. The features were strong and regular, though drawn by the ravages of illness. Boothe had not seen his nephew in seven years and in that time boyhood had given way to adulthood, but there was no way he could have failed to recognize his sister Katherine's son.

"Jim Kincaid," he said softly. "My God and Savior."

Boothe laid his hand on Jim's forehead. It was cool and damp, and his breathing was regular. The worst of the danger appeared to have passed.

Jim stirred at the touch and opened his eyes heavily. His gaze was puzzled and unfocused.

"Jim," Boothe said. "It's your Uncle Boothe."

Jim's eyes drifted closed. "Kitty sent me looking for you," he mumbled. "Fort Bridger, she said . . ."

"You found me. Is something wrong at home? Does Kitty . . ."

Jim shook his head back and forth, growing agitated. "No. They're after me. Kill me if they can. Sarah says . . . watch out for wolves . . ."

Boothe felt a chill go down his spine.

A flap of blanket was lifted, admitting a momentary square of evening sun as Star entered. She held a tin cup in her hand, and she went straight to Jim.

Boothe watched as she placed her hand on his forehead and murmured something soothing and unintelligible to him. Boothe watched her face, the tenderness of her movements, and she watched the way Jim calmed beneath her touch. The worried frown on Boothe's features deepened as he sat back on his heels.

When Jim's breathing was deep and even again, Star said quietly, "It is best for him to rest now."

Without looking at Boothe, she slipped the pendant over her head and placed it next to Jim's sleeping form. "I do not steal," she said firmly, and started to rise.

"Morning Star Woman," Boothe said formally, "I did not mean to dishonor you. I know you didn't steal."

She hesitated, but still did not look at him.

"The cross has belonged to my people since the beginning of time. I did not expect to see it in this place. I feared it meant the death of one of my own."

Slowly she nodded her head, understanding.

"This is the son of my sister," Boothe said, gesturing toward Jim. "He is much loved, and I owe his life to you. I am grateful."

Now she cast him a hesitant look. "You will not take him back to the army men?"

"No. He is my sister's child, and I will keep him safe."

Star looked at him for a long time, those dark eyes taking his measure soberly and with care, finally judging him to be an honest man. She carefully lifted the blanket that covered Jim's leg, revealing to Boothe the trouser leg that had been slit to the knee, and the poultice that had been applied to his calf. Around the poultice the flesh was yellow, but the swelling that had produced the discoloration had already dissipated and the wound was healing.

"He will walk in another day or two," Star said matter-of-factly, and covered the wound again. "Now he rests."

She rose, and Boothe followed her out of the shelter.

MacVane was stirring up the cookfire and appeared to have completely forgotten their previous altercation. "What'd I tell you?" he demanded cheerily. "Right as rain, ain't he? You takin' him in?"

Boothe shook his head, still frowning absently. "He's my nephew. Says he was sent looking for me."

"Well, ain't that a wonder? And you end up finding him!" MacVane chuckled to himself, feeding sticks into the fire.

Boothe looked at Star. "Did he say anything at all about why he is here? And why does he keep talking about the army? What kind of trouble is he in?"

Star moved toward the cookfire, shaking her head firmly. "I have no answers. Jim will rest. Soon you can ask him your questions. Now I cook."

She took the bundle of sticks from MacVane with a severe look, and the older man got up, grinning sheepishly. "Just like a woman, don't want no menfolk messin' around her cooking pot. Well hell, son," he added boisterously, "guess it ain't no hardship on me keeping him around a day or two more as long as you feed him. Meantime, I'll bet a good Scotsman like you wouldn't be caught on the trail without a wee drop or two of something to warm the innards, am I right?"

MacVane winked at him broadly, and after a moment Boothe dragged his attention away from the tent and back to the present. Whatever had brought Jim Kincaid into the mountains, whatever trouble was chasing him, would remain a secret until Jim was strong enough to tell him. In the meantime, there was nothing Boothe could do but wait.

He looked back at MacVane. "I reckon I could rustle up something," he agreed, and moved off toward his horse.

The wild barking of the dogs woke Sarah from her sleep. She was glad to wake up; she'd been dreaming about the black wolf again, and its eyes were as cold as death. She hated to sleep because of the dream.

She looked over the edge of the loft and saw Kitty making her way to the front door.

In her sister's hand was Ben's old Kentucky
rifle. The men had been gone for three days,
driving the horses to the fort to be sold to the
soldiers, and Sarah, Kitty, and the children were
alone.

"Kitty," she whispered. "What is it?"

The dogs stopped barking.

"Maybe Ben . . . I don't know. Go back to sleep,
Sarah."

Sleep was the farthest thing from Sarah's mind.
She crouched by the railing and looked down into
the big room below. Kitty, wearing her nightdress,
lit a lantern and peered out the window, rifle still
in hand. There were footsteps on the porch, and
the door opened.

"Ben!" Kitty laid down the gun and held out
her arms to him. "What are you doing here in
the middle of the night? Billy? The horses? Is
something the matter?"

Ben's voice ached with tiredness, and Sarah
could tell by the droop of his shoulders that he
was exhausted. He hugged Kitty tightly and then
broke away and slumped down in the rocker, his
head in his hands.

Kitty knelt on the floor in front of him. "Ben . . .
what is it?"

Sarah felt a little shiver even in the warmth of
the humid August night. Something was terribly
wrong. Maybe he knew something awful about
Jim . . . maybe Jim was dead. Dreams could come
true, her dreams anyway. Her stomach knotted in
fear, and she sank to the floor, arms around her
knees, praying silently to herself and listening to
the voices below.

"We're ruined, Kitty. They won't take the horses.
That's what the quartermaster said. It's over."

"No!" The word was wrenched from Kitty. "That can't be true. It's a mistake. No, I don't believe it."

Ben held Kitty's face in his hands. "It's true, Kitty. Every word. Do you think I'd make up a story like that? Do you think I could?"

"Why, Ben? Why? Tell me."

"Because of Jim. Because of your brother and Captain Lyndsay and the deserters."

Ben sounded angry, and Sarah shrank back in the shadows of the loft, hoping that they wouldn't remember she was listening.

"Jim? What does he have to do with our horses?"

Ben's voice was grim now. "That's the question I asked Sergeant Moore, and when he couldn't tell me, I went to the top. To Kearney. We're under investigation, along with Jim and Lyndsay, until the matter is resolved."

"Jim never killed anyone," Kitty said. "How could they believe . . ."

"I don't know what they really believe; I only know what they told me. Lyndsay has disappeared and Jim's on the run, and there're no other witnesses to the massacre of the deserters."

"Didn't you tell Colonel Kearney the truth? That the captain is the murderer?"

"Of course I told him, Kitty," Ben snapped. "He listened, but I don't know if he believed me. After all, it's Jim's word against Lyndsay's."

"But now that Lyndsay's running . . . isn't that a sign he's guilty?"

"Or determined to bring Jim in and prove he's guilty. For now, Kearney chooses to believe Lyndsay, or that's what he told me. I guess the army protects its own," he said bitterly. Ben got up and began pacing. Kitty remained on the floor, crouched in the glow of the lamp.

"What can we do?" Kitty raised a tear-stained face to her husband.

Sarah wanted to cry, too. She'd never seen her sister in tears.

"We can't do anything. The army's not going to buy any more horses from us until their investigation is over. It could be months...or years. Until then we're still under suspicion for harboring a dangerous criminal. Kearney's got details out looking for Jim and Lyndsay, he told me, but so far no luck."

"Dear Lord, I hope the soldiers find Jim first," Kitty said.

"Lyndsay has a head start."

Ben's words cut like a knife to Sarah's heart. From her dreams, she knew the black wolf was getting closer and closer to her brother, but now the wolf had an identity and a name and a deadly purpose that meant death to her brother. What if Lyndsay found Jim first? She shook her head violently. She wouldn't let herself think such things. Jim was on his way to find Boothe. Boothe would save him, she had to believe that, but who would help Kitty and Ben? Who would help her family?

Ben was telling Kitty about the horses. "Billy has them grazing in a valley an hour or two from here. We stopped at nightfall, and since I couldn't sleep, I rode in to tell you. I'll go back at daylight to help him."

"We can sell the horses somewhere else," Kitty said. "In Weston or Westport. People always need horses."

"Overlanders use oxen and mules, Kitty. Not horses. Oh, sure we can sell a few. Five or ten.

But that's not enough to keep us in business. We had all our money in trade goods for the Cheyenne. If we don't sell these horses . . ."

"We have nothing."

"Well, we have horses," Ben said. "Forty head of them to feed this winter."

"There must be something . . ."

"We can go back to Cairo. I can farm. We can be near our families. At least we'd have that."

"No!" Kitty got to her feet and slipped her arms around Ben's waist. "We can't give up. You hate farming; you'd be miserable. This is what we dreamed of . . ."

"Dreams don't last, Kitty. You know that."

"We aren't going to give up, Ben. We'll do something. I'll go back to the fort and talk to Colonel Kearney. I'll beg him. I'm not ashamed to beg when we're fighting for our lives."

"It won't matter, Kitty. Not until this thing with Jim is finished. Lyndsay is a treacherous bastard, but he's one of them. Not like us. Outsiders. We have no one, Kitty. No one on our side."

Her voice was muffled in his shirt. "We have each other, Ben. And the children and Billy and Sarah."

Ben sighed deeply. "It's not enough. Family's not enough now."

"I'll think of something . . ."

"I'm tired of thinking, Kitty. I need to sleep and then head out of here before sunrise. Billy needs help with the horses." Ben sounded weary beyond his years.

Sarah eased back on her pallet. She heard Kitty and Ben go into their room and the door close. Maybe Ben could sleep, but she couldn't. Kitty was crying. Kitty didn't know what to do. That didn't seem possible. Kitty always knew what to do.

Sarah couldn't take it in. Not her big sister, not the brave, indomitable Kitty, talking of giving up and going back to Cairo, and Ben sounding hopeless and beaten. Sarah didn't like Kansas, and she hated the horses, but that didn't matter. What mattered was that her family was in trouble. And there was no one to help them.

They thought they were alone.

But they weren't. Suddenly she knew how to help. It was something she had to do all by herself. If she asked Ben or Kitty, they'd tell her no, to mind her own business, to stay out of it, that she was doing the wrong thing. So she wouldn't ask them. She couldn't help Jim or protect him from the danger of the black wolf, but she could help Ben and Kitty.

She tried to sleep, but excitement and nervousness kept her awake. Just before sunrise, she heard Ben leave, slipping out quietly without waking Kitty or the girls. She waited as long as she could and then dressed quickly in riding boots, an old skirt, and a gingham blouse. She crept down the ladder from the loft, expecting Kitty to awaken at each telltale creak of wood. Moving in slow motion, Sarah crossed the floor to the door. Kitty's hat was hanging on a peg; Sarah took it for good luck. Then she opened the latch and was outside. With the dogs in pursuit, as if her early morning flight were part of a game, Sarah ran through the morning dew toward the barn.

Snow, Kitty's pony, snuffled softly in greeting. Sarah led him out of his stall and threw a blanket across his back. Her hands were trembling as she saddled the little white horse. Sarah knew she wasn't brave or strong or smart. She wasn't the kind of person to have great adventures, yet here she was getting ready to ride off into the dawn all by herself.

The path should be easy to follow. There were wagon tracks and the trail that Vertie had made. All she had to do was ride north and keep the morning sun on her right. It didn't sound too hard, she reassured herself. Snow was a good, sure-footed pony. If any mount could get her there, Kitty's pony could.

Sarah led Snow from the barn and shut her eyes and said a little prayer. She climbed into the saddle, kicked Snow with her heels, and rode away from the ranch.

Chapter Fifteen

"I'll bring some broth for him," Star said. "I think seeing you has made him stronger."

By morning light Jim did look stronger. He had recognized Boothe as soon as he opened his eyes, and had even managed to prop himself into a semi-sitting position as they talked.

His eyes followed Star as she left the shelter and then moved back to Boothe. "I still can't believe it," he said. "I just figured I dreamed seeing you last night."

"My gran always said there were stranger things in heaven and earth than we'd ever dream of." Boothe shrugged. "On the other hand, with you being headed toward Bridger's place and me headin' from it, only makes sense we'd hook up sooner or later."

"Maybe." Jim's head sank back tiredly against the pile of blankets Star had arranged for him. "I sure gave up hoping it'd ever happen though, I'll tell you that."

Boothe regarded him soberly. "Looks to me like you've got a powerful lot to tell me. Why don't you start with why you're running from the army, and who's trying to kill you?"

Haltingly, in words that sounded strained and awkward even to his own ears, Jim related the story of the horror that had haunted him across the plains, that had pursued him day and night even into the foothills of the Rockies. His throat ached when he finished and he was exhausted, but still the horror clung to him, and the miasma of disbelief.

"I know they were deserters, Uncle Boothe. But still that gave him no call to shoot 'em dead in their sleep like that. And that other officer, the one who came riding up, he must have thought so, too. I mean that *can't* be right. And then he shot his own officer. I never would've thought that. I couldn't believe it when I saw it, that he shot him right through the belly without blinking an eye. He would've shot me, too, but I guess I must've startled him. He forgot to reload."

Boothe's expression was sober. "What was that name you heard again?"

"Lyndsay. Captain Lyndsay. Do you know him?"

Boothe shook his head thoughtfully. "I know his kind, though."

"A mad killer." Jim closed his eyes, weary clear through.

"No. Nothing mad about him, from what you told me. He made his plans, thoughtful-like, and carried them out. A smart man, a careful man. He made a greenhorn mistake, not killing you, but that just shows lack of experience. Next time he won't make that mistake."

Jim opened his eyes. Beneath the pain and fatigue there was no surprise, just simple acceptance of the truth. "You think he'll come after me?"

"He's tracking you now," Boothe said flatly. "You can bet on it. Like I said, he's not experienced and that's to our good, but he'll learn fast. This Lyndsay, he makes his own rules, puts himself above the law. And once a man does that, he puts himself above everything. He thinks he's invincible, and he'll do everything he can to make sure it's so. You're a real danger to him, son, and he has to get rid of you. It's as simple as that."

The blanket flap lifted and Star came in, bearing a cup of broth. "Enough talk," she said. "Eat. You need your strength."

Jim levered himself up on his elbow to accept the broth, smiling at her. "I'll be up and about in another day; you can count on that."

Star laid her hand lightly across Jim's forehead, her face impassive. "Perhaps," she said. "Eat."

Once again Jim's eyes followed her as she left the tent; once again Boothe noticed the softening of his expression.

"She's beautiful, isn't she?" he said.

"She belongs to another man."

Jim's lips tightened briefly then relaxed. "She saved my life," he admitted. "I guess they both did."

He lifted the cup to his lips and drank. As the steaming broth settled through him, some of his strength seemed to be renewed. After a moment he spoke again.

"Ma would've wanted me to go to the fort," he said quietly, "and tell what I'd seen. Four men were murdered and I know who did it. I guess I'm a pretty big coward."

"Your ma would've wanted you to stay alive," Boothe said firmly. "And there ain't nothing cowardly about doing what you have to do to stay alive."

Jim lifted his eyes to Boothe. "What am I going to do now, Uncle Boothe?"

Boothe put his hand on Jim's shoulder. "Well, boy, there's only one thing we can do. We've got to find this Lyndsay before he finds you."

Meg rubbed the aching muscles in the small of her back. She'd been on her feet most of the day, and she felt stiff and sore. She hadn't thought the Kincaid-Gerrard Trading Post would be so busy in August. The flow of overlanders had finally stopped, at least those going west into the Rockies, and now the post was serving the failures, those who'd gotten past Fort Laramie or Fort Jim Bridger and then for whatever reason had turned back toward Missouri. Some were families left bereft by death or decimated by disease. Other settlers had gotten too late a start and were warned that if they kept on, they'd more than likely die in the winter snows of the Rocky Mountains. Whatever the reason, many of them had passed through Ash Hollow.

At first Meg had been alarmed. Some of the stragglers had money, but many didn't. She'd told Gerrard in no uncertain terms that she wasn't planning on running a charity for people who couldn't afford to pay, no matter how hard their luck. He'd laughed and agreed; he put those with no money to work and paid them with food and whatever goods they needed to make their way home. Stragglers had built the store and were now working on a house for Henryk and Anna. Gerrard was supervising the building, giving orders and watching every log that was put in place. Meg had to hand it to him. He was always thinking about ways to make more money and put more by.

She thought of the strongbox filled with cash, hidden under a floorboard in her room, and smiled. They'd done well over the summer, selling out most of their goods. A thousand overlanders had come to Ash Hollow, and most of them had had trouble with their wagons or draft animals or both. Henryk had been busy at his makeshift blacksmith shop, too, resetting wagon wheels and reshoeing mules and oxen. Sheldon and Meg allowed Henryk to keep half of the fees he charged. The Polish couple seemed content and in no hurry to move on. Meg was glad; she needed a woman she could depend on.

Meg pulled out the journal in which she kept records for the trading post and began to do her sums. She wasn't as fast as Gerrard at adding, but she worked hard and was determined to learn. Her concentration was broken when Sheldon pushed open the door and stepped into the store.

The change in him in the last months was nothing less than amazing. He now wore a handsome brown coat he'd bought from a passing traveler, a well-tied cravat, and a clean white shirt. Anna was more than pleased to do his laundry for the dollar a week he paid her. His trousers were spotless, and his one boot was shined to a bright sheen. Meg looked up from her books and bit back a smile. Sheldon Gerrard played the role of successful shopkeeper to the hilt.

He looked around the store at the almost empty shelves and nodded approval. He liked nothing more than to keep his goods moving off the shelves. Next he looked at Meg and frowned. "I thought we agreed, Miss Meg, that you'd lie down for a while. I can see the door of the store in case a customer comes along."

"I'm not tired," she said stubbornly, ignoring the nagging backache.

"You need rest," he argued.

"It's my baby, Mr. Gerrard," she snapped back. "Let me be the judge of that."

Sheldon looked at her measuringly. "I know what you think of me, Miss Meg, and you've made it clear I'm not to interfere with you and your child, but you also know me well enough to know I have to have my say. And I'm going to. It's my responsibility to see that you and your child are safe."

"No, it's not." Meg knew that she sounded petulant and ungrateful; as usual Sheldon took no offense.

"Well, we have differing opinions about that. Now go lie down for a while. I've got to get back to the men, but I'll keep an eye on the store. And leave those books 'til later."

"All right," Meg lied. "I'll be fine."

"Henryk and Anna are going to have a fine house, Miss Meg. A fine house," he said on his way out the door.

She stepped toward the back of the store where she and Sheldon slept in two small rooms, and then as soon as he was out the door, she turned back to the counter, pulled out her stool, and settled herself again. She was five months pregnant, but she wasn't about to be treated like an invalid. Having a baby was perfectly normal. She'd told herself that a hundred times, but still couldn't quite believe it. Thank God for Anna. Thank God there'd be another woman close at hand when her time came.

And, as much as she hated to admit it, thank God for Sheldon Gerrard. She'd blurted the news out to him about the baby weeks before. "I'm having a child," she'd said almost defiantly. "My husband's, but he's never to know."

She'd thought Gerrard would cut and run then; she'd thought he'd take his share of their profits and be on the trail by morning. But he wasn't. Instead, he said very softly, "He won't know, Miss Meg. At least not from me. Now tell me what you're going to do."

She had no idea.

"Go home maybe. To Cairo," she ventured.

"It's a long trip, Miss Meg. The baby might be born before you get to Cairo."

"I know." Tears had blurred her eyes and she looked away quickly. She didn't want pity from anyone, especially Sheldon Gerrard.

He hadn't given it. Instead there was a plan, rough and quickly thought out, but still a plan. "We can winter here; the house will stand the cold. We'll have company—trappers and traders coming down from the mountains. Anna can help with the baby. When's this child going to arrive, Miss Meg, if I may ask?"

"Sometime in December."

Sheldon nodded, thinking as she spoke. "Then in the spring I can go back to Bellevue for another load of goods. We need a man we can trust to take our money and our orders down to St. Louis—but that's no concern of yours. We'll be fine this winter. We can trade with the Indians for food and barter with the trappers. This is as good a place as any to spend our time."

Meg wiped away her tears with the back of her hand. "You're planning to stay here? To stay with us?"

"Where else do I have to go?"

Meg knew the answer. Sheldon Gerrard had nowhere else to go, and neither did she. Caleb O'Hare could find her at her mother's, and she couldn't bear the thought of him knowing about this child. This was her baby, hers and hers alone, and she would rear the child as she saw fit. As a Kincaid.

No doubt she'd have trouble with Sheldon about that. Already he'd become very proprietary about the baby; even though she argued with him and snapped at him, inside she was pleased at his interest and concern. Her little baby needed all the love it could get, and she, strange as it seemed, needed Sheldon Gerrard. She needed his protection, his shrewd business sense, and his cunning.

Without him, there would be no trading post at Ash Hollow; without him, her baby might not have a place to live. Meg didn't feel beholden to him though. What he gave he got back from her. She had no doubt that she'd given him a reason for living, a reason to get up each day. His pride. Whiskey—or his need for it—hadn't been mentioned since she'd told him about the pregnancy. She knew he hadn't had a drink of liquor since the trail.

They were an unlikely pair, a middle-aged one-legged man, his face ravaged by time and hardship, and a young woman with her life stretching out before her. But Meg didn't care what others thought. Survival was no longer a consuming passion. She had survived, and she had prospered. She was alive and a new life stirred inside her.

Because of Sheldon, she'd begun to dream again of what her life and her baby's might be, and that was the greatest gift of all.

The sound of hoofbeats and called greetings caused her to look up idly, mentally bemoaning the arrival of yet another straggler, dead broke, no doubt. And while a certain amount of barter was certainly acceptable when there was so much that needed doing around here, Meg had much rather see coin in the coffer. Besides, it was getting late in the year and if they weren't careful they were going to be stuck feeding this crew of misfits through the winter. They had to draw the line somewhere, and Meg decided this might be a good place to start.

She slid off the stool and then stopped, studying the newcomer through the open door. This was no ordinary traveler. He wore a U.S. Army uniform and bore himself with authority as he dismounted and looped the reins of his horse around the hitching post. An army officer this far from a fort? Meg's curiosity was only slightly offset with anxiety. He could have come to warn of Indian troubles or bring other bad news; it was almost a certainty he had not simply stopped by to chat.

Standing in the doorway staring would not give her the answers she sought. Meg squared her shoulders and went out to meet the stranger, cheering herself with the thought that for whatever bad news he might bring, the soldier at least was not broke.

Marcus had been hearing about the new trading post since he crossed the Platte, and since the first mention of it he had turned his horse on a direct course for it. The trading post itself was not much to take note of and no more than he had expected: a couple of hastily constructed buildings and a few wagons cannibalized of their usable parts; the bark was still green on the logs and the paint was hardly dry on the sign: Kincaid-Gerrard, Trading Post.

Kincaid. That was the name that had brought him here.

He had been given to understand that the Kincaid portion of the partnership was a woman, which was surprising though hardly material. Whether sister, aunt, or cousin to his prey, it was the name that attracted him. And, no doubt, it had lured his quarry as well.

Sheldon Gerrard was a neatly dressed, well-spoken man with one leg. Had Marcus been a different kind of person, he might have wondered what had caused a man such as he to end up in a trading post on the edge of nowhere. But his impatience made even polite conversation a strain, and the moment the woman appeared in the doorway he lost interest altogether.

Her deep red hair was caught up in a net behind her ears and immediately identified her as Jim Kincaid's blood relative. She wore a plain blue dress that was a little faded and somewhat tight around the waist, and over that a bleached muslin apron. She had a strong, steady gaze and a proud tilt to her chin.

Marcus swept off his hat to greet her. "Ma'am," he said. "Captain Marcus Lyndsay at your service. You must be Miz Kincaid."

She showed no recognition of his name, but her expression remained coolly curious. "Captain," she replied. "What can we do for you?"

He came up the steps, smiling. "A cool drink, perhaps, and a chance to rest my horse and freshen my supplies?"

"The only cool drink we have is spring water, and that's the only thing we offer free of charge. I hope you are carrying cash, Captain?"

"I am indeed, ma'am."

"Then please come in and look around."

Meg gestured him inside before her, then cast a questioning look over her shoulder at Sheldon. He murmured instructions about the care of Lyndsay's horse to one of the nearby men, then followed the two of them inside.

Marcus toted up a respectable sum on his bill, which left Meg kindly enough disposed toward him to offer him coffee in addition to the spring water and a slice of Anna's fresh berry pie. The three of them sat down at the counter. Sheldon made no pretense of disguising his curiosity as he said, "What brings you this far out by yourself, Captain?"

Marcus had his story prepared. "I'm acting as a forward scout for my unit, sir, on a routine mission. We'll be escorting a survey team come spring, and it's my job to mark out the route."

"It's getting late in the season," Meg commented, watching him over the rim of her cup. "I hope you don't have much farther to go."

"No, ma'am." He took a bite of the pie, complimented it profusely, then added, "Actually, I have a confession to make. I heard the name Kincaid, and I rode out of my way to find you."

He saw her stiffen up; the veil of caution descended on her eyes. Idly he wondered what this woman was hiding. Another time he might have been very interested indeed.

He added ingenuously, "Jim Kincaid is your brother, isn't he?"

He took a chance in saying that, but his gambles almost always paid off. And he knew he'd guessed right when she relaxed visibly, surprise springing into her eyes.

"Jim! Good heavens, how do you know him?"

Marcus smiled. "We're old riding buddies from Kansas Territory, back when I was stationed at Fort Leavenworth. I heard he was out this way and I was hoping to hook up with him before I had to head back."

Meg frowned, clearly disturbed. Marcus wondered if he had taken one chance too many. "Jim— in Kansas?" And then her face cleared and she laughed self-consciously. "Of course—he must've been living with my sister Kitty and her husband. I keep forgetting how long it's been since I've seen him. I still think of him as a child too young to leave home."

A look of nostalgia settled on her face, and frustrated impatience stabbed at Marcus. "He hasn't been by here, then?"

Meg looked at him, prompted out of her reminiscences. "Good heavens, no. But then . . ." She glanced at Gerrard. "We haven't been here very long, and if Jim *is* this far west I'm sure he'll find us before winter."

Marcus thought about that for a moment. Every sign he'd managed to pick up indicated that Kincaid was headed toward the Rockies, and it only made sense that he would go to his sister for refuge if he could find her. He didn't think the woman was lying; Kincaid had not been here yet. Therefore Marcus's choices were clear: he could continue his search on the last known trail, or he could winter here, hoping Kincaid would appear. If he did not, the trail would be lost forever.

"He might not know you're here," Gerrard said.

Meg frowned a little. "That's true. We got set up so late. If he crossed the Platte even a month or two ago he might not have heard we were here."

Marcus tried to hold back his frown. "Where would he go?"

"Fort Bridger?" Sheldon suggested.

"Of course!" Meg exclaimed. "Jim Bridger is an old friend of my Uncle Boothe's, and if Jim were going west, *that's* who he'd go to."

Marcus smiled thinly, his heart beating slowly and powerfully, his mind plotting. He could smell victory in the air.

"What a shame I missed him," he said mildly. "I'll probably be back this way in the spring. Maybe we can meet up then."

"But you're not leaving now," Meg objected as he started to rise. "Can't you tell me the news of my sister Kitty and her family and all that's happening back in Kansas Territory? And Jim— what does he look like now? What possessed him to go west? Surely you'll stay for supper!"

Marcus hesitated, then smiled. "Well, ma'am, thank you. Maybe I can."

Now that he knew where he was going, he had plenty of time.

Jim slept the whole night through and woke the next morning feeling better than he had in days. His fever had broken, he had the appetite of a bear, and just seeing his Uncle Boothe Carlyle had infused him with hope and strength. When Morning Star Woman entered the tent at sunrise, Jim was struggling to his feet.

"No, no. Too soon to get up." She ran to his side and laid a restraining hand on his arm.

"I'm going to eat outside this morning by the campfire with the other men," he announced.

"No," she said firmly. "You will eat here and then wash and sit with the others. Please, Jim. This is our last time to talk. I think soon you will be traveling on with your uncle."

Jim sat down again on the blankets. She was right; he was still weak, but he would not let her know that. He sat down because she said this would be their last time to talk, and he wanted more than anything to talk to her. He had never dared dream she might want to talk to him.

She left the tent and returned quickly with a tin mug of hot coffee and a bowl of rabbit stew. "The coffee is from Mr. Carlyle and the rabbit from last night."

"And still good." Jim wolfed down the meal. Star sat quietly beside him, her head lowered, her glossy braids lying against the print calico of her dress. He'd never known a woman who could be as still as Star. He remembered his sisters, always talking, moving, pushing, shoving. They were nothing like this woman, nothing at all.

Just looking at her made his throat tighten up, and he had to shift his gaze away, swallowing hard. "Tell me about MacVane. Is he your husband?"

She looked at him, her face still and calm, not betraying any of the emotion that was in her voice. "He is not my husband; he took me from my people. He stole me away."

Jim felt enormous relief wash through him. She wasn't staying with him of her own choice. He had known she couldn't be.

"Then you'll leave him," Jim said. "We'll take you with us when we leave. You don't have to worry any more. We'll take you back to the Cheyenne if you want to go."

For a long time Star simply looked at him with her grave dark eyes. "You make it sound so simple, Jim Kincaid. As though wanting can make it so."

She shook her head dolefully. "You don't understand. I want to go home, but I can't. I have disgraced my mother and my father. My uncle, High-Backed Wolf, is chief. He is disgraced, too. No Cheyenne woman can lie with a man before marriage. Don't you see? That is why I stayed with him. I have nowhere else to go."

Jim's jaw tightened. "I see that MacVane ought to be horsewhipped and left out here to die. None of this is your fault. Your parents will understand what happened."

She was stubborn. "You don't know the Cheyenne. You don't know our ways. I will not be forgiven. I will never be able to marry or have a child. I will be an outcast. It is better to be here, away from the shame."

"No, it isn't." Strength infused him, born of anger at the injustice. "What's best is for you to come with me and Boothe. We'll take care of you."

In a rush of courage, he reached out and grasped her hand. "I'll take care of you, just the way you took care of me." He tightened his fingers on hers; she didn't pull away. "Listen to me, Star. You gave me back my life. I can't repay that. But what I feel for you is more than gratitude. I can't leave you here with him. Come with me, let me show you—"

She wrenched her hand away and surged to her feet. Her eyes momentarily flashed contempt. "And should I trade one white man's bondage for another's? You make me no bargains, Jim Kincaid."

And then she gave a brief, sad shake of her head. "I belong to MacVane now. It is meant. I must stay." She pushed back the flap and ran out of the tent.

Jim struggled to his feet and followed her outside. He crossed the clearing to his uncle. "Where'd she go?"

"Took off into the woods like a scairt rabbit," Boothe said. "What did you say to her?"

"Too much," Jim muttered, looking around for Andrew.

Boothe nodded toward an area beyond the shelter. "He's off getting an early start communin' with the spirits. I never did know a man that could out-drink a Scotsman. Now what did you say to her?"

Jim scowled. Andrew had been dead-drunk or half-drunk since Boothe had arrived. "I told her that she needed to leave the old fool and come with us. He stole her, Boothe. He clean stole her."

"I know that," Boothe said calmly. "Does she want to leave him?"

"She says no, but I know she does. How could she stay with him? We could take care of her. *I* could," he amended.

Boothe looked thoughtfully at his nephew. All the signs were there. He was bright-eyed and talking wild, and it wasn't from fever; at least not the fever of sickness. "She don't know you, son. She knows Andrew and what to expect. She's been stole away from her family and home by one man; why do you think she'd go running off with another?"

"Because . . . because," Jim said passionately, "I love her."

Boothe didn't laugh or even smile, as Jim had half-expected him to do.

Instead he answered seriously. "I reckon she'd be an easy woman to love. And all that time she spent taking care of you . . ."

"It's more than that," Jim insisted fervently.

Boothe nodded. "But just because you love her don't mean she's going to run off with you and leave another man. You've still got a mite of learning to do about the ways of the world, Jim."

Jim turned his frustration on his uncle. "You think I'm just a greenhorn kid, don't you? Well, maybe I am, but a few things I know about and one of them is my own feelings! I can take care of a woman. I can take care of Star. And you can't tell me any different!"

"I ain't gonna try," Boothe agreed quietly. "But there's something else I think you ought to consider. This ain't no Sunday stroll by the river we're on. We've got a job to do. You and me have a killer to hunt down, and we can only hope he doesn't find us first. You don't want to bring a woman into that kind of danger; I know that."

Jim sobered. "No, I don't."

He turned toward the woods into which Star had disappeared, and he was quiet for a long time, wrestling with his inner pain. At last he turned back to Boothe. "I think I can ride by tomorrow."

Boothe shared with him a silent moment of sympathy and understanding before he nodded.

"Good," Boothe said. "If Lyndsay is coming for you, he's coming up the trail. Only a greenhorn from Cairo, Illinois, would wander through the woods."

That coaxed a smile from Jim.

"There's something I haven't told you. Your sister, Meg, is in these parts."

"Meg! But she's in St. Louis."

"Nope, not from what I hear. I hear she's got a trading post near the Platte. With an old friend of mine." He let the name drop quietly on the morning air. "Sheldon Gerrard."

Jim had been only a small boy when his uncle started dealing with Gerrard, but he knew the family story as well as any Kincaid. "No," he said. "Meg would never tie up with Gerrard."

"That's what we're aiming to find out."

They both looked around as Star reemerged into the campsite, looking as calm and composed as though she had never left. Boothe felt a tug in his chest for the pain that darkened the younger man's eyes.

"We'll be headin' out at first light," he said quietly. "Better say your goodbyes today."

Jim looked at him bleakly. "There's nothing to say," he answered simply, and walked away.

"Holy Mother of God." Emilie Gallier crossed herself and turned away from the window in her bedroom. She moved quickly down the big staircase, her skirts flying around her ankles, and as she ran, she called out instructions.

"Dorcas, come with me. I may need help, and Vertie, go find Mr. Charles. Now!"

By the time Sarah reined in Snow on the Gallier's graveled driveway, Emilie was by her side. Sarah gave a little moan and fell out of her saddle into Emilie's arms. "I made it, Miz Gallier. I didn't think I could . . ."

Emilie lowered Sarah to the ground. The girl was soaking wet with perspiration and she was weak with exhaustion. Her red hair frizzed out from beneath her broad-brimmed hat, and bits of leaves and sticks clung to her skirt.

"I only got lost once," she whispered through dry lips. "I remembered all of the signs—the funny rocks that look like an owl, and the ford at Sandy Creek, and the meadow with all the blue flowers. I only missed one turn, but then I remembered when I was here before we passed a tree that was struck by lightning and it looked like a skeleton and so then I saw it—"

"Sarah, *cherie*, is something the matter with your family? Are they ill? Or worse? Dear child, what is it?"

Sarah pushed herself up on her elbow. "Miz Gallier, I need you to help us. It's the horses—"

Charles appeared, his face red from running from the orchard. He wore a big straw hat and was in his shirtsleeves. He looked just like Ben when he was working, Sarah thought. Just like one of us.

He echoed his wife's shock. "The Kincaid girl? My dear Lord, what's she doing here?"

"Let's take her inside, Charles. Dorcas, get some cool cloths for her forehead and brew some of my camomile tea. Heat water for a bath, and Vertie, see to that little horse."

With Charles and Emilie supporting Sarah on either side, they made their way into the house.

"I'm fine, really," Sarah said from the sofa as Emilie hovered, dabbing at her face with a damp cloth.

"My dear child," Charles said, "what made you ride over here alone? That's not something a young lady should do. Does your family know? What an extraordinary thing."

Sarah took a sip of the tea that Dorcas brought in and smiled. "Yes, it is quite . . . extra . . . extraordinary. But I had to come. We need help, and you're the only friends we have."

Emilie sat beside Sarah and took her hands. "Of course, we are. Now tell us everything."

Stumbling and repeating, Sarah finally got the story out. "If they can't sell their horses to the soldiers, then they'll be ruined. I don't care about the horses myself," she said with a burst of honesty, "but Kitty loves them. It's what they've worked for for seven years, and now this terrible Lyndsay man is ruining their lives. Jim didn't hurt anyone! Lyndsay killed those men, not Jim. Someone's got to help us!"

"There, there." Emilie patted Sarah's shoulder and looked up at Charles. She raised her eyebrows quizzically. Charles nodded.

"Sarah, does your family know you're here?"

She shook her head. "I knew if I asked, Kitty would never let me come."

"They must be worried to death," Charles went on. "Vertie and I will ride over immediately and tell them where you are."

"And tell Mrs. Adamson that Sarah will be staying for a day or two. I think she needs some coddling."

"I probably should get home...Kitty needs me..." Sarah said halfheartedly.

"Mrs. Adamson can handle things for a few days, I imagine," Charles said dryly. "She impresses me as being a very competent young lady. Vertie and I will be late, but we will be back tonight." He came over to Sarah and took her hand. "Young lady, you are quite a heroine. I know your family will be proud of you."

Sarah wasn't at all sure of that, but she loved the praise. "Kitty told me once that everyone should have at least one adventure, especially a woman, something to tell my grandchildren about. I guess I've had mine."

Charles bit back a smile and dropped a kiss on his wife's forehead. "Take care of our guest, my dear."

"Travel safely," Emilie called after him. She turned her attention back to Sarah. "Do you feel like eating? Ham biscuits? Fruit?"

Sarah realized she was starving; still she felt a little guilty about abandoning her sister. "Maybe I should try to go home."

"Nonsense," Emilie said. "Not for a day or two. You're going to have a nice hot bath and then change into some clean clothes—"

"I don't have any."

"We'll alter something of mine; I have too many dresses anyway."

"Well," Sarah said slowly, "I guess it will be all right if I stay." She was thoughtful, and her blue eyes were all innocence when she smiled at Emilie. "I do feel a little faint . . ."

Emilie smiled back, two women who understood each other perfectly.

Kitty was half out of her mind with worry. Ben hadn't come back and Sarah—God knew where Sarah was. Snow was gone, and Kitty's hat, too, so obviously the girl had taken off, but where? After Jim? Maybe the foolish child had a harebrained idea of rescuing him. But of all the inconvenient times for Sarah to decide to become a heroine, Kitty thought, banging pots and pans as she tried to get together some food for the children.

Like most children, Carrie and Hilda were quick to pick up a parent's mood, and both girls were fussy and irritable, crying first for their father, then Sarah, and now even for Billy. Kitty was so frustrated she thought she'd scream. She heard the dogs barking in their wild and undisciplined cacophony. Surely, they had enough sense not to bark at Ben again.

She left the girls squabbling over a rag doll and went out on the porch. The dogs kept up their baying, which let her know the approaching horses belonged to strangers. She was just going back into the house to get the rifle when Charles Gallier hailed her.

"Mrs. Adamson. Hello. We've come to tell you that your sister is safe with us." Charles swung down from his horse and approached the porch.

"She's with you? That little minx. Lord, I've been worried, but why did she come to you?" Kitty's relief was mixed with irritation.

"On a mission," Charles said with a benevolent smile. "Before we talk, Mrs. Adamson, may Vertie water our horses—and I'd appreciate a drink myself."

"Of course. Yes. Please." Kitty was suddenly flustered, thinking of the disarray of the cabin and the two little girls clothed only in their underwear. Kitty led Charles into the cabin, ushered him to a seat, and poured a cup of water for him. "I'm sorry. That's all I have. I could brew up some coffee."

"Water is fine, Mrs. Adamson."

Hilda and Carrie stopped their squabbling and hid behind their mother's skirts. "You remember Mr. Gallier, don't you, girls?"

"Hurt. Knife," said Hilda. She stuck out her lower lip defiantly.

"Not today," Charles answered with a smile. "No knives today. May they have some candied fruit, Mrs. Adamson? When I knew I was coming, I prepared myself. I want them to think of me kindly."

The girls were coaxed forward to take the candy and then, quiet for a while, crawled under the table to eat.

Kitty sank down on a kitchen stool. "Thank you for letting me know about Sarah. When my husband returns, someone will ride over and fetch her."

"Not any time soon, I hope. My wife's invited her to visit for a day or two. I hope you'll let her. The ride was exhausting for her."

"I can imagine," Kitty said. "Sarah doesn't like hardships of any kind and to think of her taking off on Snow . . ." She frowned. "Why did she ride over to see you? I can't imagine—"

"To call on us as neighbors. To help out."

"Help out?"

"Sarah told us about the army not buying your horses."

"She told you that! What did she think you could do about it?" Kitty was indignant.

"She simply said we were the only friends you had, and she was asking advice. At first I wasn't sure what I could do, Mrs. Adamson, but on the long ride over, I've had a chance to think. I *can* help you. In several ways."

To Kitty the situation seemed unreal, almost like a dream. Charles Gallier, a fine gentleman in his tailor-made riding clothes and expensive boots, was sitting in her kitchen, talking about helping, while her two half-dressed children peered out from under the table, their faces sticky from sweets.

"What ways?" she asked suspiciously.

"First, I can take the horses to the fort. My contacts there are impeccable. I don't think any friend of Senator Benton's is going to be treated poorly. I shall sell your horses and deliver the money to you."

"You'd do that for us? You hardly know us, and my husband . . . well, he wasn't that polite—"

Charles raised his hand to stay her words. "Your husband is a man of honor and principle. There are few of them in the world today. I appreciate men like Mr. Adamson. It seems very simple; I can sell your horses and you can't. We only have one another out here on the frontier, Mrs. Adamson. We must look out for our neighbors. It's that simple. 'Do unto others,' as our Lord advised us."

Kitty thought carefully. It was a perfect solution, at least for now, if she could convince Ben. But what about the future? "What about next year and the next? Will you continue to sell for us?"

"If necessary, but by then this whole matter may have blown over. Your sister tells me your brother is innocent. Surely he'll be cleared of any wrong-doing."

"I don't know." Kitty shrugged. "Sometimes evil has a way of winning out."

"But not always," Charles responded. "Not in this case."

"All right," Kitty agreed. "I'll talk to Ben."

"Good, good." Charles smiled. "Now for the next part of my plan. I want to go into business with you, Mrs. Adamson."

"With me? I can't imagine—"

"Oh, yes, you can. We can imagine together. I want to ride out with you and see those horses of yours. I want us to pick out the best and keep them, and I want us to breed them."

Kitty couldn't deny the quickening of excitement she felt. "Breed horses?"

"Why not?" Charles asked. "I know something of horses; you know more. We need to start thinking of a new kind of animal, bred just for the West."

"I wouldn't know where to begin," Kitty said.

"Of course, you would," he chided gently. "If we were living in South Carolina, we'd breed our horses for racing and fancy riding. In New England, we'd want sturdy fellows who could pull carriages through the snow—"

"But here we need a horse with endurance," Kitty said. "A horse that can travel the plains and even go up into the mountains. A horse with a brave heart, like my Snow."

"We have the ingredients, Mrs. Adamson. Beautiful Spanish horses, whose blood is not yet diluted by stock brought from the East Coast of the United States. We can create the finest horse the world has seen."

Kitty's heart beat faster. "If . . . if we did this, how would it work?"

"You and I would work on a breeding plan that we both thought would succeed; you and your husband would rear the horses, and when they are sold, we divide the profits. One-fourth for me, the rest for you. How does it sound?"

Kitty stood up. "Ben and Billy are driving the horses in today. Let's go meet them so you can see what we have. There's a wonderful stallion I had my eyes on and some fine mares—" She stopped in mid-sentence. "I can't leave my children."

Charles rose to his feet. "Vertie will mind the children, unless you object."

"I'm ready to ride anytime you are, Mr. Gallier."

"How difficult will it be to persuade your husband, Mrs. Adamson?" he asked.

"Very," was her answer, "but I will, in time. Ben may be stubborn, Mr. Gallier, but he's not stupid. You are our only hope of surviving, and we are going to survive. You can count on that."

Chapter Sixteen

A late August fog lay over the mountain when Boothe and Jim started out at dawn, misty folds settling into the valleys and shrouding the hollows like the drape of a woman's gauze shawl. The echo of the horses' hooves was eerily muffled, disassociated from the ground on which they traveled. That was the way Jim felt: removed, disassociated. Somewhere ahead of him a man was looking to kill him. Somewhere behind him was a woman he had known for only a handful of days. Why should the latter weigh so much more heavily on his mind than the former?

He had lain awake all night imagining the tender good-byes he would share with her. But he had been right before—there really was nothing to say. She had saved his life through skill and attention; it was no more than she would have done for any other man. The smiles she sometimes shared with him, which seemed to hold such secret promise, were doubtless no more than the result of her own kind and generous nature. She had not asked to come with him. She would not miss him when he was gone.

And so when they were packed up and ready, Jim simply stood before her and said, "Thank you, Morning Star Woman. For everything."

There was nothing readable in her quiet dark eyes as she replied, "Good journey, Jim Kincaid."

MacVane was bleary-eyed and already half-drunk, but in good humor nonetheless. He shook their hands heartily and cheerfully invited them to look him up if they were ever back by that way.

Boothe tried to persuade him to move down the trail before winter closed in, and MacVane just laughed. "Down? Down, he says? Why, the best leavins are yet to come—*up* the trail, my boy! Up!"

Grinning, Boothe just shook his head. Jim knew his uncle would have tried harder to change MacVane's mind if he thought there was any real danger, and Jim tried not to worry about Star. MacVane was a seasoned mountain man, and if anyone knew how to take care of herself, it was Morning Star Woman.

He worried, nonetheless.

By midmorning a breeze blew up and chased the fog into a glum gray sky. With the wind came a cool crisp bite and the definite taste of autumn. Boothe commented he wouldn't be surprised to find frost on the ground come morning.

After a time Jim spoke heavily. "You were right, Uncle Boothe. I am just a greenhorn. First thing I did, before I even got into Kansas Territory good, was let a Pawnee brave steal my supper and my gun. I sat there with my knife in my hand and that brave close enough I could've whacked off his topknot, and I let him take my gun and walk off with it, laughing."

"Good thing you didn't go for his topknot," Boothe remarked mildly, nudging his horse around a spill of rocks. "They'd've cut you out of your skin before you knew what for. There ain't no such thing as a dead hero, son. You remember that. Especially when what you're really fighting for is nothing more than your pride."

Jim knew his uncle was trying to cheer him up. It didn't occur to him there might be any truth to his words.

He shook his head. "I never should've left Ma and the girls. They need me. But I kind of felt like I ought to be following Pa's footsteps—and yours . . . I thought it was going to be such an adventure. It never struck me I'd have to be at least half the man you and Pa was to follow in your footsteps."

"Looks to me like you done all right."

Jim shook his head bitterly. "I messed up everything I touched. I let my horse go lame. I crippled up myself because I was clumsy and wasn't watching where I was going. I would've starved if . . ." There he stopped, and swallowed hard. "If them three hadn't found me. And how do I pay them back? By running off when I should've stayed and faced down their killer."

"And just how would you've done that?"

Jim didn't answer. He knew as well as his uncle that by the time he had put his hands on a weapon the killer would have grabbed his pistol and fired, and at that distance one shot would have been all it took.

Instead he muttered, "I should've gone to the fort. Now no matter what happens, no one will believe me."

"True enough," Boothe agreed. "Which ain't to say you wouldn't have been shot on your way to the fort in the first place."

Jim hadn't thought of that. After a moment he released a long breath. "I wish I could be as sure of things as you are, Uncle Boothe."

"If there's one thing I've learned, it's that there's nothing I'm sure of. I just do the best I can, just like you do." He glanced at Jim. "Seems to me you done pretty damn good for a greenhorn, at that. You got yourself all the way to the Rocky Mountains, which is more than I did my first summer out."

Again Jim shook his head. "Only because I followed the wagon tracks of a bunch of pilgrims. At night I'd camp in sight of their fires."

"Smart thinking. Good to have company in case of trouble."

"Until I turned off for Fort Bridger and let that rattler crawl in my blanket. I remember waking up so sick I figured I was dying, then I don't remember anything. If MacVane hadn't happened along . . . I should have stayed at home. I never should've thought I could just light out on my own like that."

"Hell, son," Boothe replied mildly, "everybody's got to grow up some time."

"Yeah," Jim agreed morosely. "It just don't look like it's my time yet."

He would have said more, but stopped. Boothe had brought his horse to a halt atop a small rise, and the look on his face was intent and alert. "Smoke," he said, scanning the landscape.

Jim turned in his saddle, and they both spotted the dark tendrils rising above the treeline at the same time. They wheeled their horses and rode back the way they had come, moving fast.

They both knew what they would find long before they reached the camp. By that time the blaze had long since died away and only a few of the low branches of surrounding trees were still smoldering. Morning Star Woman stood in the middle of the rubble, her shoulders bowed with fatigue, her blue calico dress streaked with soot and dirt.

Jim swung out of the saddle and ran to her, catching her arms, whirling her around, searching her face, her hair, her torn and damaged clothing with his heart in his throat, and yet joy singing through his veins simply to find her alive. Her face was calm, and she met his eyes with no surprise. Neither did she try to pull away from his grasp.

"I was gathering berries," she said. "I smelled the smoke. I came quickly, but not quickly enough. I could only free the horses and fight the small fires to keep them from taking the woods."

"Where was MacVane?" Jim demanded hoarsely. "How could he let this happen? He—"

"Jim."

Jim looked up to see Boothe turning away from what appeared to be a bundle of blankets on the ground. Jim thought it odd that one bundle had not burned up, and then he realized it was Boothe's blanket, and that he had just draped it over something unidentifiable.

"He must've been asleep," Boothe said. "Or drunk more likely. That wind came up awful fast and all the junk he had piled around here was just like kindling." He looked at Star. "Morning Star Woman, I think he went quick, and didn't suffer."

Star simply turned away. "I will go catch the horses," she said.

The morning was done by the time they finished burying the remains of Andrew MacVane. Boothe began casting uneasy looks at the clouds and talking about moving on. Jim didn't stop to listen. He went looking for Star. She was kneeling by the fire, all her attention on the berries that she was pounding into a fine paste. The rock in her hand rose and fell in rhythmic precision.

He wanted to talk to her, but her face seemed closed and distant. Finally he cleared his throat and said the first thing that came into his head. "You've changed your clothes."

"These are *my* clothes," she said. "I had them hidden in my saddlebag. He didn't like them, but I do." She looked up, and Jim saw defiance in her dark eyes.

"I like them, too." He knelt beside her and reached out his hand to feel the leather. "Deerskin?"

The dress was soft and supple, a tubular garment that hung straight from her shoulders to below her knees. Along the neck and sleeves were finely sewn ornaments of blue beads and small feathers. She was wearing her deerskin moccasins, and she'd bound her braids with rawhide strips. Between her ankle and knee he could see the bare expanse of her leg, tantalizingly smooth and silken.

Jim dragged his eyes away from her leg and looked at the berries she was pounding into a mushy paste. "Is that for us?" It didn't look particularly appetizing to him, but he'd never say that to Star.

"For you and your uncle to take on the trail. It's pemmican. Something my people take with them when they travel."

"Looks like some kind of berries to me." Jim settled beside her, glad that she was talking to him. He didn't care what it was about; he just wanted to be near her.

"Chokeberries. They were all I could find here, but we make pemmican with cherries, too." She picked up the rock and continued her pounding. "I'll mix the berries with fat and buffalo meat." She pointed to strips of dried jerky by the fire. "I'll make little cakes and dry them in the sun. Then you and your uncle won't go hungry."

"That's very kind of you, Star." He wanted to tell her that she'd be traveling with them, too; that she'd be sharing the pemmican and whatever else there was to eat on the trail. They couldn't just leave her here in the wilderness; didn't she know that? He was afraid to talk to her about the future. He wished he knew what to say to her. "Are you sorry about Andrew?" he blurted.

She stopped her work and looked at him. "No, I'm not sorry at all. He did a bad thing when he took me; I can't forgive him for that."

Jim said what he'd heard at funerals all his life. "Well, I guess he's at peace now."

Star frowned and her dark eyes were thoughtful. "I'm not sure. I know little of the white man's afterlife. I watched when we buried him. I looked for his *tasoom*—"

"His what?"

"*Tasoom*. His soul," she explained to Jim as if she were talking to a child. "At death the soul leaves the body; sometimes mourners can see it; then it travels up the Hanging Road—"

"I don't know about that either." Even though they were speaking English, Jim felt as though they were conversing in an unknown tongue.

"The stars that make a path in the night sky." She was very patient.

"The Milky Way?" Jim tried to remember what his mother and father had taught him of the stars.

"Milky Way," she repeated, shrugging. "That is a strange name."

"I guess it is," Jim agreed. He'd almost seen a smile on her face and he wanted to keep talking. "So when the soul travels up the Hanging Road, where does it go? To heaven?"

"I heard Andrew talk of this heaven," she said slowly. "He said the streets were made of gold and winged creatures flew about and sang."

"They're called angels."

"It is not what the Cheyenne teach—these flying angels and golden streets. For Cheyenne, the soul goes to live in the land of the Wise One Above."

"God, you mean."

Star shook her head. "I mean the Wise One Above. He is not a god, but a spirit. The Cheyenne know many spirits. There is also the Wise One Below, but he has nothing to do with the *tasoom*. There's the spirit who rules the summer and the one that gives good health. There are spirits all around us. It is not like your Christianity at all."

"Oh." Jim was beginning to see that it wasn't easy to make comparisons between the religion in which he'd been reared and spirit world of the Cheyenne, but he desperately wanted to be closer to Star and to understand her and her world. "What's it like when spirits go to the Wise One? I mean, what do you think it's like?"

Her answer was unhesitating. "It is much like life on earth. The people hunt and camp and even make pemmican," she teased. Her smile flickered briefly and Jim felt his heart quicken. She was even more beautiful when she smiled.

"But Andrew will not go there," she said matter-of-factly. "He was not a Cheyenne and there was no *tasoom*. Perhaps Andrew will go to your heaven with streets of gold."

"I don't think so. He belongs somewhere else." In fact, Jim thought to himself, hell was too good a place for a man like Andrew MacVane, even though the old man had helped save his life. He formed his next question carefully. "Will you go back to the Cheyenne now that Andrew's dead?"

"I told you before, Jim Kincaid, I can never go back. I am disgraced." Her expression shifted and saddened, and her lower lip trembled slightly; Jim thought she was going to cry. If she cried, could he reach out to her? Could he hold her? Would she let him?

Star's tears shimmered in her eyes. "I miss my family very much; I think of them every day." Her voice trembled, but she didn't cry. "Did you have a happy childhood? Did you have sisters and brothers? Do you miss them?"

Jim nodded. "I miss all my family, especially my ma. I have two older sisters and two younger and a brother. We grew up on a farm. We lived near a big river, near two rivers in fact. In the summer we used to play on the bank of the Ohio; willows grew all along the edge and we'd grab a branch and swing back and forth, back and forth, and then when we were out over the river—we'd let go. It was real nice on a summer day." Only now, he thought, those carefree summer days seemed a million years ago. He missed his family with a dull, heavy ache.

"We have rivers with willows, too, a favorite place for camping," Star said. "On hot days our mothers would let us play in the water; it felt so cool."

"You see, there are lots of things we have in common, Star. I'll bet if we had a chance to talk and know each other—"

She looked at him almost fiercely. "You can never be a Cheyenne, Jim Kincaid, just as I can never be white. You know nothing of our spirits or our taboos or our customs or ways of rearing children, and I know little of your ways. I thought I would always live with my people, marry a Cheyenne brave, have his children, and die as an old woman among my grandchildren." Anger flickered in her eyes. "And now I can never have that. I can never be a Cheyenne wife or live in a Cheyenne village. Andrew MacVane took that from me."

"Star . . ." He reached out and stroked her hair. It was smooth and soft. He wanted to say something that comforted her, something that could give her hope. He would offer her his whole world. "There are other ways to live, Star. To be happy. There are other men you could marry."

"You don't understand, and you never will." Her look was stubborn, and her face was closed and guarded again.

"I could learn, Star. If you would help me. I want to be with you and take care of you." He didn't mean to plead or beg, but he couldn't help himself. He loved her; he knew it as certainly as he knew the sun would rise the next day.

She turned away from him. "Your Uncle Boothe is by the horses. I think he needs to speak with you about the trip, and I have work to do."

Her profile was as hard as if carved from stone.

"Star—" he tried.

She kept her face deliberately turned from him and would not answer.

With a sigh, Jim got up and went toward his uncle.

"She's right, son. A white man can never really understand the red man's life." Boothe was running his hands along the mane of his big spotted horse, picking burrs and bits of twigs out of the shining hair.

"You were listening." Jim was both angry and embarrassed.

"Don't get riled up. I only heard the last part. Listen to what she says, Jim."

Jim was still angry—at his uncle, at himself, and at Star. "We're not that different," he argued. "I bet we'd get along fine. Someone has to take care of her; we aren't just going to leave her out here."

" 'Course we're not. She knows that as well as we do, but just because we take her to Meg's or somewhere else doesn't mean she wants to be with you."

"I think she does," Jim said stubbornly. "And after this army mess is cleared up, I can go back for her and we can be together."

"We need to take one day at a time, Jim. We'll ride out this afternoon and head down to Ash Hollow." He looked up at the sky. "I don't like the way those clouds are looking over the mountains."

"Too early for snow, isn't it?"

"Never can tell in the mountains. We'll take this stuff to Meg—" His arm swept around the campsite. "I doubt Star wants it. I see she couldn't wait to get back into her own clothes. You don't think that's a sign, Jim, that she misses her old life?"

"I know she misses her family, but it's not the end of her life."

"Well, in a way it is. The end of her Indian life, of living like a Cheyenne. She can never do that again."

"None of us can choose the life we have, Uncle Boothe. If we could, do you think I'd have chosen this one? To be chased by a madman and the U.S. Army and be running for my life?" Jim asked. Bitterness colored his words, and his expression darkened. "But this is the life I have."

Boothe put his hand on his nephew's shoulder. "You're a fine man, Jim Kincaid. Your ma and pa would be proud of you just as I am. And you're right. Sometimes we can't choose the path we follow, and sometimes we can. And you can choose right now not to make Star fall in love with you."

"But—"

"Now listen to me. I know you love her, and she may love you, but she doesn't know it yet. It will be a lot easier on both of you if she never knows."

"I don't know what you're talking about."

"In her village, an Indian girl is the daughter of a chief or of a great warrior. She has respect and a place in that tribe, but when she takes up with a white man, married or not, and lives in his world, she's nothing but a squaw, Jim. That's how people see her. An Indian squaw. It's not an Indian word. It's a white man's word and it isn't one of respect. Do you want that for her?"

"It won't be that way for Star and me," Jim argued.

Boothe took Jim's arm. "Come on and walk with me. I want to tell you a story."

Jim looked longingly back at the campfire and Star.

"She'll be there when we get back," Boothe assured him.

They walked a little distance into the fragrant pines and firs. Squirrels scurried in the branches above them; their coats were already thick with cold weather fur. Airy, delicate ferns grew in the shadows of the giant trees, and a thrush, unafraid of intruders, picked its way through the underbrush, tossing aside dried leaves and needles in its search for food. Boothe touched Jim's arm and pointed. A fox stood frozen in their path, and then with a flick of his tail vanished into the undergrowth.

Boothe and Jim sat on a big hardwood tree that had fallen across a clearing. Orange and brown mushrooms clustered in bright patterns along the decaying wood.

"Nothing like the peace of the mountains," Boothe said.

Jim took a deep breath of the cool, pine-scented air. There was a tang in the breeze that he couldn't identify. "Yep, but you didn't bring me here to talk about the mountains."

Boothe smiled a little uncomfortably at his nephew. "No, I didn't. I brought you out here to tell you what I've told only one other living soul, and that was your pa."

Jim felt his chest swell with pride. "You trust me that much."

"I do, and I know you would never betray my trust."

"Never, Boothe, never."

"Then I'm going to tell you something that happened a long time ago, before you were born, and I think it will help you understand what I said about you and Star. When I was a few years older than you, I was trapping up the Missouri, just like your pa used to do. It was a hard life, but one a man could learn from."

"If you mean learning by mistakes, I know about that."

Boothe laughed. "I made plenty of mistakes too, son, and I took a lot of foolish chances, like the day I came up on three Sioux braves shooting arrows into a young Indian boy. Now I didn't know at the time that the boy—no more than thirteen or so—was a Crow, a mortal enemy of the Sioux. I only saw three men ganged up on one, so I rode in—"

"You rode in on three Indians?" Jim was filled with shame when he remembered his own embarrassing encounter with the Pawnee and the deer.

"Well, I had the advantage. I carried a rifle and the Sioux didn't. When I fired a few shots, they knew well enough to hightail it back to their camp. I got off my horse and looked at the boy. He was in bad shape, I could tell. I did what I could for him, tried to stop the bleeding and get the arrows out. I talked to him, mostly sign language and pointing, and finally figured out he wanted me to take him back to his village. Home. And so I did."

Boothe's voice changed, the timbre lowered, and Jim knew his uncle was reliving that long-ago time. "He was a brave little fellow; I can still see him trying not to show pain or cry out. He lasted 'til we got to his village. He died just at sundown in his father's arms, never a whimper despite all the pain." Boothe broke off for a moment.

"I didn't know what would happen to me—if they'd blame me for his death or torture me or kill me. I didn't know."

Jim sat quietly, intent on Boothe's story.

"It turned out they thought I was a hero for bringing the boy home. His father, White Elk, was a brave warrior and an important man in the tribe; he had many coups against the Sioux and the Blackfoot, and he asked me to stay a while. He wanted to hear again and again about how brave his son was and how he fought the three Sioux who killed him. Now White Elk had a daughter—"

"Oh," Jim said, understanding.

"She was the most beautiful girl I'd ever seen. Like Morning Star Woman with long black hair as shiny as a crow's wing and eyes . . . her eyes were dark as the night. Her name was Burning Bright, and—"

"And you fell in love with her."

"I did. I loved her very much, and being a young man and filled with dreams and hopes and thinking nothing was impossible, I wanted to marry her and take her home with me. Back to civilization."

"Why didn't you?" Jim asked. "Because Miss Caroline was waiting for you in Cairo?"

"It had nothing to do with Caroline Adamson," Boothe said. "She wasn't part of my life then; she was busy raising her children and giving no thought to me. It was part of being young and thinking I could take any path I wanted in life. But White Elk changed my mind."

"I thought he liked you."

"He did, but he was a very wise man. He knew what would happen to Burning Bright if she went into the white man's world; our children would be half-breeds, not accepted in either world, white or Indian. She'd be a squaw, cut off from her own kind and not accepted by mine."

"Ma would have taken her in, and Pa. You know that," Jim said defensively.

"Maybe she didn't want to be taken in, Jim."

"So you rode away? You just left her?"

The remembrance of pain, untempered by years, resonated in Boothe's voice. "It wasn't that easy, but, yes, I rode away, and I didn't look back."

"You never tried to see her again? To find out what happened?" Jim was incredulous. How could Boothe ride away from the woman he loved?

"Once the decision was made, there was no going back, Jim."

"You could have stayed with her," Jim argued. "You could have lived with the Indians."

"Mebbe," Boothe said slowly. "Some men can do that. I don't know if I could—"

"I know what you're telling me, Uncle Boothe, but it's not the same with me and Star. She's already left her tribe. It's not the same," he repeated stubbornly.

Boothe sighed. "I hope you don't believe that you're going to make her life better by taking her into civilization. Lord above, Jim, all these Indians out here on the plains have civilizations so complex no outsider can ever understand them. I've been here almost thirty years, and I know this much." He held his thumb and forefinger an inch apart. "Do you know what the name of Star's tribe really is?"

"She's Cheyenne."

"We call the tribe Cheyenne. They have their own name, *Tsistsistas.* The People. The Crow don't call themselves by that name. That's the white man's name. They're the *Absaroke*, the Bird-People. It has nothing to do with crows. They have their own names, their own ways—"

Jim's mouth tightened, and he knew his voice was high and tense with anger when he interrupted his uncle. "I know what you're trying to do, but it isn't going to work. I love her."

"Do you know what's taboo in her tribe? Do you know a Cheyenne can never point a knife at a wolf? That's taboo. Do you know a Cheyenne will eat a dog, but a Comanche won't—"

"I don't care!" Jim faced his uncle, eyes flashing, face flushed with anger and determination. "I know it's going to be tough, but I can learn her ways. I love her, and she's going to love me. She'll stay with Meg where she'll be safe, and once I clear my name with the army I'll come for her. If we can't live in the white man's world, then we'll live someplace, but we'll be together."

Boothe shook his head in resignation. "God knows you're a Kincaid—and a Carlyle; no way you could be any more stubborn, is there?"

"I know what I want," Jim said evenly, "and I know what's right for me no matter how it might look to someone else."

Boothe threw his arm around Jim's shoulders and pulled his nephew close. "Then I guess you're on your way to being a man, son."

Boothe's eyes looked sad and Jim didn't know if it was for what had been in the past or what lay ahead. Even when Boothe smiled, his eyes still looked sad and far away. "We'd better get about our business, Jim, and get out of these mountains while we can."

Chapter Seventeen

When they awoke the next morning, the ground was dusted with snow. Jim wanted to believe it was a freak occurrence that would melt away as soon as the sun was up good, but one look at Boothe's face told him his uncle did not share his opinion. They barely took time to eat a cold breakfast and did not wait to heat coffee; they packed quickly and silently and moved out. Still Jim waited for the sun to burn away the chill in the air and give them back the late summer day.

But the sky remained leaden, broken only by gusts of wind that grew colder rather than warmer as the day progressed. By late afternoon the drop in the temperature was dramatic; it was as if a cold, icy hand clamped down on the back of Jim's neck and wouldn't let go. He shivered and turned up the collar of his jacket. There was still a good hour or two until sundown, but ominous gray clouds were pouring out of the mountains, blotting out the sun.

Jim saw that Star had pulled a blanket around her shoulders and over her head. She rode astride, sitting the horse as easily as his sister Kitty, who Jim always thought was the best woman rider he'd ever seen, but Star rode bareback with only a blanket across the horse's broad back. There were two extra horses in their little caravan, Andrew's and the sturdy pack-horse. Boothe led the way with Star following and Jim bringing up the rear, leading the riderless horses.

He was glad they were on their way; action, any kind at all, seemed better than waiting, and the sooner he and Boothe took off after Marcus Lyndsay, the sooner it would all be resolved and he could get on with his life, which included a future with Star. Boothe had told Star they were taking her to a place where she'd be safe and have time to make up her mind about what she wanted to do. She'd nodded and begun to pack her belongings; Boothe had frowned at Jim and warned him with his eyes not to say anything else. Jim had choked back his words, but that didn't mean he'd changed his mind about wanting to be with Star.

Snowflakes began to fall, big fat drops that swirled eerily in the gusty wind. Boothe cast a worried look behind him; the sky was dangerously gray, and the wind blowing at their backs cut like a knife. Boothe knew the high mountain passes well enough to realize that this wasn't a flurry that would blow over in an hour or so; this was a full-fledged storm that would drop snow as high as the horses' bellies. They needed to take shelter and none was in sight. To their left were sheer rocky cliffs and on the right the land slanted upward in a tangle of trees and fallen rocks.

The path curved around a craggy outcropping and doubled back on itself. Now the wind blew full into their faces; Boothe noticed that the texture of the snow was changing, falling faster and more heavily, driven by the frigid blasts of wind. He glanced back anxiously at the others. Star was huddled down in her blanket, her chin lowered against the onslaught of snow and wind. Jim's head was lowered, too, the brim of his hat already white with snow. Boothe gave his attention to the trail. He knew there was nothing to do but keep on going until they found a place to shelter.

If they found a place.

There was a part of Boothe that had always known this would happen, sooner or later, once again. After all, he had come into the mountains eight years ago to die, hadn't he? He had never really expected to leave this place alive.

But neither had he expected to be the cause of the deaths of his nephew and an innocent woman.

He kept trying to tell himself this was not like that other time. But he had no more luck with that than with convincing himself that what had happened in '35 had not been his fault.

They had started across the mountains filled with dreams and greed, ready to claim a new land and build an empire. Maybe they would have succeeded, too. Maybe Sheldon Gerrard and those who shared his grandiose schemes would have changed history . . . but for one minor lapse of judgment.

Boothe had tried to tell them it was too late to try to cross the mountains. These days he wondered if he had tried hard enough. He wondered if there hadn't been a little something in him that was thinking about empires, too . . . that was thinking about being the first to claim that wide-open Oregon Territory. Or just being the first.

Maybe that was why he was condemned to do it all over again.

The snow fell fast and furiously, clinging to tree limbs and rock crevices with icy tenacity. Whatever doubts he had nurtured about this being a passing freak storm were gone. The wind was bitter and raw, and now blew directly into their faces; the horses lowered their heads almost to the ground and plodded on. This was no freak storm. This was settling in to be a full-blown blizzard.

Boothe was in the lead. The wind stung his eyes and the snow, though not thick yet, was falling so fast it formed an icy curtain through which it was hard to see. It would be easy to wander off the trail into a gully or up a dead-end mountain pass. And it would only get worse.

They had to find shelter and find it soon.

Jim struggled to keep the pack horses in line. His hands tingled with cold, and the rawhide tether cut painfully into his palm. He could barely see the outline of Star in front of him, and Boothe was invisible in the swirling snow. Jim knew they couldn't keep on like this much longer, and he had a terrible premonition that they were going to die, lost and frozen in the snow.

Suddenly Boothe was beside him, his words lost on the gusty wind. He was pointing to a break in the trees. Blindly Jim followed, his eyes half-closed against the blowing snow.

He felt his horse stumble and fall to its knees. Jim rolled off, fighting to keep a grip on the tether that held the pack animals. For a moment he lost the others in the screen of whirling white, and then he saw them ahead. Leading the horses, he plunged forward, fighting the drifts.

A circle of firs broke the worst of the wind, and Jim knew then what Boothe was planning—to shelter the horses here in the wind break and then look for some kind of sanctuary for them. Boothe and Star were off their horses now, battling wind and snow to pull off blankets and saddles. Boothe fought his way through the snow and put his mouth close to Jim's ear.

"Stay here with Star. There's an outcropping of rocks just ahead. Maybe—"

Jim nodded and led his horses toward Star. Her blanket was glistening with snow and all that he could see of her were her dark eyes, worried and watchful.

"It'll be all right. Boothe will find us somewhere to hole up, and we've got plenty to eat. Pemmican? Remember?"

He saw no answering smile in Star's eyes.

They stood frozen and weary, shoulders hunched, heads down while they waited for Boothe. They didn't hear him approach, and when he touched Jim's arm, Jim jumped and whirled around. Boothe looked like an apparition with snow powdering his hat and icy tendrils clinging to his hair.

He leaned close. "There's a ledge on that cliff that will give us some cover and a stand of firs that will shelter the horses. We'll be all right, Jim. Let's get moving."

Jim nodded numbly and followed Boothe and Star toward the cliff, which appeared and then vanished as the wind whipped the snow into swirling eddies of white.

Marcus was caught off guard by the snow. He was heading directly into the wind, and when he saw the first flakes, he wasn't worried; it was only a late summer flurry that would soon blow over. He kept on climbing, plotting his course toward the smoke that he'd seen earlier in the day. No matter how hard the weather was on him, his prey would suffer equally, and Marcus held the belief that he was stronger and smarter and more likely to prevail no matter what the circumstances.

The trail gradually disappeared, covered by a drifting, shifting carpet of snow, but Marcus didn't consider stopping to make camp. He dug his spurs into his horse and urged him on. The horse, a big roan with a mind of his own, whinnied and threw back his head. The snow was blinding him, and he danced erratically, trying to get his head and turn away from the wind. Marcus pulled at the reins. The big horse bucked frantically and plunged into a snow-filled ditch.

Cursing, Marcus slid from his saddle, thigh deep in wet and clinging snow. He fought his way out of the ditch and then began the long process of urging his horse up the slippery side and onto solid ground. The horse fought him every inch of the way, and when the animal was finally out of the ditch, both Marcus and his mount were heaving and panting with exhaustion. It was hard to catch his breath in the high altitude and cold, and each time he took in a lungful of air, it cut his chest like an icy knife.

He knew then that he had to find shelter or he would die.

They dragged the blankets and saddles off the horses in the relative calm of the wind break. Without being told, Star hobbled the riding horses in the Indian way, front leg to back, giving them enough room to maneuver but preventing them from running away.

Boothe made the first trip to the relative shelter of the rocks, bent low against the wind and the weight of a pack on his back. When he returned, Jim was struggling to unsaddle the riding horses, and Star was helping. The wind had snatched away the blanket she had used like a shawl, and the deerskin chemise she wore was not made to withstand such elements.

Boothe shouted above the wind, "Get the pack goods inside first! We'll need everything we've got if we're going to make it through the night."

Jim nodded and began to unload the animals. Boothe called to him again. "Hobble them first, Jim. I'm taking Star into the cave."

Boothe did not know whether Jim had heard him or not. The roar of the wind was so severe he could barely hear his own voice, and the snow was falling so thickly that when he turned back toward the cave he was momentarily blinded by a screen of white; he couldn't see the rock wall a mere ten feet before him. A gust of wind cleared the way, reestablishing his boundaries, however briefly. He shouted to Star and forged forward with her by his side.

Their arms loaded with blankets and bundles, Star and Boothe lowered their heads and battled their way through the snow toward the cliffs. The snow lifted for a moment like a curtain, and Jim saw them clearly, and then the wind shifted and they were lost to him. He bent down to hobble the horses and as he attached the tether to the first one, he remembered that he'd dropped the reins of the other horse, as well.

Heart pounding, throat dry with fear and dread, Jim stood up. The other pack horse had vanished.

Boothe had been optimistic when he'd called the indentation in the rocks a cave. A projecting ledge protected a small area from snow, and a pile of fallen rocks gave shelter from the blustering wind. It wasn't ideal, but it was better than being caught in the open.

The rock overhang would provide enough ventilation to start a fire, and the nearness of trees overhead suggested there might be wood to be found beneath the snow, and pinecones for kindling. Already Star, shivering beneath a blanket she had snatched from the pack, was kneeling at the edge of the shelter, digging away the snow. Boothe nodded silent approval. For whatever failings his nephew did or did not have, he knew the value of a woman.

Boothe went quickly through his own pack, where he found a pair of gloves and a strip of wool with which to tie down his hat. He couldn't have turned his back for more than fifteen seconds, but when he turned back toward the cave entrance, he was amazed and sickened to see nothing but a curtain of white. He immediately snatched up a heavy coil of rope.

"Stay inside the shelter!" Again he had to shout to make himself heard as he neared the entrance. "Stay dry! We'll be back as soon as we can!"

Boothe pulled his hat low over his eyes and stepped back into the storm.

Jim couldn't believe how quickly it had happened. How could he have let the pack horse wander off? Blankets, food, and dry clothes were packed into its saddle bags.

They needed the supplies to survive. Bending low, looking for tracks, he moved away from the horses. The animal couldn't get too far. It was probably just a little spooked and would soon stop. Too dumb and scared to go far.

There were no tracks. Maybe there had been and the wind had erased them. Maybe they had already been filled with snow. Maybe the horse had gone in the opposite direction entirely and left a perfectly legible set of tracks, but how could Jim know? Jim squinted and peered into the gloom. Dark was coming on fast and the world was painted in tones of gray and white—a blanket of white so thick and steady that moving through it was like not moving at all.

The horse might be three feet in front of him and Jim wouldn't see it unless he stumbled into it. He was beginning to realize he had made a big mistake.

Another one.

Boothe counted his steps and stopped. There ahead of him were the shapes of four of the horses, heads bent low, stoically facing away from the wind, enduring because they had no choice. But there should have been five horses.

"Jim!" He cupped his hands around his mouth. "Jim!"

His voice was snatched away by the wind, and nothing but the wind answered.

It was plain to see what had happened, and the truth was worse than any nightmare Boothe had ever dreamed. One of the horses had gotten loose and Jim had gone after it. Jim, who in his seventeen-year-old confidence wouldn't think to do anything else. Jim, who had no idea what a blizzard was, or what it could do to a man who was lost in it.

Jim, who was as good as dead.

When Boothe appeared out of the snow, a specter covered in white, Star came to him swiftly. "Jim Kincaid? What's happened to him?"

"Gone with the horse." Boothe's breath was ragged, his beard, already white, was snow. He moved close to the tendril of a fire Star had built inside the cave and stretched out his hands, flexing his fingers, which had grown stiff even inside the gloves. "Lost in the snow."

He could feel the girl's stillness as comprehension settled over her. It was the stillness of grief and terror.

But her voice was quiet. "You will go for him."

Boothe looked at her. "I have to," he said simply. "He's my sister's child."

She nodded. Her face was calm, and Boothe knew that she understood completely. She was on her own now. The chances were not good that either he or Jim would ever come back.

He moved quickly to the pack again, selecting another coil of rope, a lantern that would be useless until the wind died down enough to permit a flame to burn, and a flat metal flask of good corn whiskey. The latter he tucked inside his shirt, and as he spoke he knotted the two lengths of rope together.

"My niece's name is Meg Kincaid. Her trading post is east of Fort Laramie at a place called Ash Hollow. Just tell her what's happened; she'll know what to do."

Star's expression didn't change nor did her eyes waver, but Boothe heard the faintest tremor in her voice. "You will find him, Boothe Carlyle. You will return safe."

Boothe wanted to answer, but he couldn't. He merely looked at her for a moment, and knew she would do what had to be done.

Then he secured one end of the rope to a rocky point, and held out his hand to Star, who knotted the rope tightly around his wrist. Lastly, he turned and picked up his rifle.

He said, "Jim's a lucky man to have known you, Morning Star Woman. I reckon we both are."

Then he turned and plunged back out into the snow.

* * *

The snow was so thick that just looking at it made a man wonder that if there could be any air left in all that snow, how would it be possible to draw a breath without choking on it. Sometimes Jim did feel as though he were choking, as though he were drowning in a sea of thick white crystals, as though he were being crushed by them, pelted to death by them . . .

He had long since lost the feeling in his fingers. His face felt so raw and lacerated he imagined rivulets of blood freezing on his skin. Now his face, too, was growing numb. When he tried to focus his eyes, he realized that tears formed by the wind had frozen and glued his eyes half-shut.

He knew it was foolish to keep walking. How could he hope to find the horse and then make his way back to the camp when he couldn't see a foot in front of him? He should have let the animal go, but losing a horse packed with food and blankets was about as serious a blunder as a man could make. It wouldn't have happened to his Uncle Boothe or his pa. How many more chances would he get?

The whiteness was disorienting, in an odd way that was both comforting and terrifying. He couldn't tell east from west, up from down. Yet he couldn't stop moving. Some part of him must have known that if he stopped moving he would die.

Hell, son, a voice echoed in his head, *everybody's got to grow up sometime.*

And he knew something else. The wind was at his back, pushing him along, and he had to believe the horse would go in the same direction. Animals faced away from wind when they could, and the pack horse would do the same.

He kept moving.

What Jim knew about animal behavior he had learned from his pa and his sister Kitty, and they had taught him well. He knew the horse would follow the direction of the wind, and he also knew that, in the disorientation of the storm, it would not go far. Still, he could actually feel the warmth of the animal's body before he could see it, and he considered it blind luck to have stumbled upon the horse at all. If he had wandered even a foot off course, he would have missed it entirely.

But he hadn't. The horse stood there, head down and feet planted, as cold and dispirited as Jim was. Jim leaned heavily against the beast, drawing in its warmth, but dared not rest for more than a couple of breaths. He felt for the bridle and, at the familiar human touch, the horse responded—reluctantly, but he followed.

Jim's hands were painful and felt frozen at the joint, but he managed to hold on to the bridle, tugging the horse along. He was facing the wind now and every step was a struggle. Snow drifted up around his knees. The wind cut off his breath and drove needles into his skin. He could not keep his eyes open and didn't try. Fiercely he concentrated, counting his steps and knowing that as he fought the wind, his stride would be shorter, and knowing that if he veered off course by even a degree, he would be lost forever.

But Star was waiting for him. And if he was gone much longer his Uncle Boothe might be forced to risk his own life to come after him. Never before had his actions threatened harm to anyone but himself. Not since he had struck out on his own had anyone depended on him.

Perhaps that, in the end, was what made a man.

The wind hit him full force; it surged and rushed around him, pushed him, slapped at him like a living thing. It seized his hat and blindly he floundered after it. His hat was lost. He put his head down and yanked at the bridle. He was completely disoriented now, nothing but wind and whiteness everywhere he looked. Grimly he pointed his feet straight ahead and continued to count his footsteps.

A tremendous gust of wind howled down from the cliffs and momentarily lifted the veil of snow. A shadowy form loomed before him—a man. Jim staggered into him.

Wordlessly Boothe took the bridle from Jim's frozen fingers and placed his nephew's hands around the rope that was bound to his own wrist. Together they struggled back toward the cave.

All told, Jim had moved less than a hundred yards away from the camp.

Jim hardly knew when it was over. There was snow, and then there wasn't. There was wind, and then it wasn't so loud or so strong. There was a woman's voice, movement all around him. Blankets piled around him, a blur of color that he later realized was a fire. His legs collapsed beneath him; he sank stiffly to the ground on his knees. It was a long time before he realized that the insane frantic clicking sound was the chattering of his own teeth.

Star pressed a cup of something hot to his lips and folded his hands around the cup, holding them there with her own. He drank, spilling and slobbering like a baby, but he drank. And as the hot liquid spread through his veins, Star's face became clear, and her face was the whole world. *This was what it was for,* he thought. *Just this. Just her.*

Star turned away with quiet, efficient movements to take care of his Uncle Boothe. Consciousness returned to Jim in slow, scorching breaths. He didn't think he would ever be warm again. His fingers and toes stung and burned. Star made both men take off their boots and socks and soak their feet in a pan of snow she had melted to lukewarm water over the fire. Jim was too exhausted to find this either embarrassing or ridiculous, and he did as he was told.

"I think you will be fortunate," Star said, examining his fingers. "You will get to keep your fingers."

Jim closed his hand around hers. The movement caused a multitude of small explosions of pain in his joints, but he scarcely noticed. What he noticed was the surprise in Star's eyes, the warmth and strength of her slim fingers, the mere nearness of her. He saw something else, too, in her eyes; something he hardly dared trust, though it seemed perfectly natural, perfectly clear.

After a moment she dropped her eyes and pulled her fingers away, though not ungently. She turned back to the fire, which she had somehow built to a respectable blaze and shielded from the wind with stacked bundles of Andrew MacVane's booty.

Jim looked at Boothe. "The horses?" he said hoarsely.

"I got them to shelter. They ain't likely to wander off in this storm. If it lets up in a day or two, they'll be all right."

Jim looked at him soberly. "Do you think it will?"

"I've seen it happen before." That was all the reassurance Boothe could give.

And then he asked Jim, "How'd you do it anyways? How'd you find that animal and start back here like you did without getting yourself lost?"

"I followed the wind," Jim answered simply, "and counted my footsteps."

Boothe looked thoughtful for a minute. "That's using your head," he said, more matter-of-factly than approvingly. "The one advantage God gave us over nature, you know—our brains. Glad to see you figured that out."

Jim smiled faintly. For the first time since he'd set out from home, it occurred to him that his pa might have been proud of him today.

They dried their feet and pulled on several layers of dry socks while their boots toasted before the fire. Their wet outergarments, too, they replaced with layers of clothing belonging to strangers on some now-distant wagon train. Outside, the snow was slanted and whipped by the wind, falling so thick and fast that already drifts had piled up against the windblock Star had made and were beginning to creep into the cave.

She started dragging more bundles forward, and Jim went to help. Boothe moved outside the cave a few feet, searching beneath the snow for more wood. Even for that short distance, he kept the rope tied around his wrist.

Jim and Star reached for the same bundle at the same time; their hands touched. This time Star did not pull away. She looked at him with large grave eyes and said, "You were a fool, Jim Kincaid, to risk your life for a beast of burden."

"I think you were worried about me," he said gently.

"It is forever the task of a woman to worry about her man."

Jim's breath caught. "Her man?"

Star's grave, quiet expression did not waver or change. "I am yours, Jim Kincaid," she said. "If you want me."

Jim did what he'd wanted to do for days. He bent his head and kissed her. Despite the cold, her lips were warm, and he could feel her breath soft against his mouth. She didn't pull away from him, and he felt a joy he'd never known before. He didn't care if they were in the middle of a snowstorm and it was the last night of their lives. He was holding Star and kissing her and she was kissing him back as if she cared for him. That was enough to live on forever.

They moved apart only when Boothe returned, dumping a small armload of wood beside the fire.

"We'll have to take turns going out for more," he said. "Don't search too close to the cave. We'll have to save what's there for an emergency."

Jim and Star turned back to work, knowing that it would take all of them working together to survive the night.

Never had survival seemed so important, nor life so precious.

Chapter Eighteen

They woke to the smell of smoke.

Ben was out of bed first, pulling on his clothes as he made his way through the cabin to the front porch. He saw Billy running from the barn toward him. Billy stopped by the porch and pointed west toward the early morning sky, gray and hazy with smoke.

"Prairie fire," Ben said. It was something that everyone who lived near the plains expected—and dreaded.

Kitty joined them, her face pinched and tight with fear. She saw the smoke and she, too, knew what it meant. "How long?" she asked Billy.

Billy Threefingers sniffed the air like an animal, his head tilted back, his eyes closed. He took three deep breaths and let the air out slowly before he opened his eyes and answered. "Depends on the wind—how fast the fire comes. One hour. Maybe two. Maybe it will turn and not come here at all. Maybe it might burn itself out in the meadow."

Maybe. Only maybe. Ben and Kitty looked at each other, desperation and fear etched on both their faces. The wind was blowing toward them from the west, straight into their faces, carrying the acrid odor of smoke. The Adamson ranch was in the direct path of the fire, and the surrounding woods would burn like dry sticks in a campfire.

Kitty remembered what her Uncle Boothe had told them about prairie fires when he'd led the missionary caravan across Kansas. Fires came in the spring or late summer and autumn when the high grass was limp and dry. Sometimes the fires were started by a careless traveler or trapper at his campfire; sometimes a bolt of lightning set the prairies burning. Either way, it could be deadly.

"Boothe said to light a backfire," Kitty said quickly. "Burn the grass around you so the fire won't have fuel—"

Ben shook his head. "It won't work here, Kitty. The wind's too strong, blowing right toward us. There are too many buildings to protect, too many animals." He waved his arm toward the well-tended homestead. "A man alone on the prairie can burn out a space for himself, but not here. Not in the hills with all these trees—"

"Then what, Ben?" She fought to keep the panic from her voice.

"A firebreak. Billy and I'll start cutting and clearing down there at the bottom of the hill below the house. If we can make it wide enough, maybe the fire won't jump it. You get Sarah and start clearing the brush around the creek. It should give us protection on the north side."

If the fire jumped the creek or the break, their house, barn, and animal pens would be directly in its path. Everything they'd fought so hard to build would be destroyed. The stream wasn't very wide, and Kitty wasn't sure that it could stop a prairie fire, but she didn't hesitate. They couldn't stand by and see their world go up in smoke around them.

At a run, Kitty headed back toward the house. Sarah stumbled out onto the porch, rubbing her sleep-filled eyes. Her hair was a tumbled mass around her shoulders, and she still wore her nightdress.

"The children?" Kitty asked.

"Asleep. I just looked. What—" The scent of burning wood and grass reached her.

"Prairie fire. It's moving up the hills. Get dressed," Kitty ordered curtly. "We've got to pull the brush away from the creek. Hurry!"

"But Carrie and Hilda—"

"Let them sleep for now. I need you with me, Sarah. Move, girl!"

Kitty hurried toward the springhouse where the stream that curved around their property began. Oh, Lord, she asked, why did this have to happen? Why with forty head of horses in the pens waiting to be traded at the fort? Why, with everything for once going right? Why, Lord, why?

The horses were already frightened and anxious, tossing their heads and neighing nervously, trotting from one side of their enclosure to the other. If the fire jumped the break and the creek, Kitty knew what she had to do. Let all the livestock loose while she and the others rode the fastest horses toward the river and safety. But it hadn't come to that yet; they still had a chance. Maybe. Maybe.

An hour later, the sky to the west was glowing red, and they could hear a distant roaring—not the sound of the wind, but of the fire itself, like a giant animal stalking through meadows and up the tree-filled slopes of the Flint Hills, devouring everything in its path with its voracious appetite.

Kitty had pushed Sarah and the girls into the springhouse. It was made of stone, and its cool dampness gave refuge from the smoke and ashes that swirled in the air. That would be protection until the fire jumped the break, and then there would be nothing left but to try to outrun the flames.

Kitty wet cloths in the stream and ran toward Billy and Ben, who were still frantically cutting a firebreak between the oncoming flames and the Adamson ranch. Kitty's eyes stung with smoke, and she choked on the smell and taste of it. It was in her nose and in her hair, pervasive, suffocating. She could see the fire now as well as hear it, and the sight of it struck terror in her. It was fierce and formidable, and when she saw Billy and Ben silhouetted against the glare—two tiny figures fighting valiantly to turn back a monstrous wall of flame—she wanted to weep. Not even David fighting Goliath had been given such a task, and it broke her heart to see their bravery . . . and futility.

She wrapped the lower part of her face in the damp cloth as she charged down the slope toward the men.

Ben's face was black with soot and streaked with sweat. His hands were cut and bleeding from dragging logs and deadfalls from the path of the fire. He took the cloth from Kitty and stopped work for a moment to wipe his face.

A flock of quail flew overhead, their wings beating heavily on the thick, smoky air. A rabbit burst out of a thicket near Ben and dashed wildly back and forth, too confused to know in which direction safety lay. The dogs, which had taken refuge near the springhouse, were barking hysterically, and their howling yelps mingled eerily with the high-pitched panicked whinnies of the horses and the incessant roaring of the fire. If this wasn't hell, Ben thought, it was the closest he ever wanted to get to it.

The flames were eating their way through a stand of trees below the house. Tongues of fire danced and arched from bush to tree to bush almost joyously, glowing orange and red at the edges and at the center blue-green. Limbs snapped and cracked, and whole trees vanished in bright spurts of fire, leaving only charred smoking remains behind.

"It's too late, Ben!" Kitty screamed over the crackling roar. She could feel the heat on her face, and she was terrified by the immense power of the fire. They couldn't fight it; they had lost. "We've got to make a run for it—now." She tugged at Ben's arm. Billy had retreated and stood seemingly mesmerized by the fire, his axe clutched in his hand, but Ben wouldn't move. He stood defiant.

"I think we can hold it off, Kitty. The wind is shifting. I can feel it. If we can widen the break—"

"It's too late! Please, Ben!" The words were torn from her raw, burning throat. She moved away up the hill, toward the springhouse and her babies. If they left now, their horses could outrun the fire, but they dare not delay any longer.

Finally Ben, his shoulders sagging in defeat, turned and started toward her, his back to the fire. He didn't see the spurt of flame leap from a hickory tree to an eighty-foot cottonwood at the far side of the break. He didn't see the tree catch fire like a piece of kindling, and then slowly, almost majestically, begin to topple toward him.

Kitty saw, and she had time to scream her husband's name only once before the tree fell.

By morning the storm was nothing but a distant nightmare. The sun shone in a blue and cloudless sky; endless stretches of snow glittered and gleamed with a reflection so bright that Jim had to narrow his eyes against the glare. Boothe had gone to check the horses, and Star had already started a fire and was brewing up a pot of coffee. It was a glorious day, a wonderful day, and Jim realized he'd never been happier in his life.

On thinking about it, he decided that last night was the best of his life. He'd gotten lost in the snow, that was true, but he'd found his way back, and he'd even been a hero of sorts. He'd been tested against the elements, and he'd prevailed, and that made him feel good. But what was better was spending the whole night with Star.

She'd slept next to him, her head on his shoulder, her hip nestled against his. She'd gone right to sleep after they ate a cold supper, but Jim had stayed awake just looking at her, staring into the darkness watching her sleep. She'd looked young and vulnerable, someone very much in need of taking care of. He'd awakened this morning surer than ever that he and Star were meant to be together.

He saw Boothe wading back through the snow-drifts and went to meet him.

"Horses all right?"

"They all made it; 'course they're hungry this morning and mad as hell I didn't have any food for them. But if we get an early start, we can probably ride out of this snow by afternoon and find some forage down in the lower meadows."

Jim squinted up at the cliffs. "Looks like that sun's melting the snow pretty fast."

Boothe's eyes followed Jim's gaze. "Yep, that might cause us some trouble if we don't move out before midmorning. That snow and ice might just slide down on us."

"As soon as we eat and load up the horses, I'm ready to ride. Lord, what a fine day." Jim spread his arms out and took in the whole panorama, deep blue sky, brilliant golden sun, and snowcapped mountains gleaming like diamonds all around them.

Boothe stifled a smile. "Glad to see you in such a good mood, son. Ummm, smell that coffee that Star's brewing up. I could drink about a gallon."

Blinded by the snow, Marcus had lost his horse in the storm early on. With his mount gone, he knew it would be foolish to continue. His rifle had been strapped on his horse along with all his food and supplies. He had nothing but the clothes on his back and a pistol tucked into his belt. Being stranded in a wooded area with no rocks, no caves, not even a crevice for refuge, would have daunted a lesser man, he thought, but he knew he could survive. He had to. The chase was not yet ended.

He remembered everything he'd read as a child about soldiers stranded in the wilderness and facing the unknown. Julius Caesar, Hannibal crossing the Alps, Alexander the Great . . . all had met their tests, withstood their trials by fire and emerged victorious, just as he would.

The wiliest had endured by taking a lesson from nature. Marcus was no less a man than they. He knelt in the snow and, using his hunting knife, began to dig.

He made a burrow, wrapped himself in his army coat, and crawled into the hole. It was a long and cold night, but he'd survived it. His body heat had made a cocoon of warm air, and the barrier of snow had kept out the cold.

The next morning he clawed his way out and, bleary-eyed, gazed at the sun. Marcus didn't stop to give thanks that he'd survived; he believed he owed that to himself. No supernatural power had saved him; it had been his own cunning, intellect, and instincts that had brought him through the blizzard. His mind was the power. With it he could warm his body, slow his breathing, increase his strength and endurance. He was the superior contender in this battle against man and nature. He would not only survive, he would triumph.

The storm would have been as devastating to Kincaid as to him, and his prey was still out there, possibly weakened, certainly unwary, not even imagining he'd be pursued through a snowstorm. Staggering, falling, sometimes crawling, he made his way out of the thicket of trees onto higher ground. From there he had an unobstructed view of the mountains. To the west, not far from where he'd holed up for the night, he saw a faint trail of smoke against the intense blue sky. Someone had built a campfire.

Willing himself to take a step and then another and another, Marcus struggled through the snow, the thin line of smoke his beacon.

An hour later he had them in his sight. An Indian woman was clearing up around a campfire, and the two men were loading the horses a few dozen yards away. He recognized Jim Kincaid and instinctively knew that the other man was Boothe Carlyle.

If he was going to take them, it would be now. The woman would have to die, too; he felt no pity about that. Like Jim Kincaid at the deserter's camp, she was in the wrong place at the wrong time.

From the looks of the camp, they would be riding out soon; he needed to act now while the girl was alone.

* * *

Star was alone at the campfire when she heard the man approach. She looked up in surprise but without fear. What she felt, in fact, was concern, even pity for the man who appeared like a ghost out of the snow. He staggered and seemed about to fall; she moved toward him, wading through the knee-deep snow that Boothe and Jim had not yet cleared.

It was working even better than Marcus had planned. He stumbled and pretended to fall, and the Indian girl came to him quickly, helping him to his feet. He feigned weakness as they struggled through the snow to the cleared area around the campfire.

Already he had assessed the area; he knew what was available and what he had to do to get it. He knew the dangers and what he had to do to avoid them. When he heard the crunch of a footstep on the snow, he was ready.

He stiffened his muscles and turned swiftly, pressing Star against his body and holding her there like a shield with a forearm across her throat. Her fingers came up, nails clawing ineffectually against the wool of his jacket as small strangling sounds came from her throat.

He drew his pistol from beneath his jacket and pressed it against her temple even as he heard the click of a rifle bolt behind him. All this took mere seconds, as he was in the process of turning, and he was surprised and a little disappointed when he saw the man who faced him down the length of a rifle barrel.

"Think carefully, sir," Marcus said quietly. "I've no compunction against killing this squaw, as you might already have guessed. Kindly throw down your rifle and tell me where Kincaid is hiding."

Boothe did not lower his rifle, although he knew

holding it there was foolish. If he fired he would hit
Star; if he so much as twitched a muscle, the killer
who held her would put a bullet through her head.
There was something eerily familiar about the whole
situation, some dark dread recognition, as though he
had lived it . . . or dreamed it . . . all before.

"He's not hiding," Boothe said calmly. "He's right
behind you."

Marcus just smiled. "I am a soldier, sir, and not so
easily tricked. Never mind." His finger tightened on
the trigger. "He will come out soon enough when he
hears the gunfire."

It was all Jim could do to stay still, crouched in
the shadows of a snowdrift that had piled against
the cliff wall to the height of a man's shoulders. He
could clearly see everything that was happening. Star,
held helpless and terrified by the throat, her nostrils
flared with the effort of taking small, shallow breaths
while her fingers dug futilely into her captor's arm.
Boothe, with his rifle aimed but equally as helpless to
use it to defend himself or Star. And Marcus Lyndsay,
calmly holding a pistol to Star's head.

Jim's rifle was useless in his hands. He could no
more fire it than Boothe could fire his, not without
the risk of hitting Star. All he could do was wait,
curse God and himself for bringing this danger to
the people he loved, and try desperately to think of
what to do.

Boothe was talking, low and easy, and Jim tried
to listen over the pounding of his heart. "So you're
Captain Marcus Lyndsay. I had no idea you were so
close to us."

"I would have found you last night if it hadn't been
for the snow."

"You survived alone in that storm?"

"You sound surprised. I assure you I would have

endured ten times worse to get to Kincaid. You see, he has become something of an inconvenience to me, and he must be dealt with before he becomes a serious problem."

Jim's eyes went from Marcus to Star and back to Marcus again. He saw Star narrow her eyes and cut them sideways at Marcus, and he could tell from the look on her face that she wasn't going to stand by helplessly much longer. Jim knew if he could distract Marcus for even a second, Star would act. He felt a great surge of affection for her, coupled with pride and a fierce protective instinct. He had chosen well, and he had chosen forever.

Boothe had been thinking much the same thing. He kept talking, hoping to distract Marcus, though he had little hope of lulling such a sharp mind into complacency. He knew his time was running short; the man had come with killing on his mind and wouldn't waste many minutes on idle conversation. Boothe made his move then, a little half-step forward that caused Marcus to focus the gun on him, aimed at his heart.

Boothe saw the flash of metal on Marcus's hand, and his eyes were riveted there. The wolf ring.

The rifle went slack in his hand; he couldn't have pulled the trigger had all the hounds of hell descended on him.

This was the moment he had lived a hundred times. This was the dream. He had never understood it before; now it all made sense. A horrible, unreasoning sense . . .

He raised his eyes slowly to the other man's and saw his destiny there. "Who the hell are you?" he demanded hoarsely.

Jim saw his chance and knew it had to be now or never. If ever Lyndsay was to be caught off guard, it was at this moment. His uncle's odd behavior, the flicker of curiosity that crossed Lindsay's face, the slight lessening of his grip on Star's throat. This was Jim's chance.

He stepped out from behind the snowdrift, drawing back his rifle bolt and swinging the weapon to his shoulder in the same motion.

"Lyndsay!" he shouted.

Everything happened just as he expected. Star broke from Lyndsay's grip and flung herself away. Lyndsay swung around and aimed his pistol at Jim. Jim lurched to the side, and the shot he fired missed.

And then things stopped happening the way they should have. Boothe should have raised his weapon and fired. At that range he couldn't have missed. Lyndsay wasn't even looking at him. Boothe should have fired.

Instead, he walked slowly forward, his rifle held slackly at his side. Jim screamed at him and discharged another shot, which exploded off the side of the cliff. Boothe kept walking toward Lyndsay.

Everything was clear to Boothe. He knew it was time and he was filled with peace, the first he'd felt since he'd dreamed of the black wolf and his death in the high mountain passes of the Rockies. So, it was to be now and it would be at the hands of Marcus Lyndsay. He knew with a clear certainty that there was nothing he could do to change the hour of his death, but he didn't want Star and Jim to die with him. All he could do was hope and trust that their instincts to survive were stronger than Marcus's will to destroy.

Boothe had never felt so calm in his life. He took a step toward Marcus and then another. "It's time," he said.

Jim was yelling at him, and Marcus was smiling, the cold brutal smile of a man without a conscience. Marcus swung his pistol around and fired point-blank.

Blood blossomed in the snow like the petals of a red rose. Boothe staggered back. Marcus fired again. Boothe fell and lay still.

Jim rushed down the slippery incline, struggling to reload as he did, unable to believe the horror that was unfolding before his eyes. A heartbeat, and Star was free. A heartbeat, and Boothe was dead. A heartbeat, and Marcus turned the pistol on Jim with a clear shot.

And all the while Star was moving, rushing toward the fire, reaching down . . . now straightening as she hurled a flaming faggot into Marcus's face.

He screamed and staggered backward, his finger convulsively pulling the trigger once before it fell. Jim fired too, but he never knew if his bullet hit the target.

The echo of the gunfire joined Marcus's screams of agony and didn't die away. The echo only reverberated, louder and louder until the air itself seemed to vibrate with a terrible rumbling, a thunderous roar that sounded as though the whole earth was tumbling down around them. Jim looked up at the cliff, and his heart stopped for a full long beat.

"Avalanche!" he screamed at Star. "The shots have loosened the snow. Avalanche! Run, Star."

With a strength he didn't know he possessed he picked up his uncle's lifeless body and stumbled toward the shelter of the ledge. Star was running beside him. The first huge pieces of ice began to fall and crash around them, exploding into a thousand prisms of light.

"Go on," Jim yelled at her. "Go on, don't wait for me."

He saw her leap toward the cliff just as a huge, jagged fragment of ice crashed from above. Jim gave one final lunge, Boothe a dead weight in his arms, and fell against the wall of the cliff.

He and Star clung to each other as tons of ice and snow plummeted down the cliff, obliterating the camp and covering the now still body of Marcus Lyndsay.

After the terrible roaring stopped, there was a deathly stillness. Even the wind was quiet. The whole world was covered in snow and ice. To Jim it was as if the world had ended. He couldn't move or think or act. All he could do was huddle by the lifeless body of his uncle and pray some miracle would bring Boothe back to life.

It was Star who took charge and tramped across the mounds of fallen ice and snow toward the stand of fir trees.

"Two of the horses are dead," she told Jim when she returned. "But the trees broke the worst of the snow so three are left. I think we can lead them out."

"Boothe's horse?" Jim managed.

"He is alive."

"Then we can take Boothe out on it, take him to Meg's and bury him—"

"No." Star shook her head. "We must bury him here, Jim. It's too long on the trail. We have to leave him here; you know that."

Jim's eyes filled with tears. "No, Star, I can't. I can't just leave him."

She sat beside him and slipped her arm around his shoulders. "I did not know your Uncle Boothe well, but I know that he was a man of the mountains, Jim.

He will be at home here and he will be at peace. He would want to rest forever in the mountains that he loved."

Jim laid his face against her shoulder and wept.

They covered Boothe's body with a cairn of stones. Jim knew he ought to say something though the words were hard. He thought about the funerals he'd been to in Cairo. He thought about when his pa and Miss Caroline, Ben's mother, had died. He wished he had his family with him now, his ma and Kitty and Ben and Meg. He wanted all of them beside him, all the Kincaids that he loved and who had loved Boothe Carlyle.

He looked at Star standing bravely beside him, strong and unyielding. He looked out across the mountains and hills and valleys of the Rockies, and the words came to him.

"Yea, though I walk through the valley of the shadow of death . . ."

They packed the few supplies that hadn't been buried and started the long trek down the mountain, leading the horses behind them. Jim knew that Boothe's big Appaloosa would be his horse now; he would have Boothe's horse and saddle, and maybe if he was lucky, a part of his uncle's courage and spirit as well. Maybe someday he might be half the man that Boothe Carlyle had been.

It was as if Star could hear what he was thinking. She walked stolidly beside Jim, not complaining, keeping up with him stride for stride. "I saw his soul, Jim. I saw when Boothe Carlyle's *tasoom* left his body."

Jim felt the sting of tears against his eyelids again. "You did?" he asked, his voice gruff with emotion.

"Yes," she answered calmly. "And I know it will travel up the Hanging Road to the Wise One Above. Boothe Carlyle is at peace with his fathers."

Jim reached out and took her hand, holding it tightly as they began their journey home.

Like shadows they moved across the white expanse of snow. They were Crow, fierce and proud warriors of the Northern Plains. The leader of the small scouting party raised his hand and stopped the others. He pointed to a movement against the whiteness. Something or someone was alive.

The Indians dug their heels into their horses and rode forward.

Chapter Nineteen

April 1844

Meg remembered the community gatherings in Cairo when she was growing up with a kind of wistful reverie. Although there wasn't a churchyard in Ash Hollow, nor did willows grow along the riverbank, the idea of having the people she cared about all sitting at the same table was enough to cause her to sing softly to herself as she set out her mixed collection of plates and cutlery. Henryk had placed planks across two sawhorses to make their table, and Anna with Meg's and Star's help had prepared a meal of roast venison, sweet potatoes, rice and gravy, dried apple pie, and loaves of hot, crusty bread. One of the travelers had left a cow, and Meg was pleased that she could offer milk and butter to her guests.

A year ago she had never imagined that she would share in this kind of family gathering again. And a strange family it was, too: Anna and Henryk, foreigners who barely spoke the language; Sheldon Gerrard, a fallen man and outcast; Star, cut off from her own people; and Jim, the brother she had never thought she would see again.

And Fiona Carlyle Kincaid, four months old and thriving on this first fine day of spring. This was her family, and Meg had more to be grateful for than she had ever dreamed.

Jim and Star had arrived that past autumn, worn and tired, bringing the news about Boothe. But even that sadness couldn't dampen for Meg the joy of seeing her brother again.

Before he'd fallen into an exhausted sleep, he'd told her about Marcus Lyndsay and Boothe, but her uncle's death seemed unreal and far away. She couldn't think of him as dead; instead, she told herself he was on another adventure, the biggest of his life, and she refused to mourn openly. This was a beginning for them all, not an ending. Boothe would have wanted it that way.

Star had helped Meg when she went into labor, and sharing the intimacy of motherhood with another woman had made Meg feel as close to Star as a sister. Having Star with her, in fact, made her miss her own sisters a little less, though still she fantasized sometimes about them all being together again. Perhaps here, on a beautiful spring day like this, gathered at a trestle table beneath the trees . . .

Her reverie was interrupted by Jim's voice. "That girl of yours," he said, "is sure a Kincaid all right. She got hold of a chunk of my hair and pulled herself out a handful before she'd let go." He rubbed his scalp tenderly. "That's the fighter in her."

Meg smiled. Star was sitting on a blanket on the ground, bouncing Fiona on her lap. Sheldon, as usual, was hovering over the baby with a stuffed doll in one hand and a wooden ball in the other, while

Anna was loudly giving instructions on how to best stimulate the child's interest—in Polish, of course.

Jim followed Meg's gaze, and his expression changed, his tone quietened. "Listen, Meg. I know it ain't none of my business but . . . Sheldon Gerrard. Of all the men in the world to be the father—"

"Good heavens, Jim, the baby's not Mr. Gerrard's."

He looked stunned. "But—why didn't you say something before?"

"You didn't ask," she replied calmly. "Although you might have noticed the child's last name is Kincaid." She shrugged. "It is a convenient story, of course, and I don't mind it getting out that Sheldon is the father. He does dote on her, doesn't he?"

Jim had to admit that he did.

Meg touched her brother's arm, sympathizing with his confusion. "The baby is Caleb's, and I pray he never knows of her birth. He was a terrible man, I made an awful mistake, and I'm lucky I'm away from him. If I hadn't left St. Louis, he would have killed me or I him."

"You and Gerrard." Jim shook his head in consternation. "Who'd ever have thought you'd hook up? Boothe didn't believe it, and I guess I don't either, even though I've seen it with my own eyes. Running a trading post with Sheldon Gerrard . . ."

"He and I helped each other through a bad time, Jim."

She didn't mention Matoon or his death; it was a secret that she and Sheldon would share with no one else and carry to their graves. "Are you so disapproving?"

They stopped under the shade of an ash tree that was just coming into bloom. Jim smiled. "Hell, no. He's been good to you and that's all that matters.

Whatever was between him and Uncle Boothe is over now, gone for good. Not many of us get to choose the path we take—" The smile faded, and his eyes grew distant. "I was saying those very same words to Boothe not so long ago, and I guess they've proven to be true."

Meg nodded. "Lord knows, I didn't choose to be living in the middle of nowhere with Sheldon Gerrard and having another man's baby, but it's not a bad life, all in all. As a matter of fact, Mr. Gerrard and I are doing quite well. We're looking to take on extra help. We might even open a ferry across the Platte this summer . . . if things go as we expect and the overlanders keep on coming."

"So you're planning on staying?"

"Why not? There's work to be done and money to be made. Oh, I miss Ma and the children; I'd like to see them, but I can't go back to Cairo now. Why, I'd be stifled, Jim, and so would you, and so would Star." She glanced up at him out of the corners of her eyes. It seemed strange to think of her little brother being in love.

Jim sighed. "I've been thinking about that . . . Maybe we'd best stay out here, west of the Mississippi. Maybe with Kitty and Ben—"

"Kitty and Ben?" Meg made a dismissive gesture with her hand. "Kitty doesn't need you the way I do." At his look of surprise, she went on. "Yes, I need you to help with this business. Mr. Gerrard and I need someone we can trust to go downriver to St. Louis, order our supplies, and then get everything back to us. He could do it, but you'd be better. We really need you, Jim."

"Have you talked to Gerrard about this?"

"Not exactly," she said airily, "but he'll go along. He did say we needed someone we could trust, and who more than family? Who more than a Kincaid?"

Jim did not know why he hesitated. Star was happy here with Meg and the baby. So was he. And whatever else Gerrard might be, he was a shrewd businessman; the trading post was already beginning to prosper. This was a good place in which to build a life.

Meg followed the direction of her brother's gaze to Star. "Naturally," she said briskly, "you'll be wanting to have a word with the first preacher that comes by, and I daresay that'll happen before summer's over. After that, Star can travel with you or stay here with me. It's up to you. Before next winter comes, we can put up a little cabin for the two of you."

Jim grinned at her. "You've got it all figured out, don't you?"

"Why not, Jim? We're family and we need each other."

"You always were a bossy one."

Meg looked at him, her flippancy gone. "Stay, Jim," she said gently. "Please."

He reached for his sister and hugged her against him. "I'll stay, but I need to see Sarah. I have a terrible feeling something bad has happened to her. I'm worried about her."

"Then go see her. Bring her back with you. The more Kincaids together, the better for all of us." She smiled at him, and Jim realized how young and pretty Meg was and how much he loved her. He couldn't believe that his spoiled sister had changed into the strong, determined woman he saw in front of him, offering him a chance to make a life of his own in the West.

"I need to get things cleared up at Fort Leavenworth, though I'm not sure if they'll believe my story about Marcus Lyndsay. I can do that when I . . . when Star and I visit Kitty."

"You have to try, Jim."

"I know." He took her arm again and they walked on through the small glade of trees toward the trading post.

"Who was Lyndsay?" Meg asked after a moment. "I know he wanted to kill you because you witnessed the murder, but when he was here he seemed so *normal.* Such a gentleman. How could anyone seem so nice and be so evil? Who *was* he?"

Jim's steps seemed to falter, but only for a moment. He was still disturbed by memories of that day, and Meg did not talk to him about it often.

"That's funny," he answered quietly. "Boothe asked him the same thing, just before—he died. He looked at him, and he said, 'Who the hell *are* you?' He could have fired then, but he didn't. It was like . . . it was almost like he *recognized* Lyndsay."

Meg stopped walking and looked up at him thoughtfully. "It's possible, I suppose. Uncle Boothe knew a lot of military men."

Jim shook his head. "No, it was more than that. He saw something there at the end . . . I guess we'll never know what. And then he just walked into the bullet."

Meg shivered in the sunlight. "But Lyndsay is dead now, isn't he?"

"Buried under the snow," Jim said. "We didn't even bother to dig for the body and bury it. We left his carcass for the wolves and the buzzards."

"Good," Meg said. "I wouldn't want a man like that to have a decent burial." She was thoughtful for a moment. "But I like the idea of Uncle Boothe being in the mountains. Ma would like that, too."

"She's probably got our letter now. I know it'll be hard on her. She was awful close to Uncle Boothe."

He slipped his arm around Meg's waist. "Boothe and Pa . . . there'll never be men like them again."

"They were special, first and last of a kind, I guess." She cast a fond glance toward Star, who was lifting a laughing baby high into the air over her head. "Without them we wouldn't be where we are and have what we have. They cleared the way for us. But there's a whole new generation, Jim, and plenty left that needs doing."

Jim grinned at her, knowing this was just another pitch for his help with the trading post, even though he'd already promised he'd stay. "I reckon we'll get it done then."

Meg returned his grin and pressed her cheek briefly against his shoulder. "You bet we will. After all, we're Kincaids."

The Following is a Selection from
BOOK FOUR:
WESTWARD WINDS
Taylor Brady's
Next Book in THE KINCAIDS Series
Coming Soon
from Avon Books

1851

It was still early in the summer, and snow clung to the high Sierra Nevada peaks. It decorated the crevices between boulders and lay like creamy white frosting on flat jutting buttes, crunching beneath the wagon wheels on shady parts of the trail. Jim Kincaid had traveled through the mountains half a dozen times in the past eight years, but he never passed this way without thinking of the first time. And the snow always made him melancholy.

His first trip west had been through the Rockies. He had entered the mountains in search of his Uncle Boothe when he was a young man, when the land had been as raw and untried as he was. Only a few hardy pioneers had braved the high passes of the Oregon Trail in search of the Promised Land, and the California Trail wasn't even heard of.

The wagon ruts were deep even at this time of year, the trail worn flat by the tramping of a thousand feet. Jim gave a little shake of his head, a reflection of the wonderment he felt whenever he thought about the number of people going west. His Uncle Boothe wouldn't have believed it. It was probably best he hadn't lived to see it.

The irony was, it all had happened because of men like Boothe Carlysle, men with wandering feet who set off down the Ohio and across the Mississippi in bark-hewn canoes, who crossed the Great Plains on foot and climbed the soaring mountains and brought back tales filled with glory and awe. They broke the trails for the dreamers to follow.

John Augustus Sutter had been one of those dreamers. He had heard stories of vast unclaimed acres, of fertile valleys and forest cathedrals and endless sunny plains; and he, like many before and since, took the notion to build himself an empire. Past experience had not proven him to be much of a businessman, but he was still smooth enough to talk the governor of California into granting him 50,000 acres or so just east of the San Francisco Bay. He spent the next ten years carving out an estate that was well on its way to doing justice to the feudal empires of Europe after which it was modeled.

Then in January of 1848, James Marshall was supervising a crew that was building a sawmill on the south fork of the American river, where Sutter intended to set up a timber-cutting business. He left the sluice gates open all night to test the millrace, and when he checked the millrace the next morning he found tiny specks of what he was convinced was gold clinging to the bottom. The crew laughed at him, but he scooped up the deposits in his handkerchief and showed them to Sutter the next chance he got.

"I believe this is gold," he said, "but the people at the mill called me crazy."

Sutter looked at the material in the handkerchief

carefully and agreed. "Looks like gold to me. Let's have it tested."

And that, so the story was told, was how it all started.

The word spread by ship, first to the Sandwich Islands and then around the Horn to the East Coast, and by foot, mule, and horse across country. By July San Francisco was a city of women and children, and there was scarcely an adult male to be found in any hamlet or village in California. A stream of eager natives poured off the first ships back from the Islands; Mexican laborers, accompanied by their wives and children, livestock and household goods, flooded across the deserts of Arizona and toward the mountains filled with gold.

By December, when newspapers across the country carried the story of President Polk informing Congress of the "abundance of gold" to be had for the taking in California—accompanied by an impressive display of 230 ounces of California gold—the fever was out of control. Men, women, and children had left their plows in the field, their stores unlocked, their stock turned out, and had piled everything they could carry into wagons, sold the rest for ship's passage, and set off for gold country. It was the nature of humans always to be looking for something better, and most often that search turned their eyes west. Jim Kincaid understood that. His folks had always been the wandering kind.

Eight years ago, Jim and his Cheyenne wife Morning Star Woman had set up housekeeping on the South Platte River within the shelter of the trading post Sheldon Gerrard ran with Jim's sister, Meg. At first Jim started out by building and operating a ferry across the Platte, and it had done right well. Whole trains went past the Kincaid–Gerrard post just to take advantage of the ferry, and while they were there they reprovisioned generously out of the store.

In early summer of 1848 a passer–by brought word of a ship load of potatoes some fool had bought in Panama and was planning to sell in San Francisco. They'd all had a good laugh over that because there were a lot quicker ways to get potatoes to California— even assuming *Californios* were too stupid not to grow their own—and if the cargo wasn't eaten up with rot by the time it reached the bay, it sure would be by the time it was sold. They made jokes about the smell and how much they each figured a shipload of rotten potatoes would be going for or how much a body would have to pay to have it hauled out of the harbor, and about the stupidity of greed in general.

Jim took off that night, on horseback, with all the ready cash they had stuffed into his pockets, praying he could reach San Francisco before the boat did, praying the potatoes weren't rotten, praying he could make his deal before anyone on board heard about the hungry gold miners less than a hundred miles away.

Jim arrived in San Francisco a mere three days before the *Christo Maria* did and offered two hundred dollars for the cargo, sight unseen, before the stunned captain even had a chance to set foot off the deck. He let the captain talk him up to three fifty, all the while leading the bewildered man to believe he had discovered a new formula for whiskey and was going to set up a distillery.

Less than one quarter of the potatoes were rotten. The remainder Jim sold to starving miners whose pockets bulged with ore, to eager hoteliers looking to lure those miners into leaving some of that ore behind in their establishments, to passersby on the street, to enterprising peddlers and, at last, in the gold camps themselves. Total income from the sales amounted to over two hundred thousand dollars.

Jim had never seen so much money in his life. He had never counted anything that high before, and even trying to comprehend it was more than his brain would take without aching. He assayed the gold out, divided it up between the vaults of the three safest banks in San Francisco—figuring the chances were good that one of them might get robbed or burn down, but not all three—and started back home in something like a daze.

There were some fundamental differences between Jim and his sister. Jim had seen the madness with his own eyes, he had held the gold in his hands and been dragged down by the weight of it in his saddlebags, but he still didn't fully believe in it. He surely never thought about going after more. Two hundred thousand dollars was more money than he had known there was in the *world* six months earlier. It was more than any of them needed in this lifetime, in several lifetimes. Why would anyone want more?

But Meg looked at the insubstantial written receipt, and her eyes lit up like hills on fire. And she said, "This is only the beginning."

Within the month, Sheldon, Meg, and little Fiona were packed up and on their way to San Francisco, where they opened up a mercantile that was making money faster than they could count it. Jim and Star stayed behind to run the trading post and had almost more than they could do, outfitting the people that streamed by daily, headed for the California Trail.

Then Meg had the idea to open up some kind of "fancy house"—or at least that was what Jim called it, earning a slap on the hand in reprimand from his wife every time he did so. Meg called it an "opera house", and claimed she had gotten the idea from a ship's captain who'd just come back from France. She intended to have singing and play—acting and dancing women who showed their legs, and that sounded like a fancy house to Jim. Whatever it was called, Meg claimed the newly—rich miners would eat it up, and in that Jim had to admit she might be right.

Whether they'd appreciate the bolts upon bolts of red velvet cloth and the crystal chandeliers that filled the two wagons Jim was taking across the mountains into San Francisco was another matter. At least, he thought, and grinned a little as he clucked to the team, they didn't have to worry about Indians. They weren't hauling anything on this trip that any self-respecting Indian would be caught stealing.

Though Jim laughed at Meg's fancy house, he was glad of the trip. Star had been feeling downcast since Meg and the little one had left, and he had been thinking for some time that he might take her out for a visit. He found a couple of fellows to help him with the wagons and put Henryk, the blacksmith who'd been with them since the trading post started up, in charge of the store. He figured to have a pleasant trip across country, and a fine time showing his wife the sights of San Francisco. According to Meg, the town was something to see by now.

But when they got to the Sublette cut—off, his two drivers absconded with their hiring—on wages, apparently deciding they could get to the gold fields faster if they weren't driving two wagons loaded down with goods. Since then, the pleasure trip had been nothing but hard work, with Star driving one wagon and Jim the other. Still, there'd been good in it simply because Star was with him.

Jim turned on the wagon seat to look back at

her, grinning and doffing his hat. She sat as straight–backed as a missionary, her hair coiled into a jet black bun beneath her calico bonnet, her coppery skin glowing in the sunlight. When Jim first married her she had disdained white women's clothing, but a year or so with Meg had changed all that. Now she wore the muslin petticoats and gentle calicoes with the grace of one born to them. Even now, driving the wagon with the quiet strength and easy competence of a wrangler, she had never looked more beautiful to Jim. He loved her with all his heart.

"There's a cut off up ahead," he called to her. "We'll stop for the night."

She smiled and raised her hand in acknowledgment.

Jim settled on the wagon seat and urged the team on, aware of a contentment spreading through him that was as clear and pure as a mountain stream, dispersing the melancholia as surely as sun melted snow. In less than two weeks they would be in San Francisco. He had crossed half a continent without a major mishap, the end of the journey was in sight, and the only woman he had ever loved was by his side. He couldn't think of another thing in this world he wanted.

They called him Lobo. He wasn't certain when it had started or why, though he suspected it had something to do with the chewed-up side of his face, which rumor credited to an attack by wolves in high plains country. Lobo wore the appellation, as he did his scars, proudly, a symbol of the metamorphosis he had undergone on the way back to life from death.

He had survived the lean hard years by learning to hunt like a wolf, run like a rabbit and stalk like a cat. He had the patience of a snake on a sunny rock and the quickness of a darting lizard. Some lessons he had learned from the Indians, who had rescued him from the snow and for a while given him sanctuary, others he had observed for himself, when understanding those lessons made the difference between life and death.

Parts of those eight years of learning he'd spent living in caves like an animal, eating what he could catch with his bare hands, crossing the desert at night, killing or using whatever happened to cross his path. Sometimes what he killed was human. Sometimes what he took was spending money or jewelry or other valuables. More often, it was food and blankets, or a new pair of boots. He killed because he enjoyed it, and he stole because that was his right. Soon he became expert at both.

Lobo was an analytical man given to careful thought when it suited him. He therefore could not fail to realize that those early years, when put into the broad perspective of a man who was destined to leave his mark on history, were a necessary period of testing and proving, an ascension into manhood, a trial by fire. All of it was in preparation for this time and this place, when he would at last come into his own.

The long lonesome trails, the vast deserts, the high mountain passes, which once had been his to command with the quickness of his wits and the cleverness of his skills, were now flooded with the greedy and the desperate. They swarmed across the mountains in hoards, driven by the lust for gold. Many of them never made it to their destination; many more were doomed to disappointment once they arrived. But some of them returned along the same trails by which they'd first come, their pockets bulging, their pack beasts staggering under the weight of their burdens.

Those were the men who interested Lobo.

He was not the first man to realize that it was a great deal easier to steal from the miners than to work a claim himself. He might, however, be credited as the first to realize it was even easier to steal from the thieves.

The first time, he simply watched from a canyon rim as a robber swooped down on a departing miner, relieved him of his gold, and was on his way. Lobo met up with the thief half a mile down the road and put a bullet through his head.

The next time he stole and allowed the thief to live. And so an idea was born.

Hundreds of thousands of dollars worth of gold left the fields and camps of the Sierra Nevadas every month. One man acting alone could hope to claim only a small portion of it—and risk getting himself killed in the process. The miners weren't all as dumb as they looked; they were beginning to travel with armed guards, or hire toughs to take the gold out of the mountains while they stayed back at the camps or traveled with empty pockets. There were fortunes for the taking, traveling down those trails, but trying to take it alone was risky business.

There was strength in numbers. And the key to success lay in organization.

There were five battalions under his command, each composed of four to six men. Between them they could cover most of the trails leading in and out of gold country. Working together, choosing their targets carefully, they were almost invincible. Already Lobo was a rich man, and those who rode with him had more money than their poor imaginations had ever dreamed. Some might even have liked to quit, to retire and live the kind of life they had only been able to fantasize about before now. Sometimes they even talked about it. But few ever did anything about it. Lobo's method of maintaining discipline was very simple and very effective. No one ever left his employ alive.

Lobo did not ride out as much as he used to, only enough to keep his hand in and make his presence known. It was not superstition, he told himself, but a higher power that convinced him to take the Donner Pass that day. It was a plain and unshakable belief in Destiny.

"Cap'n, we spotted him."

Charlie had been one of the first to join him and had since earned a goodly portion of Lobo's respect, if not his unquestioned trust.

"And were you right about him, Charlie?"

Charlie looked smug, which wasn't easy to do with his face distorted by a jawful of chewing tobacco. "Yessir, the fella's got himself a target all right. Couple of wagons headed down the trail." He chuckled. "Damn fool can't figure out nobody carries gold *in* to the fields, I reckon."

"Nonetheless, it doesn't do to dismiss any opportunity."

Lobo's reply was absent, for as he turned his horse in the direction Charlie indicated, he caught a glimpse of the wagons and his curiosity was pricked. They were camped midway down the trail, overlooking Donner's lake, and he saw no indication of a family group. Those could only be supply wagons, so maybe their would–be thief wasn't as stupid as he seemed. These days, as anyone who had ever returned from gold country could testify, there were things a great deal more valuable than ore.

Two of his men were already in position at three

and nine o'clock, so well concealed in the bushes that only Lobo could have spotted them, waiting for the thief to make his move on the wagons. From the looks of it, they wouldn't have to wait long. The man was on foot, creeping through the woods toward the wagons—a miner gone broke, unless Lobo missed his guess, lean and hungry and desperate. Unless the driver was a complete fool, the would-be thief was destined to get himself shot before he got within thirty feet of the wagons, and that would spoil it for all of them.

Lobo watched for a moment, then shook his head in disgust. The idiot wasn't even going to wait for dark, and nothing those wagons contained was worth a prolonged shoot out when the pickings were so much easier up the road. They were wasting their time here.

He started to turn his horse, then stopped, muscles frozen, eyes riveted on the man who came around the side of the wagon.

"Stop him!" he hissed to Charlie without taking his eyes off the wagons. "*Now!*"

Charlie knew better than to question, or to hesitate even a moment between the order's delivery and its execution. Almost before the words were out, he was moving down the slope, barking quiet orders to the other two men.

Lobo didn't move. He sat astride his horse, watching the red-headed man until he moved out of sight.

Sarah Kincaid Deveraux studied her image in the cheval mirror and smiled with satisfaction. The deep bottle green of her new gown complimented her fair coloring and fiery hair to perfection. The low necked bodice exposed the magnolia creaminess of her shoulders, and the tight waist and full skirt flat-

tered her slender middle. The dress of silk taffeta
had been made in New Orleans, copied, the seam-
stress said, from a French original, and was adorned
with bows and flounces and ruches of lace. It was the
very height of fashion for the spring of 1851.

Sarah saw a reflection beside hers in the glass. "I
love this dress, Tante Emilie. As usual, you're far too
generous."

"You look lovely in whatever you wear, *cherie*, but I
wanted you to have something special for the party
tonight. It's a joy for me to be able to give it to you."

Sarah turned away from the mirror and hugged
the short, graying woman with genuine affection.
"Shall I take this to California with me? I know there
isn't much room for luggage on the ship, but I'd like
to have a marvelous dress to show Cade."

Emilie sank down on a little settee, her dark eyes
worried. "I wish I were as sure as you that you'll find
Cade. It's such a long way to California from here on
the Mississippi."

"There's nothing to worry about," Sarah said with
more certainty than she felt. "I know where Cade's
gold claim is located, and I know the name of the
town. My sister Meg will arrange for someone to
guide me, and *voila*—I'll find my errant husband."

Emilie, still worried, sighed heavily. "You've heard
nothing from your sister . . . nor from Cade in
months."

Sarah dismissed Emilie's concerns with an airy wave
of her hand. "Which only proves how dreadful the
mail service from California is. After I leave, long
letters will probably arrive from both of them."

"If the mail can't get through, then how do *you*
expect to?"

"We've had this discussion before, Emilie. I'm
going. You know that. You worry far too much."

"Of course, I worry. You're like a daughter to me, and my nephew, Cade, is like a son."

"Then come with me!" Sarah said with a laugh. "Think of the fun we two could have on the ship."

"Can you imagine me crossing the Isthmus of Panama on a mule?"

Sarah pretended to study the plump form of Emilie Deveraux Gallier through narrowed eyes, as if such an adventure were really possible. "Hmmmm, actually . . . I can't!"

Emilie was still fixated on the journey, which Sarah was undertaking in only two days. "I wish I knew more about this Mrs. Morgan you're traveling with."

Sarah recognized jealousy in Emilie's voice as well as concern, for she knew if Emilie were younger and didn't feel a duty to remain with her brother at Deveraux House, she would be on the ship to Panama with Sarah.

Sarah formed her words carefully. "Mrs. Morgan's letters are quite nice. She's a minister's wife from Shreveport who's going out to join her husband in San Francisco. She can't travel alone, and neither can I, so that nice ticket agent at the steamship line matched us up. It's the best of all possible plans since you can't be with me."

Emilie wasn't convinced. "Why don't you wait a month and sail with Father Leseyne and the Sisters of Hope and Charity? I'd feel much better if you were with them."

Sarah busied herself at the mirror, pushing her hair back from her face and examining what might be a freckle forming on the tip of her nose. She'd been infinitely relieved when Mrs. Morgan had written her and spared her a journey with the Sisters. Even though she'd converted to Catholicism when she married Cade Deveraux, she wasn't comfortable with the rituals of the church, or with the priests and nuns she'd met. Her new religion remained mysterious and exotic to her, and in retrospect she wondered at her eagerness to abandon the Protestant faith she'd been raised in and take on her husband's. But then, of course, she would have done anything Cade asked of her.

"When Cade left for the gold fields, I always intended to join him. It's been over a year, and the time is ripe. I can't wait any longer, Emilie. You understand." She went to her friend and knelt by the settee so that the two women's faces were almost even. "I love him so much."

Emilie took Sarah's face in her hands. "I know you love him, my sweet child. Cade is very special to me, too, but if any harm should come to you—"

"Nothing will happen to me, I promise. I can look after myself, and I think it's time I had another adventure. One I can tell my grandchildren about. Of course, unless I find my husband soon, there won't *be* any children or grandchildren!"

Emilie pretended to be shocked. "Sarah Deveraux, you are shameless!"

"And you love it." Sarah kissed Emilie on the cheek.

"I only pray that all goes well. So many things can happen . . . I've talked to Lucien about funds again."

"He's been more than generous, but I have money of my own." Sarah crossed to her dressing table and rummaged in her jewelry box. "I have one of the gold coins that Great-gran Fiona gave to Mama when she left home." It felt cool and solid in her hand.

"*Cherie*, this is a family treasure, an heirloom. You can't think of spending it." Emilie was horrified.

Sarah shrugged. "Mama used one coin to buy passage on a boat down the Ohio thirty years ago, and my sister, Kitty, used another to start up her horse ranch—so there's no reason I can't use mine to go to California." Sarah knew the coin was hundreds of years old and bore an inscription in a language she couldn't read, but the mystique and sentimentality of the family coin were of little importance to her compared to reaching California and finding her husband. "If I need to spend the gold coin, I will. So don't worry about me."

Emilie stood up, shaking her head. "A gold coin is not enough to stop me worrying about you, *ma petite*, but I can see my lectures are doing no good. No good at all."

Sarah grinned impishly. "Have they ever?"

"*Mon Dieu!*" Emilie threw up her hands. "You Kincaids must be the stubbornest humans ever born. Once you set upon a course, nothing can dissuade you."

"Be happy for me, *tante*," Sarah said softly. "I'm going to be with the man I love."

Cade Deveraux felt the steel barrel of a gun against the back of his neck with very little surprise. *Why not?* he thought. The way his luck had been running lately, why the hell not?

He was pressed flat up against a tree, trying to get a look at the campsite below without making himself a sitting duck to anyone who happened to glance up from below. It hadn't occurred to him to watch his back, but when a man was as cold and hungry as he was, a lot of things didn't occur to him. He raised his hands over his head without turning around.

"That's the time, mister," an approving voice—presumably the one that belong to the hand holding the gun—murmured behind him. "Now real nice and easy–like, you slip the strap of that there Winchester off'n your shoulder."

Cade did as he was told. There was a moment—a split-second really—while his hand was near the level of his waist, that it occurred to him to try to reach the pistol that was stuffed inside his waistband. But false heroics had never been one of Cade Deveraux's failings, particularly when such gestures were almost certain to result in a quick and messy death. He was almost relieved therefore when, a moment later, a hand reached forward and divested him of the weapon, removing temptation.

"What do you think?" A second voice addressed the first, sounding a little nervous. "Should we kill him?"

"Boss didn't say." There was a thoughtful silence. "Better not take no chances though."

Pain exploded in the back of Cade's head, blossomed blood-red, and faded to black.